Dead Man Code

A Jarvis Mann Detective Novel

By
R Weir

Copyright © R Weir 2016

The right of R Weir to be identified as the Author of the Work has been asserted by him in accordance with the Copyright, Designs and Patents Act 1988.

All rights reserved; no part of this publication may be reproduced, stored in a retrieval system, or transmitted in any form or by any means, electronic, mechanical, photocopying, recording, or otherwise without the prior written permission of the Publisher. This book may not be lent, resold, hired out or otherwise disposed of by way of trade in any form of binding or cover other than in which it is published, without the prior written consent of the Publisher. No responsibility for loss occasioned to any person or corporate body acting or refraining to act as a result of reading material in this book can be accepted by the Publisher, by the Author, or by the employer(s) of the Author. Certain images copyright.
R Weir. Dead Man Code.

This book is a work of fiction. All characters in this novel are fictitious. Any resemblance to actual events or locales or persons, living or dead, is entirely coincidental.

Copyediting by:
Gabriella West at
www.EditforIndies.com

Great Scott Editing
www.greatscottediting.net

Cover Design by:
Happi Anarky
www.happianarky.com

**To my IT friends
Lorraine, Trina, Teresa and Byron:
Crack the Code**

**Thanks to all of my beta readers,
who helped make *Dead Man Code*
the best it could be.**

Chapter 1

I was summoned to meet with a cyber security expert on a case I'd been working. He said he had vital information he needed to share, but preferred not to discuss it over the open airwaves. He was borderline paranoid about eavesdroppers, likely for good reason. We had talked before secretly, his words enlightening, though not enough to crack the case. He wanted to walk away, fear owning him, but I talked him into digging deeper. I had not heard from him for a while, but tonight he called claiming to have damning evidence to share. I trekked over to his office building near the Denver Tech Center, the darkness of the parking lot making me nervous as I waited for his reply to my text, signaling me to come up to his third-floor space.

I sat and waited; ten minutes and then twenty, singing a song or two under my breath to help pass the time, my fingers drumming a nervous beat. Staring at my phone didn't make the text arrive any sooner. I tapped the screen to make sure I had a signal and could browse the Internet. ESPN loaded promptly, showing me the Rockies had lost again. Impatient, I decided to wait no longer, and ever vigilant of trouble, I stepped out of my Mustang. Apparently, paranoia was contagious. My phone dinged, the text finally arriving, saying to come up.

Security in the building was poor: no locked front entrance, elevators and stairs easily accessed without a code to enter, or magnetic card to swipe. I rode the lift up with an uneasy feeling. My gun was sitting on my back hip as a measure of security, at the ready, covered by the tail of my shirt. The long hallway of beat-up beige walls and worn, stained gray carpeting led to his front office door where the security normally started, the sign spelling out "Colorado Cyber Border Security." But when I reached for the handle I found it ajar. Leaning back against the sidewall, I used my foot to push it open, careful of danger. Nothing happened, so I peered around the door jam, seeing nothing. I moved in low and up against the stucco, watching, and hearing anything that moved. The office wasn't large, two openings, one on each side, each with a door. The first on the left was closed, the one on the right open. The office of the man I was supposed to meet, his nameplate mounted in brass.

Creeping closer, I could hear noise now, though faint. Someone was there, but I wasn't about to call out and bring attention to myself. Caution at the situation got my heart racing. Instinctively, my gun was poised in my right hand, the left one still taped from an injury. As I closed on the final doorway, I counted to myself and on three sprung, ready to strike.

I entered, quickly surveying the scene, gun at my side. A man stood there, about my height and weight, with curly blond hair and bushy sideburns. He turned and pointed his gun at me, since I was slow to raise mine. I recognized the face. One I knew well, but didn't care for. He aimed center mass, looking as if he'd fire at any moment, his hand a little shaky. Adam King, a fellow private detective, a foe I had encountered before because of his attempts at stealing my clients, stood there nervously, sweat beads covering his pale face, appearing a bit scared. A dead body lay behind him, the cyber security expert I was supposed to meet, an apparent bullet hole in his head.

"Don't move, Jarvis," he said with a tremor in his voice, his finger on the trigger of his 9mm.

My mind searched for a snappy comeback or brilliant idea to get me out of this situation. Nothing came to mind as time froze still. There was little I could do but stand there and let him shoot me.

Chapter 2

Months earlier I was back in Denver, returning from Des Moines, victorious at the conclusion of my case, exacting revenge on the man who was responsible for my brother's death. It was a shallow victory, but I had accepted it. Yet I was a failure once again in my personal life, as I had cheated on my girlfriend of nearly a year, Melissa, and was now facing the music. Her reaction was swift and painful, as she slapped my face in anger, then pounded on my chest with the flats of her hands. All I could do was stand there and take it, for I had betrayed her trust once again. She started to cry, and I pulled her into me, whispering, "I'm sorry," though the words certainly rang hollow. She twisted out of my grip and wiped her eyes, more anger in her words.

"I can't be around you anymore, Jarvis!" she said bitterly. "You've broken my heart and I can't stand the sight of you! You must go."

I stood there staring, uncertain what to do, looking for words to find closure. Nothing I could say would change things.

"Leave!" she said again, forcefully. "I said leave, damn you!"

There was nothing more to do. Ashamed, I climbed back on the motorcycle and rode off. I was upset, too, and drove way faster than I should, traveling many miles to nowhere. Well south of town I stopped on the side of a quiet two-lane road, the afternoon sun beating down on me. I sat on the ground and put my head in my hands, cursing myself for screwing up the best thing I had in my life. I punched my chest, then the ground until my knuckles were red and nearly bleeding. Exhausted, I lay back and closed my eyes, lying there for an unknown period, thinking of everything and nothing at the same time. Pieces of the events that led to all of this. The death of my brother. The killing of the man who had orchestrated it. The drunken night that led to me sleeping with Roni. The motorcycle I now lay next to, a gift given to me by my sister-in-law and niece. It was a jumble of emotions and images I couldn't contain. Soon a car pulled up with black and blue stripes on the door, with State Patrol in black letters on the rear-side panel.

"Are you OK, sir?" an officer called out from his PA system.

I sat up and gave him a thumbs-up, standing now, my face

warm and feeling burned from the sun.

The Colorado state trooper stepped out, holster unsnapped, his hand at the ready.

"Have you been drinking, sir?" he asked.

"No, Officer. I was sitting here thinking over some things. It's been a tough day."

"Let's make sure."

He had me do a few tests, which I passed easily. He looked in my eyes and could see my pain.

"How far away do you live?"

"South part of Denver, west of the DU area."

"A long ride home. Do you need a lift back into town? You can arrange to get your bike later."

"I will be fine. Lost the love of my life today, and needed to ride and clear my head."

"Did it work?"

"Not really."

"A matter of time. We've all been through it."

"Way more often than I should have. But it's my own fault. No one to blame but myself."

"Time to make a change, then. Get your life back on track and be a better man."

"Easier said than done for me."

"Maybe. But if you want to badly enough, it can be accomplished."

He snapped his holster and headed back to his vehicle.

"Sure you don't want a lift?"

"No, thank you. I'll be OK."

"Drive safe. I know on those two-wheeled muscle machines, it's easy to drive too fast."

I nodded and as he drove away, I climbed back on and made a slower trek back home, where I found a cold beer and soft sofa. I collapsed there to sleep away the rest of the day and into the night, with sad dreams of the tear-streaked face of the woman I loved bouncing in and out of my slumber. For me the sleep was not restful.

Chapter 3

It took many days to pull myself together, flush the sadness and too many beers from my system. Knowing I had a client waiting in the wings forced me to get back to work, to put my mind on other things. Besides, she had given me a retainer before I went back to Iowa to resolve my brother's murder, and most of that money was already gone. So, refunding it would put me in the red and make for an unhappy customer, which I couldn't afford.

We met at a local sandwich shop a mile or so from home. Feeling cleaner and dressed in slacks and a polo, I was presentable, certainly more so than I'd been days earlier. When I walked in I found her sitting at a back table, drinking her tea out of a plastic cup, no food sitting before her. She was small in size, maybe 5' 3", had a nice figure covered with a knee-length gray skirt and dark blue short-sleeved blouse. Her blonde hair was loose, with waves that reached her shoulders and mostly covered her large earrings. She smiled when I approached, though sadness lingered behind her eyes, much as they likely lingered behind mine. She had hired me to find out who had killed her husband months ago, a cold case with no suspects.

"Hello, Mandy," I said while sitting down. "How are you holding up?"

"Not great, but in time we'll see. I'll feel better once I know who did this."

"Well, I'm clear now to put my full attention on this case. I wanted to meet with you to reassure you of this and to go over everything again, since it's been a while since we first talked. Determine if there are any new developments."

"Yes, it has. I was beginning to wonder if you were ever coming back."

"I'm sorry. I was dealing with a personal matter, not unlike your own. It took longer to resolve."

She looked up from her tea, her face looking pale, as if never seeing the sun.

"And were you able to resolve it satisfactorily?"

"Yes. One in the win column for me."

I left out the part about the pair of losses on the personal side.

"I'm glad. I hope you can resolve this one as well. What else do you need to know?"

"Tell me all you can about your husband. Start anywhere you want. I find it's best to learn as much as I can about all the parties."

She let out a long sigh.

"I know it's hard. Take your time."

"Aaron and I met in college, about six years ago. He was a nerdy geek and I was the pretty cheerleader. It wasn't love at first sight, but over time there was something about him that made my heart beat faster. He was shy, so I asked him out. All the other girls thought I was nuts, because they wanted the jock and couldn't see what I saw in him. Pretty soon we never wanted to be apart. About a year later we moved in together and six months after were married."

She grabbed her purse, pulled out a photo and handed to me.

"Here's a picture of him shortly before he was killed."

Looking at him, he didn't appear all that geeky to me, though he was wearing thick-framed eyeglasses. No pock-marked skin and goofy grin. He was a handsome man if you looked closely.

"May I keep this?"

She nodded her head.

"Please go on and tell me more about him."

"As he completed his degree, he had offers from several tech companies. Microsoft, Apple and Cisco all were interested in his skills. But a newer tech company came to the forefront with a big money offer, which he jumped at. They had offices here in Denver, so he wouldn't have to move."

"What was the company?"

"Waterton Albers New Networking Systems. Most in the tech industry refer to them as WANN."

"Is this who he was working for when he was murdered?"

"Yes."

"I don't think I've heard of them."

"Been around for a while now and rising fast. They have cut into Cisco's profits significantly in the last couple of years, selling network firewalls, switches and routers at a price much lower than anyone else in the industry. Breaking into the consumer market first and then the business one. Their market share is climbing, with a large number of big companies switching to their equipment and software because of the cost savings. They have razor-thin margins, but their stock is through the roof."

Stock pricing, I cared little about, or the tech world in general. It was all foreign to me. I did know that sagging profits didn't always translate into poor stock prices. But I'd have to do some considerable research to understand more thoroughly.

"What was it he did there?"

"High-level security testing. It was his job to find bugs and security holes in their software design."

"You believe he found something which may have gotten him killed?"

"Yes...maybe...I don't really know for certain. He spoke software geek-speak a lot. I often tuned him out, because I didn't understand it. All I know is something concerned him about what they were doing in their products."

"I see in my notes from before that you mentioned identity theft."

"It's a term you often hear. I threw it out there. I have no hard facts."

"So, it's not something he mentioned."

"He may have. I don't recall for certain. Again, there were times I would tune him out when the computer acronyms started flying. I wish now I'd listened more closely."

It seemed hard to imagine what they had in common, but that wasn't my place to worry about for now. Though my experience with computer nerds was, they did talk a lot of gibberish I didn't understand either. This case would definitely test my attention span.

"What else can you provide for me? Any notes or files he kept on what was going on? Anything digital on his home computer he may have shared via social media?"

"No. He never shared anything work-related on social media. He knew, working for a tech company, they would be monitoring for leaks of any kind. He would only post personal items, like pictures of us together, friends or family."

"What about friends or family he might have confided in?"

"He wasn't close to his parents. They live in San Diego and didn't even come to the funeral. Only sent flowers, which really burned me. As for friends, I can give you a few names. I'm certain they will talk with you. But I doubt you'll learn anything more than what I've heard from them."

I wrote down the names of the friends and could talk with them later. They might open up more around me than her, as they might be afraid of hurting her more. I got the parents' names as well. There might be something there that I might be able to pry out of them. To not even come to the funeral was odd.

"How about in your life? Anything going on which may have led to his death?"

She looked up from her tea, as if surprised by the question.

"I'm sorry. It's something I must ask. Sometimes people you love are hurt by things you do or have done."

I was speaking from experience. She looked as if she might begin to cry, but held it together.

"Sure, I understand. No, there is nothing in my life which should have caused this."

Her eyes were back down staring at the table when she spoke. I sensed I wasn't getting the whole truth, which often seemed to be the case with my clients. But I'd hold this in reserve for now.

"Where are you working these days?" I asked.

"Nowhere currently. I was self-employed doing various jobs, but I can't work right now. It is hard enough to get though the day."

"It's never easy to lose a loved one. Are you getting any professional help to cope?"

"No."

"I can suggest some names. People you can talk to. I, of course, can listen as well if you need to shed some of the burden. Though I'm not trained in how to respond properly, I can hear the words. Sometimes it helps to say them out loud."

"You can give me the names. I'm not sure if I'm ready to talk, but I'll keep it in mind."

With my phone I forwarded three names of people I knew could help her.

"How about financially?"

"I'm good there. He had a large life insurance policy, and his workplace paid me the equivalent of a year's worth of his salary. They said they felt guilty for not protecting their employees better on their property."

I wanted to say "hush money," but resisted.

"Anything more you want to tell me?"

Again, she looked up from her tea, a burning expression now on her face and in her eyes.

"I want them caught," she said bitterly. "No matter what it takes. Bring them to justice or kill them, it doesn't matter to me. Can you do this for me?"

I had no intention of killing again, if it wasn't necessary. But catching them and putting them in jail was what I'd strive for. Being jovial was the right expression I wanted to convey, so I kept a straight face and said as confidently as I could:

"You bet your ass!!"

Chapter 4

My first stop was at the Denver Police station down the street from me. When I walked in I figured everyone would call out my name in joyful tones, but of course it never happened. If anything, I had to jump up and down a few times to get someone's attention, as they really weren't all that thrilled to see me.

My main connection there was Bill Malone, an officer on the force for nearly twenty years, whose son I helped out of a messy jam a year earlier. He had been a reliable source of information when I needed it. But today he was out in the field working, something he rarely did because of getting shot years before, causing a painful injury which limited his physical activity. Since they were heavy in the vacation season, the department was shorthanded, so he got to spend time out from behind the desk, which he enjoyed, at least for short stretches.

April Rainn was my other contact. She was there, but busy. I got a stern look when I said "hi."

"Unless you are packing some fresh Iowa sweet corn, I have no time for you."

She was referring to payment for information she had provided me during my Midwest case months earlier. In all the chaos it had slipped my mind.

"Sorry. Circumstances prevented me from coming away with some. But a box is being shipped as we speak and should arrive by the end of the week."

"Yeah, sure. Typical man, always forgetting to bring home the goods. What do you need, Jarvis?"

"I need a case file on a murder a few months back. A computer geek, Aaron Bailey, killed in the parking lot where he worked. Waterton Albers New Networking Systems."

"I remember that case. Ruled a robbery gone bad. Who hired you?"

"His wife. She doesn't believe it was a robbery."

"So, she called you up!"

"Who better?"

April smiled.

"Well I can't vouch for that, other than what I heard. I'd send you to Mallard to get it, but he is on vacation too. Seems like everyone goes at once this time of year. Give me a few minutes and I'll see if I can pull it. But it's going to cost you."

"Beer, ribs and hot wings at Boone's."

"You are a one-trick pony, Jarvis."

"When you are good at something, keep doing it. My Boone's bribes have always worked in the past to get what I need."

"One of these days I may have to up the ante to get what I need. Take a seat and I'll be back as soon as I can."

I found a seat and contemplated what she was implying, though I was pretty certain I knew what it was. Our friendship was open, as she talked freely around me about her life. It had always been playful banter and a fair amount of flirting. Still in recovery mode from my split from Melissa, I needed to be careful not to get drawn into a physical encounter, no matter how tempting. *And oh, it was!*

About fifteen minutes passed when April returned with the file. Since she didn't want me sitting out front flipping through sensitive information, she led me back to an open cubicle where I could look over things in private. On the way we ran into a person who disliked me greatly and who was Mallard's partner. Dan Cummings was always tense around me. Maybe he was this way with everyone, but he always seemed to be about to blow a vein in his forehead during our encounters. Today was no different.

"What is this asshole doing here?" he stated straight to April.

"Working a case," she answered back, not backing down.

"He doesn't work here, and if he doesn't leave I'll escort him out forcefully."

"Cummings, you need to get laid once in a while," said April. "You're going to have a stroke if you don't blow off some of that tension you have built up inside."

His face turned red at her words.

"Mallard said to give him the info on this case, so I did. So why don't you go home for the day and nail the wife a couple of times, smile for once in your miserable life, and leave Jarvis and me alone."

Cummings turned to me, but all I could do was smile broadly, hands in the air in mock surrender.

"I'm going to call Mallard and see what he says," barked Cummings.

"Please do," I replied. "I'm sure he'll be thrilled you disturbed his fishing trip for something this trivial. But go ahead and call him."

He was caught and knew it.

"Besides, April makes a good suggestion. Go home and give the wife some of your best loving. I bet when you are worked up like this you make one hell of a lover."

He waved us off and stormed out of the room. We held out as long as we could, but both of us started laughing uncontrollably. It took a minute for us to settle down, but once I did I found a seat and started going over the file. April left me to absorb the information, after we shared a high-five.

Most police case files have an order to them. I'd seen a few in my day, and normally the most recent info was on top, chronologically going from there back to the beginning. This one was a mess, though, as if someone had dropped it on the floor and didn't bother to put it back in order. I sorted through, finding the beginning, the day Aaron's body was discovered.

A call was put into the police dispatch, saying a body had been found in the parking lot in the Denver Tech Center at around 1 a.m. Police responded, arriving several minutes later, in the nearly empty concrete structure, next to a gray four-door sedan. A WANN security person was there waiting for them to arrive, his name in the file. They closed off the area, calling for the Coroner and homicide detectives, as the person was obviously dead, apparently from a pair of gunshot wounds. Pictures of the scene were in the file, never pleasant to view, but I looked them over to confirm the information. Digging further, the identity was determined to be of Aaron Bailey, who had died of a single 9mm gunshot wound to the chest. They also found another through his right leg, with additional bruising on his face and torso, from a beating he received before he was killed. Blood was found inside the car, along with one bullet, likely from the leg wound. Another bullet on the pavement outside the car, with more blood, from the chest. No casings were discovered, though. There were cameras in the parking lot, but conveniently they were offline that night for several hours, for some unknown reason, blamed on a computer software failure.

The crime unit collected as many fibers and fingerprints as they could, but found nothing substantial to work with. The wife was questioned, as were many who worked closely with the victim. No real leads or evidence pointed to anything other than a violent robbery, as money and credit cards had been stolen, along with his work notebook computer. No mention of the plastic or computer ever being found. Reward money was offered for any leads. Denver detectives put in the time they could, but with nothing to go on, it became a cold case filed away with others, with little chance of being solved. Now it was in my hands to come up with something.

I combed through everything a second and third time, nothing more revealing surfacing. I made notes of various people involved and contacted by the police, taking pictures of pages with my phone that I could refer to later. I tucked everything back into the file, this time in the proper order, and returned it to April.

"Has anyone else been looking through this file recently?" I asked her while handing it over.

"Not that I'm aware of," she replied. "Not that I babysit the filing cabinet. Anyone in the station can get to it with the proper clearance and key. Why?"

"Just curious. The file was a mess, like someone rifled through and then got caught and put it back without cleaning it up. It may be nothing, but I was wondering."

"Let me check something."

She went to a nearby computer and logged in. After typing out a few things, she pointed to the screen. I looked and the last person, at least per the computer log, to look over the case was Cummings.

"Is this Cummings's case?" I asked.

"No, Mallard's, but they work pretty close together, so it's not surprising he would be looking it over."

"It says it was two weeks ago. Is it unusual for someone else to get into the file and not log it?"

"Not really. I'm not logging I got the file for you to look at. Certainly, others could have gotten their mitts on it. Besides, Cummings is anal with a capital A, so I doubt he'd have left the file a mess."

"Do you think he'll answer me if I ask?"

April had taken a drink of water, nearly spitting it out in response.

"After our exchange a few minutes ago, I'd say it was a long shot."

"Can't hurt to ask. He can only tell me to fuck off. It wouldn't be the first time."

April led me to his office, where he was filling out a report.

"What the fuck do you want?" he bellowed.

I turned to April. "Well, I got it half right."

"Jarvis wanted to ask you a couple of questions about the Bailey murder," said April.

"I'm not in the habit of answering questions from people I don't care for."

"The feeling is mutual," I said. "But the truth of the matter is, this case is going nowhere. Maybe I can't solve it, but I sure can give it the time necessary to come to some conclusion. Time you don't have, as I'm sure you are working ten different cases simultaneously."

Cummings leaned back in his chair, and pointed at a big stack of files.

"Thirteen. I'm listening."

"It says credit cards and his computer were stolen. Did the plastic ever get used? And did the computer ever turn up?"

"No to both."

"Did it seem odd the credit cards weren't immediately used if it was a robbery?"

"Yes. Unfortunately, that doesn't lead us anywhere. You would think, yes, they'd have purchased a ton of stuff right after stealing them. But not a single charge was made up until the cards were cancelled."

"You didn't think it was a robbery, then?"

"Deep down, no. But I have no proof beyond what my police sense is telling me. And that doesn't carry much weight. Conjecture in a police report is generally frowned upon."

"It shows you were the last person to check out the case paperwork, a couple of weeks ago. Any reason why?"

Cummings gave April a hard look. She just flipped him off.

"I always go back over cases when I have a few minutes. When you stare at it constantly key things get missed. Always good to go back over it with a clear mind."

"Did you find anything you'd missed before?"

"No."

"Did the case file look different in any way to you from the last time you'd looked at it?"

"No. Why?"

"Mostly curious. It appeared to be a bit out of sync to me. As if someone rifled through it and then dumped everything back together in a hurry."

"It was perfectly fine when I filed it away. I'm a real stickler for keeping everything in order. People around here are always messing up the files and I have to clean up after them."

I looked around his office and could tell. It was one of the cleanest offices I'd ever seen. Even the stack of files on his desk was neatly lined up on top of one another.

"I appreciate you taking a couple of minutes giving me your thoughts."

"Yes, it was a real thrill for me too. If you two can hit the road, I have other cases to hopefully find some answers to."

We walked away, with me not learning much else. But I had something to start with. As we reached the front of the station entrance, I turned to April.

"Thanks for helping me out. Dinner at Boone's this week. I'll call you when I have a free night."

April reached out her hand and I shook it. It was soft and warm to the touch.

"Don't show up without the sweet corn, or you may need to come across with something more intimate!"

I smiled, and as I walked out, pulled out my phone to call Helen back in Des Moines to ship some ASAP.

Chapter 5

Logic told me to start at the murder scene. The office was in the Denver Tech Center, west of I-25 off Belleview Avenue. Waterton Albers New Networking Systems had their own multi-storied building, all shiny glass and metal, a modern shrine they had built from their mega-revenues.

Since the weather was typical of this time of year, warm and sunny, I had zipped down on the Harley, parking in the visitor space. There was a separate lot for employees, which you couldn't access by vehicle without a magnetic keycard. But there was no issue walking in and looking around. It was four levels high, normally packed with cars, but with today being a weekend, it was only about a third full. I made my way up the stairs to the top level, where the murder had taken place. Looking around, I found the spot, a stain where the blood had flowed, still showing. It had been months, so I didn't expect to find anything, but still, I was a thorough person who liked to look at everything with my own eyes. I pulled out my phone to see the photos I had taken of the crime scene pictures. I imagined where the car sat, how the body was found and tried to play out the events in my head.

Aaron would have come out from the west-side stairwell, which was nearest to his car, either by himself, joined or led by someone, late that night. Once in the vehicle he was attacked, beaten and then shot in the leg. But why? Were they trying to get information out of him? If so, did they succeed and then they killed him? And why kill him outside the car and not inside? Did he try to escape and then was shot? Not likely, since he would have been shot in the back, whereas the Coroner says the bullet entered from the front. You would think killing him in the car would make more sense, as no one would likely find the body until morning. Of course, if it was a professional hit, they likely wouldn't care. Murdering him was possibly a message for all to see. A warning to anyone else. Mandy seemed to think he might have found something which may have gotten him murdered. Could others have known as well? Right now, it was all conjecture.

I started walking around looking for the security cameras. There were several light poles on each corner, each with a mounted camera. All had good viewing angles of the upper level, and would have revealed much had they been working. Being a networking company, they could have easily arranged them to be down, if they were involved. It was convenient they were offline that night, which was something I couldn't easily ignore. In a few minutes I might be able to ask this very question, as coming towards me was an electric motorized cart carrying what appeared to be two security guards, each one armed. They pulled up next to me, stepping out and flanking me, each with a hand on their unsnapped holster. I figured now was not an appropriate time to run.

"Don't move, sir," said the first guard, tall enough to play small forward in the NBA.

"I wouldn't think of it," I replied.

"What are you doing here?" asked the second guard, who could have only been in the NBA if he was Spud Webb.

"Looking over the crime scene," I answered. I kept my unassuming, non-dangerous smile in place.

"What crime scene?" asked Spud, his hand shaking slightly over the gun handle.

"The murder of Aaron Bailey. One of your employees. I'm trying to get a sense of what happened."

"What business is it of yours?" said the tall one.

"I'm a private detective. I've been hired to find his killer."

They each turned their heads, looking at the other. I was hoping they weren't deciding who got to shoot me!

"Call it in," commanded Spud to the other. "I would suggest you get comfortable and sit on the ground with your hands where we can see them."

I did as I was told, thankful it was a lovely day. I hoped my sunscreen was going to hold out under the dense UV rays of the Mile-High City. I heard the tall one talking on his portable radio, though couldn't make out completely what he was saying, as he turned when speaking into the microphone. Once he was done they both stood there ready to act, if I got aggressive. But I only smiled their way and after about fifteen minutes another cart showed up, with someone in a suit and tie straight off a *GQ* photo shoot. He walked over in front of the two guards and opened his coat to show me his shoulder holster, with a shiny silver gun. I guess he was trying to impress me, as if his gun was any more threatening than the other two.

"Is your gun made of the same material as the building?" I quipped. "The sun reflecting off it is blinding me!"

He didn't even blink at my humor.

"I'm the head of security, and I'm about to have you arrested for trespassing. So, you better give me a good reason not to call the police."

"May I reach into my back pocket and show you my ID?"

"Show me where it is, and I'll grab it. But if you do anything silly, I'll put you down."

I pointed to my rear cheek, and he came over and pulled it out. I wanted to do a leg whip and knock him on his ass, but the trigger-happy twins would probably shoot me at the slightest twitch.

"ID says you're Jarvis Mann, Private Detective," said the head of security. "What are you doing here?"

"Your name would be?" I asked.

"Head of security is all you need to know."

"Alright, Head. As I told your underlings, I'm here looking over the crime scene of Aaron Bailey. I've been hired to look into his murder."

I'm not sure he liked my pet name for him. But what else would I call him? I certainly wasn't going to say "sir."

"You should have checked in with us first."

"I didn't expect you'd let me on the scene."

"You are probably right."

"Walked up here on my own, figuring I'd ask forgiveness later." I paused a second, then spoke as if I were a child. "Forgive me."

He didn't seem happy with my quip.

"Who hired you?"

"I'm not at liberty to divulge that information."

"And we are not at liberty to allow you to snoop around our building. You will walk out of here, never to return."

"Gee, I'd think you'd want to find out who killed one of your employees."

"It is a matter for the police."

"For me as well. I'm licensed for this work. I will do my job, with or without your help. It will be harder, but I'll get to the bottom of who killed him. Helping me might be in your company's best interest, if you want the killer found."

"Of course, we do. It's a matter of not dragging our enterprise down in the process."

"Nothing would drag it down, unless someone at WANN was involved."

"Which is absurd."

"Maybe. Or could it be the head of security doesn't want to look bad, being he let it happen on his watch. And didn't make sure the security monitoring system was working properly. Or is that a frequent problem, it failing?"

"I was not head of security when it happened. The man in charge was relieved of his job shortly afterwards. Our company takes this type of situation seriously. The failure required changes be made."

"Or a fall guy be found. It would be good to talk with him and get his thoughts. Can you tell me his name?"

"Not going to happen."

"How about the guard who called the murder in. Is he working today? Or did you let him go too? Maybe it's one of these two strapping young lads."

"We don't work the night shift," stated Spud, before getting a tense look from his boss for saying anything.

"We will speak of this no further," said the head of security. "Now start walking out of here before I lose my temper."

I didn't need the names, since I already had them from the report. Now I needed to find them. I got up and headed towards the stairwell, the taller guard following me about ten feet behind. Once we reached the bottom the two carts were waiting, just in case I'd done something rash. I reached my bike and waved goodbye, riding off now knowing Aaron Bailey's former employer was not going to help me any. That told me something, though I wasn't sure what it was—at least yet.

Chapter 6

April had set up a rendezvous with the first officer to arrive on the murder scene. He was on duty today, but had some spare time to meet. I pulled up and waited in a nearly empty shopping center on the corner of South Broadway and West Belleview. It was empty because the Kmart that occupied a huge section of this corner had very few customers. It was hard to believe the place was still open, given the financial shape of the once-mighty retailer. I stood beside my bike enjoying the warm day. The season had been hot and dry, not unlike most summers in Denver, even though the masses complained otherwise. In about ten minutes a Denver Police car pulled up and the driver put down his window.

"Are you Jarvis?" said the baritone voice.

"I am. You must be Officer Bale."

"Yes."

"Aren't you a little out of your district?"

"Dropping off a suspect in Littleton and was on my way back. April said you wanted to talk to me about a crime scene I was first to arrive at."

"Yes. Aaron Bailey, the computer engineer for WANN systems who was murdered. Happened a few months back."

"Sure. April says you are a PI working the case for the widow. She said you were pretty cool and that Mallard gave the OK to talk with you about it."

April had stretched the truth some, but I didn't mind, especially the cool reference. I'm sure Mallard would be thrilled for my help, as always.

"April is pretty cool herself," I said.

"Yes, she is, and a sweet lady. How long have you known her?"

"A little while now. She provides me information when I need it. Normally I go through Bill Malone as well."

"Bill is a good guy too. I asked April out a couple of times, but she doesn't like going out with cops. Or so she said."

"Probably thinks two people armed with mace and handcuffs is one too many."

Bale smiled and then stopped to check something on the computer that was anchored down on the center console. After clicking away at the screen, he turned back to face me.

"What information are you looking for?"

"Mostly want to know what you recall when you arrived. I read your report, but it's always good to hear it firsthand."

"Sure. Let me call into dispatch."

He quickly called in, using one of the fancy ten-codes you always heard the police use, this one saying he was on a break or talking to a cool PI. He stayed in his car with the engine running. He filled the seat, a large black man who worked out, as his arms bulged at his shirtsleeves. If he hadn't been a multi-sport participant, I would have been surprised. He couldn't have been much older than twenty-five, and from what April mentioned had not been on the force for too many years.

"Are you looking for anything in general?" he said. "It has been a while, so the memory is a little foggy."

"No, just whatever you can tell me is helpful. Like when you first showed up, what did you see?"

"The call came in as a man down, at the top of the parking garage. I rolled and was the first to arrive. I drove up and saw the car there. I approached from the passenger side, as I recall, so I didn't see him until I got out of my unit. He was down and there was a security guard standing nearby. I asked him to step away and lie on the ground, face down until I had some backup. Another car arrived a couple minutes after me, and that is when we checked on the body and determined he was dead."

"The garage gate was up?"

"Yes, the guard said their boss told them to open it, since they knew the police were coming."

"Anything odd about the WANN guard?"

"Not really. Normal rent-a-cop type. Heavy set, carrying a gun. He said he was the one that called it in. But we needed to be certain he wasn't the killer. One never knows, and we need to cover all angles."

"How was the body positioned?"

"He was leaning against the driver's side, his back against the door. A lot of blood on his chest, leg and on the pavement. You could tell from the blood loss he was dead."

"No sign of a weapon? Or who did it?"

"Not when we arrived. Of course, once it was known he was

dead the detectives and crime scene teams took over. We get pushed back and mostly do traffic control. Once Mallard arrived he took my statement and that of the officer who showed up afterwards. Then it was mostly paperwork and making sure no one trampled on the scene."

"Did the WANN guard do any trampling?"

"As I recall, he touched the body. Wanted to see if he was alive and needed tending to. Not smart on his part, since like I said, with the blood loss it was obvious there was no hope for him. Besides, he wasn't using gloves. Crime scene folks were not happy about it either."

A car drove past us, curious about what was going on. I smiled and wondered if I looked like an informant. Or a criminal.

"Anything else you recall?"

"Yeah, one thing. I do remember someone high up, saying he was with security, showed up. He kept trying to crash the crime scene. Mallard was not a happy guy and yelled at us to take control and if necessary arrest anyone who didn't comply. This one guy was an asshole, and I about had to wrestle him to the ground to get him to back off."

"Do you know his name?"

"No. But he was dressed to the nines. Expensive suit and shoes, with a shiny gun under his jacket that he must have polished every day. But he was real concerned about the company name being smeared. Didn't seem all that bothered about the death of one of his employees."

"I think we met earlier today. Anything else you can add?"

He reached down to grab his drink cup and took a long draw though the straw.

"Sorry, that was about all I can recall. As I said, not much more than what was probably in the report."

"No, you gave me some other details. May not mean much but everything is important in a case like this. I appreciate the help. If you are ever around the DU area, stop into Boone's. If I'm there stop by and I'll buy you a beer. If not, tell the bartender and he'll put it on my tab. April even hangs out there at times. Maybe a chance to get to know her better."

"Something to keep in mind," he said, laughing. "But I'll have to pass on the beer, as I don't drink alcohol."

"How about chicken wings or ribs?"

"Wings are a vice, so yes, I'd take you up on that."

"No worse than donuts."

Bale started laughing.

"I'll take a dozen wings over a dozen Krispy Kremes any day."

"They will pull your union card for that statement," I said with a smile. "Do you have any thoughts on what happened at the murder scene? So far, they are calling it a robbery gone bad."

"Not really. Being a street cop, you don't get into the whys or how's. Just try to keep the peace and maybe occasionally prevent a crime. The detectives get to do all the heavy thinking. Be nice to catch the bastard who did this. What about you? Do have any thoughts on what happened?"

"Not yet," I said with a smile. "I'm just beginning the heavy thinking, and I hope I don't sprain a muscle."

Chapter 7

The day was winding down, so I went home. I parked my bike next to another in the parking lot, sharing the space, since parking was in short supply. Kate's Harley was similar, though a couple years newer. She had ridden a lot more miles than I had, having cycled for years. After dropping off my helmet, jacket and gloves, I stopped by the salon to say "hi."

Once she saw me Kate came over and gave me a hug. We were close friends now, thanks to the help I gave her last year, assistance which in the end saved her and her kids' lives. I now had free haircuts for life, but lately I was letting it grow out, especially in back.

"Need a trim?" she asked with a smile.

"No, I'm liking it the way it is right now. Looking for change, for some reason."

"I understand. How about we dye it blond?"

I laughed.

"No, I like my natural brown hair color."

"No gray, at least yet, to worry about like me. We women love to mess with our hair color. It's the simplest thing we can change about ourselves."

Which was true, as Kate recently had dyed hers an auburn color with some pink highlights. It seemed every six months or so, she would try something new with her color or hairstyle.

"The length is probably more about me being lazy right now. I'm not too worried about how I look at the present."

"Nothing new from Melissa?"

She knew the whole story of what happened, as I'd spilled the beans shortly after.

"No. I don't expect anything to change."

"Hard to forgive a man for cheating. I did once with Jack, but couldn't a second time."

"She has a right. I'm having a tough time forgiving myself."

"I've known you for a while now, and have seen you with some of the ladies who've worked here and you dated, if you want to call it that. It might not be in your nature to be a one-woman man."

I'd come to the conclusion myself, only wasn't certain why. If I examined it hard enough, maybe I'd find the answer. For now, work would be my shelter from the hurt. Help me to fend off the internal self-analysis. Small talk with the ladies didn't hurt either. I spent a few minutes saying "hello" to the others there, all happy to see me, the light and joyful conversation pushing the pain to one side. Once done, I returned to my home-office to make some dinner. Food options were limited, so I stuck with a ham and cheese sandwich on wheat, and a few low-fat chips, which was an oxymoron, washing it down with some lemon iced tea I'd made the day before. Once the stomach was full, I turned to my computer to begin research.

The Internet was a vast wasteland of information, which in this case would provide me with a bevy of innuendo, mixed with facts, about Waterton Albers New Networking Systems. Using various search strings, I found numerous articles and printed them out, finding the printed page easier to study than on the computer screen, since there was so much to absorb. I took to the sofa and started sorting through it all.

The company was founded nearly two decades ago by two college students, Burton Waterton and Logan Albers. Both had complementary computer skill sets. Burton's strength was in computer programming and languages, while Logan was the designer, with hardware smarts and business skills. They had been roommates in college, having clicked as friends, and soon were talking about building a business, bouncing ideas off each other, and working on concepts in their dorm room in their free time. Since their families had money to float them, they leased some small warehouse space near their campus when they needed more room. With used computers and servers, they found cheaply, they began building their networking empire, taking many years to see any gains in the industry. They first designed an operating system language, making it as lightweight and simple to use as possible, borrowing from others in the process, though not so much that they would expose themselves to lawsuits. As in many industries, borrowing in the tech world was common. The idea was to sell it to others to install on their hardware and make a killing. When few wanted it, they decided to manufacture the hardware to go with it, and slowly build the business a client at a time. Using tech conferences and press events, the two men together were impressive in front of a crowd. They were billed by many in the media as the two-headed Steve Jobs. It would seem they could turn shit into shinola. *Though that wasn't a motto or logo you'd care to have plastered on the side of your building, or printed on your marketing materials.*

Burton was the tech genius, who could code like few others. Many other tech companies tried to hire him in college and then away from their new-founded business in its early days, when it was struggling. But he stuck with it even though the company nearly folded on a couple of occasions. Logan, with his business and sales skills, worked the streets for financing during the challenging times, bringing in the needed capital when all seemed doomed. A couple of eleventh-hour deals saved them on two occasions, the last one providing an infusion of capital that put them over the top, where they never looked back. Their yearly revenue now pushing one billion dollars and seemingly growing. Though with razor-thin margins—the profits did not match some of the other big boys in the industry. Nevertheless, they were a force in the tech world to be reckoned with, as the other tech giants were leery of them, always watching in their rearview mirrors.

Down to the more personal information, Burton was married with four kids. He had a house in the Silicon Valley, as well as houses in Hawaii and Florida. He was athletic, playing tennis, racquetball and golf. His collection of antique motorcycles was extremely valuable. His wife, Judy, did lots of charitable work for the homeless and children growing up in poverty. All their kids were either in high school or college, the youngest a sophomore, the oldest working on his masters at Cal. All in their lives appeared perfect and squeaky-clean. Really too clean, as I had to wonder if this was all part of the publicity machine of a large corporation.

Logan, though, had been married for thirteen years, but was now divorced, with only one child, a girl, who went to Stanford. The breakup between him and his wife Lyndi, apparently because of her infidelity, was fairly private, but some tabloids through the Internet search played it up for a few months, with various gossip items, before tiring and moving onto something which provided more one-clicks. The biggest story was the large settlement she received, even though she was at fault. Nothing ever concrete was learned, but it appeared Logan may not have been as faithful as portrayed in the press releases. Corporate PR working in his favor. His passion, beyond the business world, was traveling to Las Vegas. He was a high roller welcomed at several casinos. Rumors again claimed he could drop many thousands of dollars playing blackjack, Texas Hold'em and craps. Now that he was single again, he was often seen at many of the Vegas shows with an entourage of young women and men, throwing around money like he could print it at will.

I then turned my attention to Aaron and Mandy. I did a blanket search of their names and found very little. Most led back to Facebook. Once there, I found Aaron's Facebook page had been removed. The caching of the search engines still held the link, but when I clicked it, said it no longer existed. As for Mandy, her profile page hadn't been updated in months, and earlier postings had only been pictures of her and Aaron out and about. It seemed they liked hiking and biking together. Various milestones, birthdays and anniversaries, were listed. It was plain and boring. Trying other searches led to nothing. Their digital fingerprint was insignificant.

I grew tired of the research, as darkness filled my windows. I checked my cell phone for text messages, but nothing was there. Somewhere deep inside, I'd hoped for a message from Melissa, saying she'd forgive me again. But it was wishful thinking. I had to get on with my life, but was struggling. I stretched out on the sofa and dozed off, as I'd done almost exclusively since the breakup, not caring to sleep in what now seemed like an immense bed by myself.

Chapter 8

Deep sleep was hard to claim, but I was off and moving the next day, after a hot, then cold shower revived my senses. From the police I had the name of the former head of security of the WANN Denver office, along with an address. Mitchell Crabtree lived in Englewood in a nice neighborhood just off Cherry Hills, where many of the city's millionaires lived. Though only a few blocks from the high tax bracket, his housing was modest and not extravagant, but still worth several hundred thousand. I decided to show up unannounced and see what I'd find. If he wasn't home, I would work from there. But he was, and stood in his driveway under the hood of his seventies cherry-red Corvette Stingray. Walking up from the curb where I'd parked my Harley, I approached him smiling.

"Good morning," I stated, from a distance so I didn't startle him.

"Hello," he replied, peering around the edge of the hood. "What can I help you with?"

"Are you Mitchell Crabtree?" I asked.

"I am."

From his bent position he stood up and began wiping his greasy hands on a towel. He was quite tall, maybe 6' 4", with a slender, solid build, dressed in dirty jeans and a dirty-white T-shirt with more holes than a prairie-dog field. He had chestnut brown medium-length hair, with sideburns trimmed to the bottom of his earlobe and a day-old unshaven face. He was likely in his mid-to-late forties, and though he looked good for his age, one could tell by his appearance he was unemployed, passing the time. He stepped around to look me over, his eyes leery of what my mission was. Maybe he sensed who I was, as he didn't stick out his hand, yet they were dirty from the engine work.

"Call me Mitch."

"Good to meet you, Mitch," I said. "I'm Jarvis Mann, and I wanted to see if you had a few minutes to answer some questions."

"Well, you certainly aren't a Jehovah's Witness," he stated. "Enough of them come knocking on the door trying to sell their religion that I can spot them a mile away. And you don't dress well enough to be a cop. So, are you private?"

I guess my jeans and T-shirt weren't much better than his. Though at least they were clean. I showed him my ID.

"I wasn't sure until you made the comment about answering some questions. The bike threw me a little too. A Harley Softail, I would guess."

"Yep. Helps clear my mind and allows me to think without phones or radio distracting me."

Mitch tossed the towel on the front grille, his hands as clean as they would get.

"Would love to ride. Been so close to buying one on several occasions, but the wife won't let me. Says they are dangerous."

"No more so than being the head of security, it would seem."

"Can't argue there. I'm guessing this is about the parking lot killing?"

"It is. I wonder what you can tell me about it."

"Not much, if anything. Part of my release from my job was not to discuss it."

"Are they paying you?"

"Yes. My full salary for six months."

"Wow, pretty generous of them."

"I thought so. I'm not poor, but it's nice not having to work too hard to put food on the table. Allows me time to find the right position. They even promised to give me a glowing recommendation."

"So why did they can you?"

He leaned back onto the padded covered front fender of the Corvette, thinking about what he could tell me.

"Scapegoat," he said.

"Had to fire someone to look like they were doing something about what happened."

He nodded.

"So why you?"

"I was in charge."

"Were you there that night?"

Again, he paused and shook his head no.

"You weren't directly responsible?"

"My team, my fault."

"How did you feel about being blamed?"

29

"Didn't leave me dancing in the aisles. The severance lessened the sting."

"Any thoughts on why the security cameras failed?"

"Technology sucks!"

I had to laugh.

"Even when used by a technology company?"

"The computer world is full of bugs. WANN Systems technology is no different."

"Did it fail often?"

Once more a pause.

"I only recall one other time."

"How long had the system been in place?"

"Long as I'd been there. Nearly six years, with a few software upgrades over time."

"Any upgrades recently?"

"No."

"Technology-wise, this system was pretty solid."

"Yes."

"Hard for me to ignore it failing during the exact moment of the killing. Coincidences do happen, but they don't lead me anywhere. Which makes me wonder if it was tampered with?"

"No comment."

"Was tampering considered? Was there an investigation?"

No words, only a frown.

"And if it weren't for the gag order, would you provide conjecture?"

This time he smiled, but remained silent. I had to believe he was agreeing with my theory.

"Any thoughts on what will happen if I continue to dig into this?"

He took his right hand and chopped down onto his left forearm.

"They have friends in low places to provide strong-armed support?" I asked.

This time he touched his nose.

"I need to watch my back?"

A very slight nod. He was telling me a lot when saying so little.

"Do you know anything about your replacement?"

"The new head of security. I would assume it was my assistant, Blake Zorn."

"Nice dresser. Definitely not off the rack."

"That would be him."

"I believe I ran into him looking over the crime scene. Wasn't too pleased I was poking into their business. Any thoughts you can share about him that won't violate the agreement."

He didn't hesitate in responding. "Asshole."

"Straight and to the point."

"Not much else I can add. He tried to undermine me every day he could. Brown-nosing for a promotion the day he started."

"How long had he worked there?"

"A couple years."

"If he was like that, why didn't you get rid of him?"

"I didn't hire him, so I couldn't fire him. I had no say in the matter."

"Well, that certainly sucks."

You could see the anger building in his eyes, but he stopped to take a few deep breaths.

"Best I not talk about him. Only pisses me off and gets my blood pressure up."

I decided to change the subject to something he would enjoy.

"What year is the Corvette?"

"1970. Mileage is low for an older vehicle. I don't drive her much."

He slid into the driver's seat and started her up. She sounded as if she'd been driven off the lot brand new today.

"Wow, she sounds perfect."

"Lots of arduous work to keep her running like this. Now I have the time to baby her even more."

"I have a '69 Mustang when I'm not riding the Harley. Though she's not in as good a shape as the Corvette, and is pushing 400K on the mileage."

"If you take care of her, she could go for some time. Those cars were built to last. Unlike the crap now you drive off the lot."

"She gets as good a treatment a detective on the go can give her. Now that I have the bike I figure she can last that much longer."

He turned in his seat, allowing the 'Vette to idle.

"I probably can guess. But who hired you for this case?"

"I have to give you a no comment on that."

"I should know better. Are you hiring?"

"I'm a single-man operation, most of the time. Occasionally I need some backup. Do you have a resume?"

He laughed.

"Not on me, but I can tell you I keep my mouth shut, can handle a gun and I'm skilled working on cars?"

It was my turn to laugh.

"I already knew this, being a trained detective, other than the gun part. Are you ex-military or worked in the police department?"

"Army eight years, working in the military police. I did a little sniper training and was pretty good, but didn't like it. After I got out I did security work for various companies before joining WANN Systems. Not the job of my dreams, but the pay was fantastic."

"If I hired you to help me with this case, could you enlighten me more on what the hell is going on?"

"No comment."

At least he was consistent.

"By the looks and sound of the Corvette, maybe I should hire you as my mechanic. What about bodywork? Can you patch bullet holes?"

"Hell, yes!" he said while revving the engine. "I'm a magician with Bondo."

If WANN Systems had the muscle he alluded to, this might be the case where I'd get to test all his magical skills.

Chapter 9

As I left Mitch's place I noticed a tail. It was a good-sized white Chevy Tahoe, and from what I could see in my mirrors had at least two people in front and one in back. There was no front plate, so my only hope of getting a number would be getting behind them. They were keeping their distance as best as possible, but in Denver traffic it was hard to hide too much, especially after I took several right turns in a row and they were with me all the way.

My initial plan had been to go home and grab some lunch, but I decided to take them for a ride. I did a U-turn and headed for the highway. I-25 was normally crowded on a workday through the Denver Tech Center, so I took the onramp on Belleview and headed south, finding my top speed quickly. The fun of a motorcycle is you can move in and out of tight traffic more easily than a vehicle, especially something as large as a Tahoe. Putting some distance between me and them, I exited at Dry Creek. I pulled over to the side and dismounted, putting my helmet and leather jacket on the grass. Up ahead was a man holding a sign asking for help, for he didn't have a job. I walked over to him with money in hand.

"For twenty dollars can I hold your sign for a few minutes?" I asked him.

"Sure. I could use a break," he replied. "I'm frying in this hot sun."

"Any handouts are yours as well. I need to wait here for someone."

"Be my guest."

He took the money and walked over to his bag and stuffed the twenty away. Sitting down, he grabbed some water and relaxed in the midday sun. His clothes were worn, but at least he didn't smell of booze.

I kept my eyes on the cars coming down the ramp. If they missed me exiting, then I'd miss my chance and would just drive on. But if they did come down I'd have a surprise for them and hopefully a plate number to work with. A couple of cars stopped and handed me some money. I smiled and thanked each one, stuffing the fives and ones in my pocket. It still amazed me how generous people could be, even in a world where terrorists kill and bomb innocent citizens for no reason, other than a warped vision of their faith.

From a distance I saw the white SUV exiting. I held the sign up to my face, so they couldn't tell it was me. I wasn't dressed much better than anyone you'd see on the corner looking for handouts, so they had no reason to think otherwise. They slowed down when they saw the bike and received a couple of honks from the cars behind them, angry they weren't moving fast enough. I walked past them holding the sign, as they wouldn't be in a giving mood. From my back pocket I pulled out the buck knife I kept in the saddle bags of the Harley, went around to the back side and cut the tire stem in one motion. They started moving forward as the light changed but didn't get too far as the tire went flat in a manner of seconds, followed by the wail of more horns by the angry cars trying to get through the snarling traffic maze. In rush hour people had little patience. The SUV was partway in the intersection when they finally stopped realizing what had happened, the tire rim on the pavement not allowing more movement. I hustled back to the homeless man, handed him his sign and money, then ran back to my bike, gearing up quickly, starting the engine with a good roar. There was no rear plate either, only a temporary tag in the rear window, impossible to make out through the heavily tinted glass. When they stepped out I quickly took pictures with my phone, so I could better recognize them later.

I roared off on my motorcycle honking at them as I drove past, leaving the trio unhappy. Their shouts echoed in my ears as I rode home, causing me to snicker as the wind blew into my face, the shield up to allow the breeze to cool me on this warm day.

At home, I pulled up the pictures on my phone and zoomed them in. Since the resolution was pretty good on my camera phone, the faces were crystal clear. I cropped the photos as best I could and made a call to Denver Police Headquarters. Bill Malone answered on the first ring, since he was back today at his desk.

"Bill, it's Jarvis, how is your day?" I asked.

"Normal busy day dealing with the dregs of society," he replied.

"Well, I hope I'm not one of the dregs. How is the family doing?"

"All is good. Ray did some spring football and is looking sharp on the field, with Raven keeping him well grounded. Monika has her first boyfriend, which I hate. And Rachael is wonderful and the glue that keeps me going. Life in general is boring and I love it."

"Good to hear. Believe it or not, I didn't call to get a family update. I need a favor?"

"I'm stunned."

I smiled. Bill was so stoic with his responses it made me laugh.

"I have a couple of pictures to send your way. When you have time can you run them through the system and see if you get a hit on them?"

"When I have time? If you want to wait until then, I'll never get to them."

"Then sometime today would be perfect."

"And what did they do?"

"They were following me. I think it's related to this new case I have."

"What is it about you that brings about unsavory people?"

"My charming personality, I suppose. Honestly, I'd prefer not to have them on my back, but I can't always choose my clients and thugs that seem to gravitate to them. When they come knocking, I need the work to pay the bills."

"OK, I can run it later today. You know our system is pretty slow, so likely won't have anything until tomorrow."

"Tomorrow will be wonderful. And worth a beer."

There was a pause.

"Sorry to hear about Melissa."

"No one to blame but myself. How did you hear?"

"April mentioned it. Not a real surprise, since it's your M.O. But still, I'm sorry to see it happen."

"Yes, so was I."

"You made a good couple."

"We did, but maybe it's for the better. With everything going on these days, it's not safe having a girlfriend to use against me. Besides, it allows me and my right hand to get better acquainted after all this time being apart."

Bill laughed out loud, which was a rarity. Strangely enough I was happy someone found humor in my personal pain.

Chapter 10

Before leaving his place, Mitch gave me his number, in case I needed to ask more questions. I called him a couple of times but didn't get an answer. After being tailed I wondered if they had seen me at his place. I had no real reason to believe they would go and bother him, other than a gut feeling. I hopped on my bike and drove back over in the afternoon heat.

From a distance I saw the flashing red lights. When I got close enough I saw a fire engine, the men hosing down the Corvette, now a charred, burnt memory of what it used to be. A classic no more. Since the street was blocked, I parked further down and walked, getting as close as I could. I saw Mitchell standing there, happy to see he hadn't been harmed, beyond a bruise on his cheek, an ice pack held to battle the swelling. He was talking with a police officer, so I stayed back for now, mingling with a crowd of neighbors watching on.

"What happened?" I asked a thirtysomething woman, standing in tight shorts and tank top.

"Some men in a big SUV showed up and assaulted Mitch," she said. "They then tossed something into his car, I think it was a signal flare, and it started on fire. We heard the commotion and called the authorities."

"Any ideas what it was about?"

"Nope. Seemed totally random."

"Mitch is such a nice guy," said the man standing next to her, also in shorts and tank top. "Hard to believe anyone would want to hurt him."

"Did you get a good look at the SUV?" I asked. "Get a plate number?"

"No plate," said the woman. "It was white and big. They all look the same to me, so I couldn't tell you a make or model."

"It was a Chevy of some kind," added the man. "Looked like three guys total. I saw two of them climb back in before his car started on fire. The driver was behind the wheel waiting. They looked dangerous, so I didn't want to step in. The type to be carrying guns."

"Description?"

"European, I would guess. I couldn't hear much. Once they left I went over to help Mitch up and get him away from the car. You could see he was hurting, though likely more about the car than the welt on his face. He really loved that car."

We stood around and talked some more, then one of the officers came over and started asking questions. Since I didn't see what happened, I told them I couldn't provide any information. But it was likely the same three whose tire I'd flattened earlier. I hung around until the commotion died down and everyone left. Mitch stayed at home, refusing to go to the hospital. I walked over to see if I could help.

"Did you know the guys who did this?" I asked.

"No."

"Any ideas on why?"

"Maybe because I talked with you."

"Talked is an overstatement. You hardly said a word, other than about your car."

"Apparently I said enough."

"How did they know?"

"Must have been watching."

I didn't immediately spill the details of them following me after I left. I had failed to pick up the tail earlier. If I had, then who knows.

"Did they mention me?"

"Yes. They said if I talked with you again it would be worse. Threatened my wife and kid."

He pulled off the ice pack, and I could see the swelling and bruising skin. It would heal but would be sore for several days.

"Sorry. Maybe I should leave."

"That might be best."

"What are you going to do?"

"Take a vacation and leave town for a while. The wife and I are due for some R&R. And my son is away at summer camp for another week."

"Anything else you'd care to tell me?"

"Watch your back. They will be paying you a visit."

"They already did and failed."

I held up my phone to show him the photos I took.

"Yes, those are the men."

"Go get packed and I'll hang around in case they come back. I don't want you or anyone in your family hurt."

"If they show up, what will you do?"

I opened my jacket to show him my Beretta.

"Possibly shoot them. A just punishment for destroying a classic car."

Though it hurt to do so, Mitch grinned.

Chapter 11

Mitch's wife showed up and gasped when she saw the Corvette. She seemed a little leery of me, even after Mitch told her who I was, giving her the details of what happened. They each quickly packed and drove away, as I made sure no one followed them. I felt better they were out of harm's way, a little concerned I had fueled the confrontation. It appeared wherever I went these days I was a powder keg of trouble waiting to be ignited.

I drove home to get my car, as it was getting late and I was scheduled to meet Bill at Boone's. It was supposed to be earlier, but since I got hung up, I called him, and he said we could meet after his dinner at home. It was around 7 p.m. when I arrived. Taking a seat at the bar, I ordered two beers and some ribs for my own nourishment. Bill showed up shortly after in street clothes, taking a stool next to me.

"Thanks," he said while sipping the beer. "My favorite brand."

"I know, anything with suds," I joked.

"So long as it's cold. You look tired and smell of smoke."

"I was near a burning classic car."

He turned on his stool to look at me.

"Hopefully not a Mustang," Bill asked.

"No, a Corvette. Cherry red, though now it's burnt red. I was questioning a witness, and someone didn't like me talking with him. Forced him to leave town."

"Wow, you sure seem to get into pickles these days. A new case?"

"Yes. Wife of the computer programmer shot and killed a couple months ago at WANN Systems over in the Tech Center."

"Sure, I remember that case. Ruled a robbery. I'm guessing someone doesn't think so."

"The widow. She says he knew of something illegal going on in the company. No hard facts, but after today I'm starting to think she is right. The boys that torched the Corvette are the same ones in the picture I gave you to identify."

"Started the search before I left. Like I said, our system is slow with facial recognition. When I get in tomorrow I'll see if it found something and let you know."

Bill had been helping me for a few years now, providing information the police had easier access to than I did. He grumbled about it, but always came through. And I'd helped his college son out of a jam, which didn't hurt either. He was probably the closest thing I had to a best friend. Of course, if I said this out loud he'd punch me.

"So how are you holding up?" he asked.

"As well as can be expected. The last few months have been tough. Trying to bury myself in work. Keeps my brain occupied."

"With all of Ray's issues last year, I worked to get through the day. When you sit around with nothing to do, you dwell too much."

"Or drink," I said, while ordering myself a second beer.

"Don't do too much of that. The bottom of a bottle is never the cure."

I knew this all too well. As too much drinking had led me down the infidelity road.

"Three tonight is my limit."

"Hold him to it, will you, Nick?"

Nick the bartender smiled, and nodded his head.

"What game is on tonight?" asked Bill.

"Yankees and Red Sox."

"Oh, boy."

"Yep, always good for ratings."

"But bad for those of us who can't stand either team. Well, if there is nothing good on tonight, I'm going home to my wife. I'm assuming you will be able to get home safely."

"If I can't, Nick will set up a cot for me in the back."

Nick turned and gave me the evil eye.

"Or not!"

"Well, thanks for the beer, Jarvis. I'd shake your hand, but it's hard to say where it's been after your comment this afternoon."

I nodded my head and smiled.

"I washed my hands since then, I think…"

"I'll call you tomorrow with what the computer finds."

Now that Bill was gone I could concentrate on my ribs. They were meaty and falling off the bone. With a couple bones cleaned off I finished the second beer. My last one of the night hit the counter without delay, as Nick was always on top of things.

As I ate a couple more bones, I thought over the last two days' events. There appeared to be little doubt WANN Systems was covering up something. The circumstances of Aaron's death certainly were looking fishy. Time to poke the stick some more and see what surfaced. The question was where to go from here. I needed to talk with some co-workers and friends, preferably those closest to him. I received a few names from Mandy, so that is where I'd start tomorrow. Looking up at the screen I gnawed off the meat on my last bone and wiped my face, when I felt a hand on my shoulder. It was April, who now occupied the seat next to me.

"Missed a spot," she said, while taking her finger and wiping sauce from my cheek, then tasting it.

"Oh yes, you like the mild flavor," she said. "You need a little spice in your life."

Maybe she was talking about something else, but I left it alone.

"Heartburn would keep me up all night," I replied. "Been difficult enough sleeping lately." I looked her up and down. "You look nice tonight."

"Thanks for noticing."

April was no skinny, small thing. She had some meat on her, most of which was firm and strong. She was dressed in jeans and a baggy Rockies jersey, with black boots. She had grown her hair out and it was bleached out some because of the summer sun. With her boots on she stood a hair taller than me. She was tough, swore quite a bit, and was overt when speaking about pretty much any topic.

"Are you here alone?" I asked.

"No. Some lady friends and I are going to sit around, drink and gossip."

"Sounds exciting."

"The fun part will be us fending off every advance from the loser testosterone crowd we seem to attract. And possibly eyeball a few hotties we'd care to get horizontal with, were the mood right."

"And where would I land?"

"Hottie, for certain. I know my friend Jessica has been warm for your form since she laid eyes on you that night we first met here at Boone's."

Smiling, I looked over and saw Jessica. She was wearing tight shorts and a lacy off-the-shoulder top that barely held her braless chest. She waved, and I raised my glass to her.

"Hard to believe she is ever lonely," I stated.

"Oh, she isn't. She goes through men pretty quickly."

"You still haven't found Mister Right?"

"Nope. But I aim to bop every able-bodied man I can find to narrow the field."

She turned on the stool, looking me straight in the eye.

"Why don't you come join us," she said. "At the least you won't be bored. At the most, who knows…? Jessica might take you for a ride you'll not soon forget!"

"Thanks, April, but no. I'm not up to it tonight. Been a long day and all has not gone well."

"I can smell the smoke on you. Care to explain?"

I told her the story as she listened intently.

"Hardly your fault."

"No. But it seems with each step I take these days, someone is always getting hurt. I know it is part of the business, but still…"

"Shake it off and join us. No one will get hurt in our group."

"Maybe another time."

"You promise?"

I crossed my heart.

"I'm holding you to it. Take care, Jarvis."

She put her arm on my shoulder, hugging me from the side while squeezing my hand.

I finished up my beer and paid my tab. I said goodnight to Nick and stepped out the door. My mind was still wandering, and I felt like taking a walk in the darkening night. The air was warm and dry, with a touch of breeze. The full moon lit up the street as I strolled down Evans. If I'd been more alert, I'd have noticed the man following me sooner. I turned around as I came to the curb, and recognized him as one of the men from earlier in the day. From behind I heard a vehicle hop the sidewalk and two doors slam. Three men surrounded me in a flash. I instinctively reached for my gun, not finding it there, since I didn't bring it, and instantly knew I was in trouble.

Chapter 12

The three men had me cornered. I looked at each of them, trying to gauge a course of action. From what I could see of their faces they appeared to be related, since their facial features were similar. All were tall, about 6' 2" and two hundred-plus of solid pounds. Each had a smile on their face of confidence, knowing they had me. I smiled back to mask my fear of what was about to happen. My options were limited.

"Jarvis Mann," said the one directly in front of me. "The man who cut the stem on our tire and left us stranded in the middle of the intersection, where we had to change it out with angry passengers in cars all around us."

"Gee, I hope you didn't break a nail," I quipped. "I know a good manicurist who would give you a fair price. File and buff them back to the beauty an enforcer would be proud of to beat people up with."

Humor often relieved my tension, but often didn't endear me to my foes. The man in front of me stepped forward and took a swing. I tried raising my arm to block the punch, but was grabbed from behind, holding my arms down. The shot to the side of the head was jarring and I would have fallen if I hadn't been held up. Though my knees did buckle. He stepped back and let my cobwebs fade. It was a good shot, and I let him know it once the ringing cleared from my noggin.

"Good punch. Got all your weight into it. You must have boxed at one time."

"I did. And you can take a punch. I felt it all the way up my arm. Of course, no one can take repeated punches, especially when the puncher's knuckles have some help."

From his pocket he pulled out some brass knuckles and slid them over his right hand. It would be easier on his hand, but not my face and body. I'd needed to come up with something quick.

"What are you wanting from me?' I asked. "Maybe I can provide some answers without losing my teeth."

"Why were you talking to Mitchell Crabtree?"

"He had a cool car I was checking out."

By his face I could see he didn't buy it.

"I was selling magazine subscriptions?"

He smacked his brass-knuckled fist into his other hand.

"Girl Scout cookies?"

He was losing patience with my stalling.

"Someone hired you to nose around in our business. Who was it?"

"Hired me for what exactly?"

"The killing of Aaron Bailey."

"You know I can't tell you. In my business clients have the right to confidentiality."

"And you have the right, or maybe better yet, option, not to end up in the hospital with tubes handling your bodily functions. So, I'll ask you one more time. And if you refuse, I break a few ribs, we put you in the car and take you somewhere, and do even worse things to you."

The man behind me, holding my arms, was strong. I'd been slacking in the workout department recently and it was showing, as I couldn't pull free. There were a couple of moves I knew I could use, but would it be enough? As I was about to act I heard the click of heeled boots coming our way. I glanced over my shoulder and saw April walking up the sidewalk. The third man in the group moved towards her, motioning her to stop.

"Sweetie, please turn around and go the other way," he said to her.

April took two more steps, looking over the scene.

"I'm not allowed to join the party, darling?" she said in sultry voice. "Looks like three strong men having their way with this handsome gentleman. Maybe I'd like to partake in the fun."

The third man looked over at the brass-knuckled brute and laughed.

"If you care to join us, I'm sure we can have an enjoyable time with you after we've finished with Jarvis here."

"What did you have in mind?"

He looked her up and down liking what he saw.

"How about those sweet lips wrapped around my dick!"

April shook her head, not bashful at all in her response, licking her lips.

"Let me see what you've got. Need to make sure it measures up to my standards and will fit my mouth properly. And my mouth can handle a lot of erect manhood!"

"Oh, it does for sure, honey…"

He looked down to grab his zipper, when like a shot of lightning she kicked him square in the groin with her right boot. Down to the pavement he went in a grunt. The brass-knuckled man moved towards her but not quickly enough, as from her purse she pulled her handgun and pointed it straight at him. He froze in his tracks, as she was all business. With the distraction, I took my foot and stepped hard on the instep of the man holding me, and then used my elbow to smash him in the head. His yelp and cry of pain got him to release me, and I stepped over next to April, thankful for the assistance.

"Those of you not already on the ground, get down now," she said. "Face down and hands behind your head. Anyone moves will get shot."

"Who the hell are you?" said the leader of the group.

"Your friendly neighborhood cop," replied April. "Trying to keep the peace and help my friend. Please don't make me have to ask you again."

He did not look happy, but did as he was told, waving for the one whom I gave the head shot to do the same.

"Jarvis, call it in please."

I pulled my cell phone and dialed 911, giving April's name and badge number, which I knew by heart. In about three minutes four squad cars arrived, the flashing red lights circling the scene. Once there the officers frisked them, finding handguns on each, saps and, of course, the brass knuckles. None of them were carrying any ID. Paramedics arrived and provided ice for my face, but left the bruised-testicle man to his pain, knowing it would soon pass. After some time taking statements, the three men were hauled away and a tow truck called to impound their SUV. Once things started settling down I was able to speak with April.

"Lucky you were coming outside," I said. "You saved my butt. Though I was about to spring upon them a kick-ass move and wipe them out. This allows me to hold it in reserve for another time."

"I'm certain you had it handled, but you are welcome. How's the eye?"

I removed the ice pack to show her.

"Nothing too serious. I've had worse. And would have if he had torn into me with those brass knuckles."

She put her hand up to touch the spot and I cringed some. Some Advil would be required to sleep.

"So, were you following me?"

April looked a little embarrassed, which was a first for her.

"I saw you leave. Since you seemed a little down I wanted to make sure you were OK. I was coming out to confirm you could drive yourself home. I wasn't sure how much you'd had to drink."

"Well, I definitely owe you big time."

"Yes. I expect more than a couple of beers and chicken wings at Boone's as payback."

"What did you have in mind?'

"A nice dinner out. Somewhere without loud TVs playing some silly game with macho millionaires running around on grass."

"The least I can do for my savior."

"I was hoping for the *most* you can do, but it's a start."

I had to laugh and maybe blush, not that you could tell with the condition of my face. Even a macho man like myself found it kind of exciting having a woman step in and save my bacon. And the hint of playfulness in her tone warmed my downtrodden heart.

Chapter 13

The evening went to nearly midnight, as I spent time at the police station finishing up my statement. I offered to take April back to her car at Boone's, but she needed to stay even later, for she had a great deal more paperwork to fill out and interviews to give, since she had pulled her gun and was off duty. There would be an investigation, and I would need to testify on her behalf. She likely wouldn't be in trouble; it was just the normal red tape for an incident like this. I thanked her again, with new feelings for her, though I was uncertain what they were.

The next morning, I awoke, my face still swollen, the bruising around my eye even more noticeable after I'd finished showering. I looked in the mirror thinking a little makeup would hide the damage. But that would be against the hard-boiled detective code. Concealer and foundation were not in my gumshoe tool bag. The black and blue markings would make me look all the tougher. Toughness certainly was going to be important once again.

After a light breakfast I went to work out, knowing I needed to stay sharp on this case. I had to hone my strength to be able to break free from my assailants. A few of the regulars at the gym noticed the damage and commented—in a less than flattering way.

"Jarvis, did your girlfriend do that to you after she caught you with another woman?" said one man on the Nautilus machine next to me. It was amazing how word of infidelity had made the rounds.

"Nice shiner. Did you run into a door?" stated another.

I laughed off each of the comments, knowing the testicles of one of my assailants would be more colorful than my face. I'd take a bruised face over a damaged groin any day.

Once I finished my workout, I stopped by the station. Bill was there, and I waited for a free moment with him.

"Into another mess, I see," said Bill at his desk.

"Not my preference. Seems I'm on a hot streak these days."

"April is on paid leave right now. Doesn't look like any real trouble for her, but she can't work until they are done investigating. I'm sure you'll be called in."

"Hey, she saved my ass. Believe me, I'm grateful and will tell them exactly what happened. I'd be in pieces if she hadn't come along. She left that one boy with damage in his privates which will take a while to heal."

Bill grabbed a folder and tossed it my way.

"Are these the same men who were following you that you wanted me to track down?"

I opened the folder up and saw pictures and some basic information. They did appear to be from Russia or thereabouts.

"It is the same three. What did you find on them?"

"All three of them are related. Two are brothers and one a cousin. The main man, the one who struck you, is Aleksi Platov. He works within some Russian organized crime group. Couldn't get the name, and the FBI isn't sharing. He appears to be pretty nasty, as the Feds list him as dangerous and not to be approached without backup."

"I wished I'd known that before I'd disabled his tire."

"You tend to act foolishly sometimes."

"But my heart is pure."

Bill sneered at my words while uttering an obscenity.

"The one who was holding you was Petya Platov and is Aleksi's brother. The third one, who April kicked in the gonads, is Jasha Platov. Aleksi appears to be the straw that stirs the drink of the three. The other two are not Mother Teresa either. All are considered armed and extremely dangerous."

"Are they new in town?"

"Uncertain. But it could be they came in just to find a pain-in-the-ass detective sticking his nose in their business."

"Just my luck. Any ideas of ties to WANN Systems?"

"Not from what little we were able to access. Need higher clearance than a Denver cop, to get more."

"I have a friend in the FBI who'll happily help me."

"I doubt he'll be happy."

I laughed, though it hurt my face.

"Their lawyer is posting bail now. They'll be out on the street pretty soon."

"Who is representing them?"

"Bristol & Bristol."

"You are kidding. Is it Tony?"

"No, his brother, Don. It's not surprising, with their current clientele. And they are extremely good litigators."

"I may have to pay a visit to their offices. See if they are willing to share anything."

"I doubt you are on their favorites list right now, after what happened with Melissa."

I couldn't argue the point. But sometimes you had to do unpleasant things in this line of work. The worse that would happen would be I'd get tossed out on my ear. Though unlikely a five-hundred-dollar an hour lawyer could do that, even on my worse day.

"You may want backup on this case," said Bill. "A call to Sparks might be in order. These appear to be some nasty men."

"I can't go running to mother every time I need help. But I'll keep it in mind."

"Your funeral."

"Can I keep these?"

"They are your copies. The Denver police have a new budget designation, for covering the costs of assisting you."

This time I resisted laughing and only smiled, to avoid the pain. I left and went back to my place, vigilant to make sure no one was following or waiting for me. Vigilance was key. So was making sure I was armed wherever I went. This included in the bathroom, where I showered with my holster within easy reach. Once cleaned up and dressed, I pulled out my cell phone and dialed an Iowa number. It was answered on the second ring.

"Jarvis Mann," said FBI agent Bart Wilson, caller ID giving me away. "I hoped to never hear from you again, but apparently I'm not going to win the lottery on that one. What the hell do you want?"

"I'm so happy to hear your voice too," I replied. "I'm looking for a local FBI source here in Denver. Figured you could put in a good word so I can talk with them. I need some information on three Russian mob enforcers I've encountered recently. Apparently, there are some secrets about them the FBI won't share with the Denver police."

"What reason would we have to share with you?"

"Because you'd put in a good word for me after all the fine work we did together to bring down The Bull."

"And why would I pass off a pain in the ass to one of my colleagues?"

"If you don't, then I'll keep pestering you."

He may have snorted, I couldn't tell for certain.

"I'm sure there is someone in the Denver FBI office you don't care for, who you'd love to refer me to, just to piss them off."

"True."

There was a long pause. Either he was thinking or looking up a name.

"Dezmond Price. He is an agent who works there in Denver. Not one of my favorites. A tough SOB and a real jerk. You'll get along great. I'll give him a call and tell him to expect to hear from you. Give it a day before reaching out." He gave me a number to call.

Before I could say thanks, Wilson hung up on me. Always nice to have close friends in the Bureau. I would be sure to add him to my Christmas card list.

Chapter 14

I was set to meet with one of Aaron's closest friends for lunch. We were meeting in a large shopping complex where the old Stapleton Airport used to operate. Northfield Stapleton had everything a shopper could want in the way of retailers to max out your credit card, and many places to eat. Aaron's friend chose Jim 'N Nicks Bar-B-Q. Hard to turn down, though a little on the heavy side for lunch. But I would make do.

Walking in the door I found a geeky-looking thirtysomething male sitting at a table. Derek Skully was in baggy tan cargo shorts and a T-shirt which said Halestorm on it, which was a hard rock band. *Sometimes I was hip to the latest artists.* Tucked into his shirt was a napkin with barbeque sauce on it; portions of it were also on the edges of his lips from the ribs he was savoring. His red hair was cropped short and standing straight up, thanks to some type of gel. He had thick-rimmed beige glasses hanging off a flat nose. His skin was pale white, as if he'd never seen the sun. He stood up, his round body never meeting a meal it didn't finish, and wiped his digits on his napkin before shaking my hand.

"Sorry I didn't wait for you," he said, with a slightly high-pitched voice. "The food smelled so good and I was starving. I hope you don't mind."

I grinned as if to say, no problem. The aroma of the place was enticing.

"You can't miss with anything on the menu. You'll be dying for seconds and leftovers."

A waitress stopped by and I ordered a Classic Pulled Pork Sandwich and a soda. No need for a heavy meal, as I needed to stay light on my feet in case I encountered my Russian friends again.

"You were good friends with Aaron Bailey?" I asked.

"Yes, we were tight. I knew him in college."

"How did you meet?"

"We had several classes together. We were teamed up on a couple of tech projects and hit it off."

My soda arrived, and I took a long drink. It was mostly ice, so refills would be needed.

"You are a programmer, like he was?"

"Yes. I can do it all. You name the language and I can write it. Mostly C++, but so many others as well."

"Was he as good as you were?"

"Oh, hell no. He had skills, but he wasn't in my league."

Derek was not lacking in confidence.

"Were you both computer hackers as well?"

"Sure, I do some on the side. But Aaron wasn't that adept. He tried to come off as a white and black hat in the hacker community, but he didn't have the kind of skill most of us had. He talked a good game, but there were times I wondered what he really knew."

"White and black hats?" I asked.

"Oh sorry, I thought you knew the lingo. There are two types of hackers, the white hats, who do it for the good of everyone. Trying to find vulnerabilities in code and turn them in, to make software more secure. They can get paid for this by software companies. The black hats find the holes, but then exploit it for their own personal gain. Usually to steal and sell information on people. Though illegal, that is where the real money can be made. Of course, there are some who do a little of both?"

"And that would be you and Aaron?"

"Aaron, I believe, tried to stay on the good side of the ledger. I go where the money is. I have to pay my bills."

"Even though it's other people's money you are stealing?"

"I raid mostly the corporate world. They can afford it. Most just write it off as any other business loss. A few pennies here and there, and these billionaires never miss it. The key is not to get greedy."

My sandwich was delivered, and I took a few bites. Derek ordered some more ribs. Apparently, he'd not eaten yet today and was loading up at my expense, or at least my client's expense.

"Were you friends with Mandy, too?"

"Absolutely. She is a wonderful gal."

"Did you know her before you knew Aaron?"

"Knew of her, but didn't know her. She was a hottie in college. Always surprised she hooked up with Aaron. Seemed like the type to go after the starting quarterback or power forward. Looks, but not necessarily the smartest person around. But hey, it was a win for our side. If he can get a pretty girl like her, there is hope for all of us computer geeks."

He could hope all he wanted, but I doubted he'd get the prom queen.

"Do you still keep in contact with her?"

"No. I've not seen her since the funeral. I told her to call if she needed anything, but she hasn't."

His next plate of ribs came, and he dug in. I stuck with the one sandwich and the chips provided.

"Mandy mentioned Aaron may have discovered something about WANN Systems and their network, which may have gotten him killed. Did he ever mention anything to you about this?"

"He said once to me he was onto something. Maybe a month or so before he was killed. Didn't give me any details. Only that he'd thought it might be big. A hack for the ages, I believe he stated. But then he never mentioned it again."

"Was it related to the WANN System network?"

"Didn't say specifically. But I wouldn't be surprised. I worked there myself until a couple years ago. Their code was quite buggy and easy to exploit. They were always putting out updates to fix things. They were good at hiding their issues. Marketing always squashed the bad press."

"Is that why you left?"

"It was a part of the reason. Mostly I found a better job, with more money, better benefits and without the crazy hours. WANN would work you to death. If you didn't put in sixty hours a week minimum, you wouldn't survive. Most there work eighty hours. It was hard on your social life."

I smiled, wondering what type of social life Derek had. I imaged him sitting on the computer playing online video games, watching porn and in chatrooms doing who knows what. His idea of an ideal date would never take him too far from his computer.

"Any more you can tell me about Aaron that might help me catch his killer?" I asked.

He polished off the second set of bones and wiped his face.

"Aaron was a good guy. He didn't deserve to die. But I always wondered if there was more to him that he let on. He seemed to have a deep, dark secret of some kind. There were times I thought he was going to spill and let me know, but he always stopped and changed the subject."

"So, you didn't press him on what it was?"

"No. If he was going to tell me, he would. I couldn't care less. We all have our secrets. Hell, I had a few of my own."

Yes, we did. Part of my job was to find them out.

"Hey, do you mind if I order some take-home. I got a girl coming over and we're going to play some *Call of Duty* on Xbox. That way we never need to leave the sofa."

I laughed as I pulled out my credit card to pay for the food. His secrets weren't hard to figure out.

Chapter 15

I had the name of the guard who was the first to arrive at the scene before calling the police. With his address I decided to pay him a visit. He lived in a small two-story house in Aurora just off Quincy. The place was badly in need of painting, yard work and cleanup, as children's toys, including a small bicycle with training wheels, littered the front. When I hit the front steps, I pressed the doorbell but didn't hear anything. I then knocked on the door a few times before someone answered.

"Is your dad home?" I asked of the male child before me, who couldn't have been more than four years old.

"No," was his only response.

"Your mom, then?" I put on my friendly smile.

He turned and left the front door wide open as I heard him yell for his mother. I probably should have explained the danger of doing this, but figured it wouldn't matter. A woman soon showed up, in tight Daisy Duke shorts, halter top, cigarette in mouth, holding a baby. I probably should have explained the danger of smoking around an infant, but again it probably wouldn't do any good.

"Yes," she said, brushing aside her long brown hair.

"I'm looking for Dennis Overland. Is he home?"

She grunted after exhaling a long stream of smoke.

"Of course not. What do you want him for?"

I pulled out my ID and showed it to her. She kind of perked up some when seeing who I was.

"Ryan, come and take your sister," she yelled to the boy who'd been at the door.

He came a-running and took her.

"What do you want me to do with her?" he said.

"What do you think? Play with her. I need to talk with this man about something."

He carried her away, trying his best not to drop her. Again, I wanted to say something...

"Wow, a real cop," she said, while stepping outside and closing the door.

"Private," I replied.

"Close enough. Better than what Dennis does. Said he'd be a cop someday, but can't pass the damn exam."

Once outside she seemed to loosen up. She brushed at her hair, put out her cigarette and threw out her chest at me, all the while moving closer. I backed up feeling uncomfortable, as if a groupie was stalking a rock star.

"I'm sure he is giving his best effort."

"I doubt it. If he worked out like you did, I bet he'd pass."

She put her hand on my left bicep. I was really getting uncomfortable now, but needed to use her fixation with me to my advantage.

"Can you tell me where he is? It would really be a favor to me."

"Why do you want to see him?"

"It's about a case I'm working on. Nothing that will get him in trouble."

"What do I get if you tell me?"

She was rubbing her thigh now with her left hand, while her right was trailing down my arm and moving to my chest.

"I will be extremely grateful."

"How about you come inside and have a drink and we can discuss in more detail."

"First tell me where he is and then we can see."

"Where he always is in the afternoon. At McCarthy's Bar & Grill. Probably chasing some tail instead of mine. Likes to dress up in his security guard uniform and get some tramp to blow him."

"Hard to believe he'd do that with the likes of you waiting at home."

She pulled her hand off me and ran them both up and down her body.

"Damn right. I'm one hot lady if you play me right. He can't see it anymore, though. Needs something different. Gets tired of the same old pussy. His loss, though could be your gain. What do you say?"

"Tempting, but I must go talk with him first. But if all goes well, maybe I'll come back and have that drink."

"You mean it?"

I didn't, but I would leave her wanting more. I took her hand and kissed it, turning and walking away. Once on my bike I drove off heading for McCarthy's, a bar on Smoky Hill Road. When I arrived, the place was quiet, the early afternoon crowd not overwhelming the place. It looked clean and well maintained, and at the bar I saw a man in uniform sitting by himself. If he was there to get laid, as his wife said, he didn't seem to be successful, at least for now. I took a seat next to him, where I could smell the beer fragrance filling the air, the mug before him nearly empty. He gave a glance my way and didn't seem to care much. I laid my ID on the bar before him, so he knew who I was. He picked it up, glancing it over and then tossed it back to me.

"What the fuck do you want?" he said.

"Came here to ask some questions," I replied. "I'd buy you another beer, but I think you've had plenty. What about some food to provide a balanced diet?"

I don't think he cared for my humor, as he took his hand and tried to push me off the stool. It wasn't much of a push and I barely moved at all.

"Leave me alone or I'll punch your lights out."

I looked him over and concluded he couldn't punch out anything. He was around my height, but probably thirty pounds heavier, with most of it in his waist and hips. His arms and chest weren't small, but didn't look firm. If he hit the gym in the last year or so I'd be shocked. Even though in uniform, he had no gun or weapons that I could see. He was overmatched, but couldn't admit it in his current state.

"Dennis, you couldn't take me on a good day," I said. "Why don't you take me up on the offer of some free food? It might help you sober up some and we can have a gentlemanly conversation."

He slid off his stool and took a long-armed sling at me. I had already moved and slipped the punch with little effort, pushing him in the back as he passed me. Straightening himself he tried again, and I blocked it with my left arm and punched him once in the stomach with enough snap it knocked the wind out of him. As he gasped I could tell he was going to lose everything in his stomach. Asking for directions to the restroom, I led him quickly where he found an empty stall and threw up. Waiting patiently, I tossed him some wet towels to clean up. I walked back out while he freshened up and spoke to the bouncer making sure he was cool with what happened. After explaining and showing him ID, he was fine so long as there wouldn't be any more trouble.

"I think all the starch in him just was flushed down the toilet," I said.

He laughed and returned to his post while I took a seat at a table and ordered two Sprites, wings and mozzarella sticks from the Happy Hour menu. After about five minutes Dennis came out and sat across from me.

"Feeling better?" I asked.

"Not really."

"In time. Food and some soda will help. It will be here shortly."

The soda arrived, and he took a long drink. I told the waitress to bring him another one to try and ease his stomach.

"Good punch," he said.

"Thanks." I could tell him I held back some and it could have been worse. But I didn't care to rub it in. Life for him now was not all roses. That was obvious from my encounter with his wife.

"How did you know I was here?"

"Your wife told me."

"Did she offer to bang your brains out as well?"

I shrugged. No need to flaunt it.

"And did you?"

"No. It wouldn't have done her or me any good. Besides your kids were there and they don't need to learn that about their mom."

"Even though he is young, I think my son already knows. Anything in a uniform she'll screw. That is how we met."

"I'm sorry."

"Yeah, no one to blame but myself."

The food arrived, and he dug in the wings as if he hadn't eaten in two days. The emptying of his stomach contributing.

"You said you have some questions for me. You are a private cop, that much I deduced from your ID. What did you want to talk about?"

"Aaron Bailey's murder."

He looked up from eating another wing, a bit of fear now showing in his eyes. He glanced around the room to make sure no one heard me. Over the music playing that was highly unlikely, since no one was sitting close to us.

"I'm not supposed to talk about that."

"Why not?"

"It will get me fired. Or worse."

"All I want to know is what you found when you arrived on the scene. You were the first to find him."

"Yeah, sure, I was. I went out to do my rounds and found him. Horrible sight to see."

"Did you know Aaron?"

"Somewhat. You know, said hi when he'd sign out at night. It was not like we were buddies."

I grabbed a couple of the cheese sticks before all the food was gone. I waved down the waitress to bring us some more wings, so I could try some, since the basket was empty.

"Did he sign out that night?"

"Gee, I don't know if I should say anything."

"Dennis, no one will know you talked with me. Look around and there is no one here even paying attention to us right now. Your wife mentioned you want to be a cop. This is your chance to help me figure out who killed him, just like a real detective would do."

He grabbed some napkins to clean off the sauce from his face and hands. He was processing what to say, and I wondered if he knew more than he would tell me. All I could do was work him.

"No, he didn't. I never saw him sign out."

"How could he have gotten outside without you knowing it?"

"Shit, that is easy. Anyone can sneak out if they want to. The procedure is to check out, but it's not like we can enforce it. Most of the bigwigs never check in or out. They are too high and mighty to. Their security cards allow them to come and go as they please."

"Did you know the security system was down?"

"Sure we did. That is why I was out walking. Normally we don't go out too often to walk the grounds because we can see almost everything from the cameras. That night the ones for the parking garage and area around it were down. I had to do a walk through every hour or so."

"Was only the parking garage security down?"

"Yes. The rest of them were working fine, covering the front area and visitor parking."

"Did that happen often?"

"Not that I recall. I mean it is technology, so it does fail occasionally. But I don't remember the last time it didn't all work."

"Did anyone tell you why it wasn't working?"

"No, they don't tell me shit. I'm just a lowly night-shift security guard. You'd think I could get the hell off graveyard, but so far, they tell me there are no positions available. At least I get some shift differential for working those god-awful hours."

The other basket of wings arrived, and this time I got my hands on a couple before he could devour them. I went over all I had learned and wished there had been more. I continued to press to see what else he might spill.

"When you found him, he was already dead?"

"Yes. There was a lot of blood, but I checked for a pulse and didn't find one. The investigators weren't thrilled I'd done that, but I had to be sure. If there was any way I could help him, I wanted to try."

"You saw no one else there at the scene?"

"Nothing. He was all alone, sitting there against the car door. I called it in to the security desk and waited for the police to arrive. They asked me a lot of questions and even checked my gun to see if it had been fired. It was a long night."

"When it was all over, your bosses told you to keep quiet about it?"

"Not to the cops. They said to tell the truth. But to anyone else I was to remain quiet. You aren't going to rat me out, are you? I really need this job."

"No, I will remain silent."

"Good. I mean, I really feel sorry for Aaron and all. I do hope they figure who killed him. But I have to look out for me and my family."

I should have pointed out to him there probably wasn't much of a family to save, but like with everything else for this group, it probably would do no good.

Chapter 16

The other friend I was going to talk with still worked at WANN Systems. Mandy had provided the name, Shaw Bentley, and I contacted him. We would meet at his apartment complex down in Lone Tree after he got home from work at around 8 p.m. Climbing the stairs to the third floor, I knocked on his door. Once inside, after showing ID, he offered me a drink as I sat in a chair at his kitchen table.

"Bottled water, if you have any," I said.

He pulled out a fresh bottle from the fridge and sat down. He was probably close to my age, but shorter and heavier. He was dressed in beige Dockers and a blue polo. His dark hair was short and thinning, with a slight curl. He had poured himself a shot of whiskey, which he slammed back and then poured a second shot, which he carried to the table.

"You said you are investigating Aaron's shooting," he said.

"Yes, I've been hired to look into it."

"The police say it was random. A robbery."

"I've not come to that conclusion. I believe there was more to it."

He looked a little nervous. Maybe why he needed the shot and one in reserve.

"Aaron was a good guy. We'd often have lunch together and talk about tech stuff."

"You still work at WANN?"

"Yes."

"What do you do there?"

"I work within the marketing group. Graphic design, logos, press releases; those type of things. We are the face of the company. What the general public sees first."

"Image is everything."

"Certainly, in the corporate world it can be. The difference between success and failure."

"I understand they are quite demanding of their employees."

"Yes, they are. I'm lucky I'm home in time to meet you. Unless you have a severed limb, you need to be at work. A typical day is 6 a.m. to 6 p.m. They give us notebooks, so then after getting home you are expected to VPN in and work some more."

"Hard on your private life."

"Why I'm living in an apartment. My wife and I split up because I worked too much."

"How is the pay?"

"If you worked forty hours a week, it's not bad. But when you work sixty-plus, then not so much. But it pays the bills and I don't have to eat mac and cheese each night."

"No overtime?"

"I'm on salary, so there is no such thing. But even hourly employees are told to only enter in forty and no more, even when working more."

"Isn't that illegal?"

"Who is going to complain? You'd get fired or worse!"

"And what would be worse?"

"A visit from one of the security people. A gentle nudge to follow the unwritten rules. Veiled threats of a cut in pay, a transfer to a less desirable position or losing your job."

"Why not get another job?"

"I have quite a few years there I'd hate to throw away. Plus, it's hard to find something when you work nearly non-stop. And you must be careful. If they find out you are looking, they've been known to fire people without severance and not pay any of your leftover vacation or sick time."

"What about Aaron? Did he mention anything to you about finding bugs in your software?"

Shaw grabbed the second shot and downed it quickly, his hand shaking some.

"Since we mostly talked at work, he couldn't say much. And our work phones are monitored, along with email and instant messaging. But we did have dinner out a couple weeks before his death and he asked me if I knew about any type of snooping or data gathering we were doing with our equipment."

"You mean internally?"

"No, he was talking about the stuff we sell to clients. Was it gathering information, tracking all the traffic on their networks."

"Was it?"

"I told him no."

"Was it the truth?"

His eyes looked down at the shot glass. He got up and poured another one. Even with his extra weight, this would soon begin to impair him.

"Maybe you should slow down some on the whiskey?" I said.

"Sorry. I'm nervous. Why I wanted to meet you here. And told you to make sure you weren't followed."

"I wasn't. You are safe. When you are ready, you can continue. No pressure."

He looked at the glass, but didn't drink. He was trying to steady himself. I found the harder you tried to relax, the worse it got. I sat, waiting him out.

"There were rumors. Nothing I can prove or say for certain. But yes, I'd heard about possible information gathering they were using."

"What types of information can they obtain, if it were true?"

"Everything. I'm sure you've been on the Internet. We put it all out there for everyone to see and hear. We buy everything using our credit cards, whether on the Internet or in a store using a credit card machine, which transmits back to servers. How often have you had to change your credit card out after a fraudulent purchase was made?"

He was right. My credit card had been replaced a couple of times because of fraud. I wasn't on the hook for the charges, but someone had to eat the cost. I doubted the culprits got caught in most cases.

"Aren't the transactions protected somehow? Encrypted?"

"Sure. But nothing is hundred percent fool-proof safe. Encryption can be bypassed. Most basic 128-bit keys can easily be broken these days."

"You sound like you have a coding background?"

"I do. I coded before going into marketing. My skills aren't what they once were, since I don't keep up. But I understand it."

"If Aaron did stumble onto something, is it possible he was killed because of it?"

"It is not out of the realm of possibilities."

"Are you aware of any links WANN has to some Russian mobsters?"

Shaw this time did drink down the third shot. Much more of this, and his head would be hitting the table top from passing out.

"The last couple of days, there were some large men making the rounds at the office. I heard one of them talk and he sounded Russian."

I pulled out my phone and showed him a picture.

"Yeah, that was him."

"And you hadn't seen them around until recently?"

"Only the last few days. So, are they criminals?"

"I haven't completely confirmed it yet, but it looks like it. They came and visited me, wanting to know why I was snooping around Aaron's murder."

I left out the part about them planning to beat the information out of me. I figured Shaw didn't need any more to worry about.

"What did you tell them?"

"Nothing more than I'm a PI working a case."

"And they left you alone?"

"A Denver cop friend of mine intervened, so I didn't have to answer their questions."

"Am I safe?"

"They won't know I've come to visit you. There is no reason to think they'd hurt you."

I'm not sure he felt reassured by my words, or that what I said was true. I wasn't even certain. If they knew of his friendship to Aaron, they might come a-calling.

"Do you have any vacation or sick time coming?" I asked.

"Sure. Why do you ask?"

I smiled and suggested he leave town for a while. Maybe Mitch and him could split the cost!

Chapter 17

At the rate people were leaving town in fear, thanks to me, I would have the city to myself before too long. Well, at least the streets would be free of traffic. Though it would take a lot more people leaving before helping with congestion that I sat stuck in trying to get to the FBI office in north Denver.

I had called Agent Dezmond Price the next day and arranged an appointment with him. He sounded a little put off on the phone when I called, but listened more closely when I mentioned the last name Platov. Once I arrived, I locked my gun away in my Mustang, chancing I could go unarmed on the walk-through security. Once inside after a thorough check of my body, and showing ID and signing in, I was told where to go. The Denver FBI office was a big step up from Des Moines. Apparently, their budget was higher, with a nicer glass and chrome building, and better furnishings. Up the elevator to the fourth floor I found Price's office. His door was open, and I walked in. He wasn't there so I took a seat and waited. His desktop was covered with computer monitor, keyboard and mouse, files, his name plate, and a picture of his wife and kids. I resisted the urge to snoop through his files. On the wall were diplomas and honors for working at the FBI, showing fifteen years of dedicated service. I heard footsteps and he walked in, dressed as all Feds, in black jacket, slacks and tie, with white shirt and shoulder holster and gun, underneath. I stood to shake his hand, but he passed by me without an effort to oblige. He was tall like an average college point guard, and appeared in decent shape. His skin matched his black hair, which was cut short and combed so no hair was out of place. When he sat down he put on some reading glasses after grabbing a file on his desk. He was silent while he read over a few pages in the manila folder. Once done he set it down, leaned back in his chair and looked straight at me.

"Interesting reading about you," he said. "Seems you got yourself into a pickle last year in Des Moines."

"Into and back out of, I'm assuming it says."

"Sounds like by the skin of your teeth. Lucky to be alive."

"Luck and skill sometimes are closely aligned."

"Seems like a reckless attitude to have."

"Sometimes you need to take chances to succeed. I'm sure Wilson told you what was accomplished by my recklessness."

"Much about you I've read in the file. What he told me is you punched him in the stomach."

"It was a love tap, to get his attention."

"Tap me and I'll lock you up."

"Fair enough. Can we get past the foreplay and get down to business? You've titillated me enough."

"Said you were a smart mouth too. That won't fly with me either."

I sighed, growing tired of the back and forth.

"Do I walk away now, or do we find a common ground and work together."

He leaned forward in his chair, standing to walk over to his small fridge. He pulled out two bottles of OJ and tossed one to me. He twisted off the top and took a drink, sitting on the edge of his desk.

"I guess it's not important for us to like each other to cooperate."

"Wilson and I butted heads plenty and still got the job done. I'll be happy to share what I know and will even start first, if you can give me information on the Platov boys. I have a feeling I'll be running into them again and I need to know what I'm up against."

"Tell me what you know."

I gave Dezmond all the details of my encounter with them, all of which started when I began poking around in WANN Systems business and the murder of Aaron Bailey. For once, I didn't leave anything out, other than whom my client was.

"You go poking around trying to solve a murder and the three Platov boys show up. Who hired you?"

"I'd rather not say. Be safer for them, the fewer people know."

"Fair enough. Certainly, no coincidence they show up after you visit WANN Systems and talk with their former head of security."

"How long have they been in town?"

"Flew in that night on a private jet."

"And you know this?"

"We watch all undesirables these days pretty closely."

"If they are undesirable, how come they aren't in jail?"

"Nothing much to hold them on. You got them arrested and saw how quickly they were out. Even if charges hold up, they likely wouldn't do much jail time. Most witnesses generally withdraw their complaints or disappear."

This was worrying to hear. April could be in danger, though from the skill she showed the other day, she could probably handle herself. Still, a word of warning wouldn't hurt.

"Give me the scoop on these three. I doubt they were raised in a church by nuns."

No smile at my humor. He returned to his chair, sipping his juice.

"They are all from Chechnya. They were born there and during the two major wars with Russia, fought for and against Chechnya, eventually integrating into the Russian forces there. In time they left the army, being recruited to join several organized crime groups. One of those groups grew in scope and power, by making deals with other crime groups and then destroying their leadership by taking complete control. This was led by the man they work for, Orell Krupski. He is powerful and ruthless. Even the Russian government fears him."

"Does his organization have a name?"

"Vlast, which loosely means control."

"So, the Platov boys work for him?"

"Correct."

"Why send them here about a simple murder case? Seems small in the grand scheme of things."

Dezmond stopped to contemplate what to say next.

"It is rumored, though never proven, that Vlast may be investing in various companies, many in the United States."

"And one of those companies is WANN Systems?"

"Yes. Though again, we've not seen any evidence of this. The money is filtered many times, through many countries throughout the world, before ending up in their hands. But on a couple of occasions WANN was out of money and on the verge of bankruptcy. The last time a few years back, they received an eleventh-hour infusion of cash in the hundreds of millions of dollars. It was never reported where it came from. A private investor was all that was said. After the tech crash, which lasted until 2002, investors were scarce. Companies weren't picky about where the money came from. Even with the smaller crashes the last couple of years, cash is tougher to come by, at least without stipulations. It is possible they have a stake in WANN they are trying to protect. The question is, what threat did a lowly software engineer present that required killing him?"

"Is Vlast in the business of stealing user information?" I asked. "Identity theft?"

"Good question. Mostly they deal in drugs, prostitution and gambling. But some of the biggest Internet theft and hacker groups come out of Russia. They certainly could have their hands in that arena. It is a multibillion dollar business."

"And all it needs is a bunch of nerds to capture the data and a network of connected machines for it to flow. WANN has all of that."

"True, but how do we prove it. As of now, the Bureau can't even begin to stop it. Most companies just write it off as a cost of doing business and don't even try to bring anyone to justice for stealing this way."

"My job is to solve a murder right now. That is the only thing that matters to me. If it leads down a road to a bigger fish, they are all yours. I can only do so much and would prefer not to be killed in a horrible fashion. The question is, can you do something about getting the Platov boys off my back, so I can work?"

"You believe you can solve the murder?"

"Yes. But I can't be looking over my shoulder constantly."

Dezmond rubbed his chin for a good two minutes, then got on the phone.

"We need to get a team together to round up three terrorists and send them to Cuba. We need this ASAP. Put your best men together and we'll have a meeting in two hours in the situation room where I'll spell out the details... Sounds good. Thanks."

Price turned his attention back to me, with a happy look on his face.

"Once we find them, we can hold them indefinitely. Probably seventy-two hours to hustle them out of the country."

"They've got good lawyers."

"Who?"

"Local ones. Bristol & Bristol. Do you know them?"

"I've heard of them. We'll do our best to keep them away, so they don't mess things up. Of course, we won't be reading them their rights or allowing them a phone call."

"Sounds illegal."

"Patriot Act says otherwise. These men are terrorists and a threat to national security."

I wasn't sure if that was completely true, but I wasn't about to argue.

"Thanks."

"I'm not doing it for you. And I expect updates on your progress."

"I always cooperate with the Men in Black."

"Wilson said you'd say that. And he said it was a lie."

I smiled.

"Well, maybe an exaggeration."

Chapter 18

Once my meeting was done, I immediately wanted to call April, but didn't have her personal number. I called down to the Denver PD and got Bill on the line, asking if he had it.

"What do you need it for?" he asked. I think he was concerned it was for personal reasons.

"After a conversation with the FBI, I need to let her know she might be in danger."

"Related to your skirmish?"

"Yes. Those three are extremely dangerous."

"Let me see if I can access the personnel records and find it."

After several minutes he found her cell and gave it to me, which I called immediately.

"Hello."

"April, it's Jarvis. Where are you at?"

"Home. I'm about to go to my martial arts class. Why, what's wrong?"

"You might be in danger. Do you have a gun?"

"It was taken from me while I'm on leave. I don't own one myself. Why, am I in danger?"

"Those three men you took down and had arrested are some bad dudes…" I went on to explain what Dezmond had told me. There was no "oh my gosh" reaction from her.

"I'm not going to hide away. If they come after me, I won't go quietly."

"I'd feel better if you had a gun. I've got an extra .38 I can loan you."

There was a lull before she answered.

"OK. But I'm late now for my class. Can't it wait until I'm done?"

"Where is the class and I'll bring it to you? Promise you'll go straight there and don't dawdle. If you see them, get somewhere safe."

"Why Jarvis, I didn't know you cared?"

"Enough not to see you dead!"

"Oh, you sweet talker."

She gave me the address and promised to be diligent. I went

home and got my extra .38 and took it to the studio. When I arrived, I found a seat as her class was already in session. She was a red belt and was very good, showing speed and agility. Several times she brought her opponent to the mat with a thundering thud. I liked what I saw and wondered if I should join to improve my hand-to-hand martial arts skills. After the sixty-minute session she was sweating hard. I was impressed with her skill set. She grabbed her bag and walked over.

"Damn, lady, I'm glad you were on my side the other day," I stated. "Maybe you don't need a gun."

"Thank you," she replied, while toweling the sweat off her face. "I can hold my own in hand to hand. But three of them would be challenging. And if they are armed, there is no martial arts move that can deflect a bullet."

"True. And they won't underestimate you this time, thinking you're just a sexy woman. They know you have some skills."

"Sexy woman. Are those your words?"

I may have blushed, but did my best to mask it with a big grin.

"There is no denying it. They certainly thought so too. But now they'll not hesitate."

We walked outside and once we reached her car, I handed her the gun. She took it, opened it to verify it was loaded, and tucked it in her bag. I then handed her an extra box of bullets, in case the six inside weren't enough.

"Gee, you'd think I was going to war!"

"Hopefully not," I replied. "The FBI are going to round them up in the next day or so. Once they are put away, then the danger should be over."

"And until then?"

"Stay home and lock the doors."

"Hell no, Jarvis. I'm not hiding."

"Then don't go out unnecessarily."

"What if a good-looking detective was with me? Would that be OK?"

I smiled.

"I didn't realize you knew any other private detectives?"

She gave me a smirk.

"Of course, I'm talking about you."

I responded with an "oh, you meant me" gesture.

"I don't normally go out on a date armed, unless the lady is dangerous. But yes, you should be safe."

"Then dinner tonight? The one you owe me for saving your butt?"

I thought it over for a minute, but what else could I say? At least I'd know she was safe.

"It's a date. You pick the place."

"Colore's. Pick me up at seven."

"Sounds good."

"Oh, and thanks for the sweet corn. I've got it stored away in the fridge. Maybe you'll have to come over for some later this week, if we live through our dinner."

I had to laugh. *Let's hope we did.*

Chapter 19

Time was short, but I needed to check in with my client. Mandy was home, so I stopped by to give her an update. She let me in wearing blue jean shorts and a tank top. Her hair was tied back, and she was wearing dark-framed glasses. This was much different than when I'd seen her the other times. At first, I wondered if I was at the right house.

"Hardly recognized you," I said, after letting me in.

"This is the casual me. The one for sitting around the house waiting with little to do."

"Not working right now?"

"No, I'm still taking some time off. Feel like I need to get this settled before I can move on."

"Money must not be an issue."

"No, it's not a problem right now."

"What do you do normally?"

She paused for a minute. Not sure if she was uncomfortable with the question. I really wasn't trying to grill her for information. Just wanted to make some small talk, though the more I knew about everything, even small facts about a client, the better I can do my job.

"I was an administrative coordinator at my last job. I quit shortly after Aaron was killed. Fortunately, we had a healthy amount of money stashed away, and no major bills other than mortgage and utilities. We weren't the type of couple to spend money foolishly."

"Good to hear you have no financial issues," I said. "I do have some news I wanted to share about how the case is going."

She pointed to a leather recliner for me to sit in, while she took the matching sofa, curling her legs under her.

"I'm all ears."

"I've concluded you may be right about the murder of Aaron. Something fishy is going on over at WANN Systems."

"What have you learned?"

Her eyes were focused on me, absorbing each word, as I filled her in on every detail of the last couple of days, other than graphically explaining about the three Russian enforcers' past of killing witnesses. She showed no emotion or fear, which was a little surprising. Maybe inside she was tougher than she looked, or good at masking her feelings.

"Can I get you something to drink?" she asked, standing up. "I have some coffee I can make, soda or some bottle water."

"Water would be great."

While she went to get the water, I stood and looked around the room. The living area was small, what I expected from an average-sized two-story home. To the back was the small kitchen and dining area, to the right, an office or workroom. The furnishings were modern, with dark mahogany hardwood floors and surprisingly no television, and only a stereo system, with well-hidden speakers, as they were hard to find. There was a bookcase with various novels, many classics and some from modern writers, fiction and mystery the common theme. One shelf was open, with framed pictures of the couple: static poses of them together. Nothing obvious as to what they did in their spare time. Only poses of them hugging or holding hands, and one of their wedding day. The place was orderly and tidy, not a dust ball in sight. Either she was very neat or cleaned to pass the time. Mandy returned several minutes later and handed me the water, a cup of coffee in her hand, the steam rising from the mug.

"You have a charming home here," I stated. "How are you holding up?"

"Thank you," she replied, after a long sip of the dark brew. "The days are better, but the nights are lonely. Sleep is hard without Aaron by my side. I'm managing as well as can be expected.

"Do you have friends to help you? Talk to?"

"One really close friend. She checks up on me pretty regularly. Takes me out to dinner and we talk on the phone. I'm not the most social person and mostly keep to myself, other than with Aaron. You would say he was my soulmate."

"Did you call any of those numbers I gave you? People who you can talk with and work through your emotions."

"I did. But I'm not quite ready yet. I promise I will once this situation is resolved."

"Don't wait too long."

Her sorrow appeared real and I was concerned. Deep and

scarred, with a long road of healing ahead. It was a pain I felt earlier in the year when I lost Flynn. In time the hurt stopped, but you'd never completely get over it.

"Do you mind answering a couple of other questions about Aaron? It's important for the case."

She grabbed a tissue from the coffee table and wiped her eyes, which were moist.

"Please do. Whatever I can do to help."

"From those I talk with, they say WANN Systems were pretty much slave-drivers. Demanding their employees work crazy-long hours without paying any overtime. Was that the case with Aaron as well?"

"Yes. He did work sixty-plus hours a week at times. He'd fudge it some and still have time for us. But there were days where he'd work sixteen hours."

"Did he work at home? Or was he always at the office?"

"No, he worked at home quite a bit."

"He would bring his notebook home then and work?"

"Yes, absolutely. Every day he carried it in his bag. It was a big powerful workhorse of a computer. The work he did demanded it."

"There was no mention of his notebook being found with him? And I found this odd."

"True. In my grief I didn't think of this at first."

"Do you know where it is?"

"No. Maybe the person who killed him took it."

"That was my thought. I'm certain it was securely protected. But still I'm curious what happened to it. It doesn't seem WANN was too concerned. Unless they were involved and did recover it. Do you know if he kept anything on there he was trying to keep from them?"

"Not that I'm aware of."

"Did he have a home computer he worked on?"

"No. He did all his work on the computer WANN provided."

"Could he have saved files on some cloud storage area or external device they weren't aware of."

"I doubt it. The computers were locked down to prevent this, I believe he mentioned once or twice."

"Do you own a computer he could have used?"

There was a slight hesitation.

"Other than my iPad, no. I'm not a computer geek like he was. Only email and browsing the Web to shop."

I'd file this away under something I'd need to look into further. Not having a home computer was not normal in this day and age.

"Maybe I can find out from WANN what happened. Someone on the inside might be able to answer the question."

"Hopefully. They are not forthcoming when querying data. I believe they hope it all becomes yesterday's news."

"I can be persuasive and sneaky when needed. The mark of a good PI."

"I'm so glad you are making progress. I was worried at first when you didn't call me back. I'm glad I stuck with you. That other PI I talked with sounded creepy."

"Who else did you talk to?"

"Well, when I didn't hear back when I first gave you the deposit, I started looking for someone else. I contacted a King Detective Agency. Talked with an Adam King."

"Crap!" I said.

"You know him?"

"Oh yes. He is extremely slimy. We've had it out once when he tried to steal my client. Not one of my favorite people."

"He was kind of creepy when I met him. He's been bugging me ever since, telling me what a slacker you are. I don't like it when someone denigrates someone in an obvious attempt to get business. I keep telling him I'm not interested, but he won't give up. I have been ignoring his calls as best as I can."

"Seems I need to pay him a visit as well. Convince him to look elsewhere for clients."

"So, you believe you can get him to stop?"

"Without a doubt!" I stated with conviction.

Though it might require a five-fingered persuasion, which I'd get a kick out of.

Chapter 20

Time was short, so I rushed home and changed quickly, and went to pick up April for dinner. I wore slacks and a nice cotton shirt with a sport jacket over it, to conceal my gun. Because of the danger she and I still were in, I wasn't going unarmed until Dezmond confirmed the Platov trio were in custody. When I arrived at her front door, she wowed me with her attire. Black, slightly over-the-knee-length skirt, polished black boots covering her calves, yellow sleeveless blouse, with a little cleavage showing. Her light brown hair flowed freely to her shoulders. I'd rarely seen her outside the office, other than at Boone's, and today she filled my eyes with her stunning looks. I took a couple of deep breaths to compose myself.

"You look pretty," I said calmly.

"Thank you. I put in the effort every now and then."

She put her arm through mine and we walked to my car, where I opened the door and she slid in. The drive to the restaurant was quiet, as the radio played some world-class rock on one of my favorite stations. I wanted to talk of other things, and not of the danger she was in or work-related items. I had a tough time coming up with something, as my mind was frozen. When we arrived at the restaurant we were seated quickly in a nice corner booth. I sat across from her and our eyes met.

"Well, that was one of the more silent drives I've been on in some time," said April. "You'd think we'd been married for several years."

"Sorry. My brain locked and couldn't come up with anything to talk about. I wanted to avoid talking shop because of the current situation."

"Was that all?"

Oh, what the hell. I might as well say it!

"Honestly, I'm a little nervous. After my recent breakup I'm a little leery of myself and dating."

"You think this is a date?"

"It had crossed my mind. I doubt you dress up like this for a causal night out."

April grinned widely.

"So true. This is one of my 'get the guys eyes to bug-out' outfits. But we've known each other for a while now, so nothing to be worried about. It would be nice to talk in a quiet environment and get to know each other better. No pressure. Have an enjoyable time and see where it leads. My intentions are purely honorable!"

I couldn't help but laugh, happy she had defused the pressure I was feeling. The waitress arrived, and we ordered some red wine and an appetizer of Burrata.

"So normally I'd say, tell me about yourself," I began. "But it seems we already know each other fairly well. I know you mentioned you had three older brothers. What do they do?"

"We come from a family of cops," she said. "My dad was a cop for twenty years before retiring. My oldest brother works for the Douglas County Sheriff's department. The other two work in Aurora. One is a detective, the other a plain-clothes officer working Vice. It's something the four of us always wanted to do."

"How does your mom feel about you being a cop?"

"She knew it was going to happen. I was pretty much a tomboy from day one, running with, into and through my brothers. I'm sure it concerned her, but she's always been proud of me. Though she worries if I'll ever find a man who can put up with my job."

"It can be a hard life for any spouse, male or female."

The wine arrived, and they had me taste it. It met with my approval, so two glasses were poured.

"Yes, it is," said April, after a taste of wine. "But she doesn't understand I like being single and free to choose. I rarely feel lonely. I'm too busy."

"You mentioned once growing up you eventually were able to kick your brothers' asses. Is that still true?"

"Absolutely. Though they'd never admit it. They still look out for me and worry too. But they know I'm not without skills."

"I've seen them, both during the class and in action on the streets. Hopefully I stay on your good side."

"I heard of your fighting skill as well. I'd rather not tangle with you either. Well, at least in a negative way."

She said it without blushing, which was normal. She was often forward with me, in a friendly way. This shouldn't be any different than any other time we had talked. Or so I kept telling myself. But somehow it did feel different.

The Burrata arrived and we dug in, enjoying the ball-shaped mozzarella with buttery cream inside. It was quite tasty and filling. For the main meal April ordered Eggplant Parmigiana, while I decided on baked Penne Bolognese.

"Do you think the latest situation will get you more time on the streets?" I asked.

"I don't think it will hurt. I was already getting out more and more, usually pairing up with a more experienced officer. My day is coming. As Bill says, as long as I'm patient it will happen."

"I'm looking forward to testifying on our behalf. I'll try my best not to come across as smitten with you, and blab on like an idiot."

"Well, if you decide to, let me know so I can get a video copy to post on the Internet!"

I had a mouthful of food and nearly spit it out laughing. We talked on a little longer about her life, where I learned a few more things about her. She was a good shot on the firing range, played basketball and softball in high school and college, and wanted a motorcycle but couldn't quite afford it yet.

"I'd love to have a bike like you have," she said. "Your jaw must have hit your chest when they unloaded it. Your sister-in-law must really care about you."

"She was a good person, and I'm so happy to have been able to free her from the burden my brother had put her under. The circumstance wasn't ideal, but I'm glad she can get on with her life."

"Your brother sounded like an ass, if you don't mind my saying so."

I couldn't argue the point. Though I was sad he was gone, I had no guilt for what the final outcome was. I had gone the extra mile to try and save him.

"He was Flynn. Not much I could do to change him."

"And what about you? Will you be able to get on with your life?"

"I have no issues with how it all came down with Flynn."

"No, I mean with Melissa."

I wasn't sure if I could answer that question. I was still struggling.

"I screwed up. It will be a while before I can forgive myself."

April reached her hand out and placed it on mine. I almost

pulled away in surprise, a twitch of reflex filling me, but held still.

"Believe or not, our failings can make us stronger. The first part is forgiving ourselves."

I had wanted to, but couldn't. Maybe in time. Deep down, I wondered if I ever could.

"Maybe if I knew if she could forgive me, then I might be able to forgive myself. I don't like hurting the ones I care about."

"Just don't hurt yourself too. And understand others care about you, including me."

She cupped my hand tightly and then let it go, when the main meal arrived. We ate while talking about happier things, with me giving her a rundown on my life. It was a good time and I did feel better. When the meal was done, the check paid, we went out to the car where I opened the door for her. She turned into me, giving me a long embrace and a kiss on the lips. My reaction wasn't of surprise, but of not wanting to kiss back. She pulled away, with a look of not hurt, but of shock.

"And I imagined you as a good kisser," she said with a mock pout.

"I'm sorry. You caught me off guard." I paused, looking for the right words. "I didn't want to lead you on. I'm not certain I'm ready."

"No worries. I had a wonderful time tonight. I wanted to make sure you understood."

"As did I. I'm not certain I want to go beyond what we already have between us. I enjoy your friendship, and who knows, in time maybe it can be more."

Once in the car we drove back to her place. When we arrived, she grabbed my hand.

"Can you walk me to my door?" she asked.

"Of course. I want to make sure you get inside safely."

"You can come in for something to drink. No pressure, of course. I enjoy talking to you. It is a nice form of verbal foreplay."

Again, I laughed, which felt good. I was considering her offer, figuring it wouldn't hurt to make sure no one had broken in and would attack her after I'd left. I had convinced myself this would be the only reason to go inside, but deep down I knew more could happen. As we strolled to her apartment door, her arm in mine, her head on my shoulder, out stepped one of the Platov men from behind a pillar. It was still light enough that I could see it was the one April had disabled. He raised his arm, gun in hand, pointing. My mind raced on what defense I should mount, knowing it likely wouldn't be enough.

Chapter 21

I tried to push April away and shield her. The first shot boomed, filling my ears and I felt her body grow heavy and pull away from me. By the second shot she was down and I lunged at him, grabbing his gun hand, pushing it downward, as a third shot went into the sidewalk.

I gripped him as tightly as I could, trying to pull the weapon from his hand. But he was incredibly strong, and we were in a standoff, neither of us being able to get an advantage over the other. I removed one hand from his arm and tried to punch at his face, but could only get a glancing blow, which did no damage. He pulled free with his gun hand and shoved me backwards; I tripped, falling back into a bush. He raised his gun hand and aimed at me. I tried to reach for my gun, but there was no time. I heard four shots in rapid succession and figured I was dead. But instead he fell backwards, clutching at his chest, blood seeping through his fingers, before hitting the ground. Looking over, I saw the wounded April had pulled out the .38 I'd loaned her, both hands steady as she expertly placed each shot in the kill zone, putting Jasha down for the count.

I went over to make sure he was dead and pushed his dropped weapon away, in case he came back to life. April had slumped backwards and onto her side, the blood seeping from her stomach. Pulling off my coat I rolled it up to put pressure front and back. She was bleeding a lot and starting to lose consciousness.

"Hang in there, April!" I said forcefully. "Don't you dare die on me!"

I pulled out my cell phone and made a frantic call to 911.

"A Denver officer has been shot! Please get an ambulance here as fast as you can." I gave them the address and her badge number.

"Damn, Jarvis, it hurts," she said. "I don't think I'm going to make it."

"You'll be fine. We have that second date to go on. And you can't skip out on me."

She had a weak smile, but her eyes were closing. She had lost a lot of blood and there was nothing I could do to stop it. I kept talking with her until the paramedics arrived. They worked on her but knew they couldn't help her enough and got her in the ambulance. They didn't want to let me go, but a couple of officers who arrived on the scene knew me and told them to allow it. On the drive over, I still was talking to her. When we arrived at Swedish Medical Center, the triage team met us outside and took her away, leaving me with another doctor, who wanted to make sure I was alright.

"Are you hurt sir?" he said, a little leery of the gun I was carrying.

"The blood is not mine. It's April's."

"We'll need to make sure. You may be in shock, so I'd like to examine you. But first we need to get your gun."

There was a security officer there, though I didn't remember seeing him. I handed him the gun and was walked over to a room where I could be checked over. Once the doctor confirmed I wasn't injured, they allowed me to clean the blood as much as I could. With a thorough washing I could clean it off my hands, but my shirt and pants were a lost cause.

Several Denver officers arrived and took my statement. Time moved slowly, and others arrived, including April's parents and two of her brothers. Bill showed up as well and tried to talk with me, but I was out of it. A couple hours passed and soon after the surgeon who worked on April came to talk with us. I heard the words but was instantly angry, the shock wearing off. I turned to Bill for his help.

"I need my gun back," I said to him. "I need to settle this. And you need to drive me back, so I can get my car."

"Don't do anything stupid. It won't change a thing."

I didn't care, giving him the sternest look I could muster. He got me the gun back and drove me to my car.

"What do you plan to do?"

"Make sure the other two don't harm anyone else."

"How do you plan to do that?"

"With the help of the FBI."

"Good luck." Bill didn't sound convinced.

Once in my car I called Dezmond on the phone.

"What do you want?"

"The other two Platov brothers. One just killed my friend."

There was silence.

"We have two in custody. The other so far has eluded us."

"He is dead. Killed by Officer April Rainn."

"Is she the one who died?"

"Yes."

"Planning on getting revenge?"

"No, I want to question them. I need answers."

"Why would I let you do this?"

"Because there is no reason not to let me. You are putting them far away, from what you told me. Let me talk with them. But they need to think I'm going to kill them if they don't talk. There is something larger involved here. Something big the government would like to know about. Possibly a career maker for you."

Dezmond was silent for a while thinking it over. I was already driving towards the FBI office. If he didn't let me in, storming the building was on my mind. *Crazy PI shot dead in feeble attempt to enter FBI facility.* I was hoping, wishing, it wouldn't come to that.

"Tell me what you want to do."

I explained on the drive over my emotionally charged plan. When I arrived, he met me at security, and signed me in to allow my weapon. We went to a lower level, where the two brothers were being held. He led me to the secure holding place, signing me in again.

"Who do you want to talk to first?" Dezmond asked.

"Aleksi. He seems the best bet to know the most."

"He is also the toughest."

"So am I."

Dezmond smiled. Not sure if he agreed I was tough, but he wasn't about to stop me. I was let into the room, where Aleksi sat in a bolted-to-the-floor chair, legs and arms cuffed to the frame. He saw my face and smiled. I stepped forward and punched him as hard as I could in the face. His mouth quickly filled with blood, which he spit out on the floor, still smiling.

"I'm guessing you are not here to make small talk," he said.

"No, I'm here to kill you," I responded, with as much vigor as I could muster.

He didn't seem too concerned. "Why?"

"Because your cousin Jasha killed my friend."

"The woman. I believe her name was April."

"Yes."

"I tried to talk him out of it. But he was shamed by her and had to exact revenge. A pity, as she was lovely."

"Yes, she was. Lovely enough to kill Jasha before she succumbed to her wounds."

"Resourceful and tough too. She saved your life before and now you plan on exacting your own revenge."

"Exactly."

"And how can this happen. I'm in a cage with cameras watching my every move. The FBI will never allow this to happen."

"Oh, I think you are wrong. They plan on losing you in Gitmo. And it costs American dollars to keep prisoners down there. With the government budget cuts, they would be thrilled with not having to feed you to save money."

He seemed fearless. I knew it would take a great deal to break him.

"Besides, the camera system is not working. Seems like a software or hardware glitch. Funny how that happens when someone is about to die."

His smile slowly ebbed from his face.

"Her blood is on me," I said pointing to my stained shirt. "I hope none of yours gets on me when I blow your brains out!"

I pulled out my gun and pressed it against his head, and pulled the hammer back.

"Now, you can either talk to me, or die. Either way I'll get what I want, because I'll have your brother brought in and I'll ask him the same questions over your lifeless, bloody body. He will not doubt my threat once he sees you. Tell me your answer, for my patience is thin, and I have nothing to lose."

I could feel him looking at me, seeing the blood on my clothes, measuring my threat, looking deep into my eyes. He could see I meant every word. A deep sigh filled the room as he nodded his head.

"I believe you. What do you want to know?"

"Who killed Aaron Bailey?" I asked, the gun now at my side. "And why were you brought in to stop me from investigating?"

"It's a long story."

"I have time."

"I don't know all the details. We were simply doing a job as we were tasked to do."

"Do you know enough to lead me in the correct direction?"

"Yes, I believe so."

"Then begin."

He started filling me in on various facts he knew. With each statement I would ask follow-up questions. We talked for about thirty minutes before I had all he seemed to know. I walked out of the cell, where Dezmond was waiting.

"Did you get all of that?" I asked.

"Yes, we recorded every word. I'm assuming you want a copy."

"Or a transcript would be helpful."

"Did you learn what you hoped for?"

"Pretty much. Still some holes, but filled in a lot of the blanks and will send me in a new direction."

"Good. Hopefully, it will help us as well and was worth the price of the death of your friend."

I grinned widely.

"Oh, she isn't dead. It was touch and go, but she will make it. Long recovery, though."

"You son-of-a-bitch. You played me."

"I needed you on board, and the emotion of a cop dying is a strong selling point. I wanted you and him to believe me. An Academy Award–winning performance."

"Wilson warned me you were a dick!"

I headed for the elevator. *Better than me punching you in the gut.*

Chapter 22

There was a pounding in my head, which I originally thought was a massive headache from the poor night of sleep. I rolled in late and collapsed on my bed still in my bloody clothing. I had stripped them off some time during the night, still half asleep, before crashing again. But the pounding didn't stop, so I determined someone was angrily knocking on my door with fists like hammers. I got up and grabbed the black robe Melissa had purchased for me, covering me up as I peeked through the window at two faces I didn't know.

"What?" I said with a grouchy disposition.

The first of the two held up a badge, which said Douglas County Sheriff's on it. I sighed, for I didn't feel like explaining anymore about the events of the night before, but opened the door anyway. He came crashing through with his right forearm on my chest, slamming me against the wall with a thud.

"I'm going to rip you a new one if you don't give me a good reason not to!" he yelled.

With all the danger I had already experienced, I was prepared. Out of the robe pocket I pulled my .38 and jammed it in his ribs. Carrying my gun, no matter what the situation was, would be SOP until this case ended. Even the pizza deliveryman would be challenged, if he looked at me the wrong way.

"Please back away," I said firmly. "You maybe a cop, but I'm pretty edgy from a few days of being beaten and shot at."

"Clay, relax," said the man behind him. "Let's hear him out before going off and doing something stupid."

Clay stepped back and gave me some room. I motioned them both to take a seat in the kitchen, while I stood.

"You obviously are Clay," I stated. "And you would be?"

"Kirby Rainn," he said.

"That makes sense. You must be two of April's brothers."

"You are correct. April has told you about us?"

"Yes. I'm surprised all three of you aren't here."

"Neil is a Vice cop and working undercover right now. We can't get ahold of him, or yes, he would be here wanting answers as well."

I tucked the gun back into the pocket and leaned against the wall.

"What answers are you looking for?"

"What the hell happened?" said Clay.

Clay was the oldest, a Douglas County Sheriff, and big. Close to 6' 4" and 225 pounds of muscle-bound anger. He was not in uniform, but in jeans and sleeveless T-shirt, which showed arms any bodybuilder would dream of. He was probably close to my age, with a few specks of gray showing on his close-cropped hair. His fingers were drumming the table nervously, and I wasn't looking forward to having him slam me against anything ever again.

"What do you know?" I asked.

"Not much. Only what my contacts in the Denver PD could tell me, which couldn't explain a whole hell of a lot. Only got your name and that she'd been shot. The specifics were lacking."

"Well, it all started with a case I'm working on…" I went into detail talking about the confrontation outside Boone's, how April kicked the man in the groin, pulled her gun and saved me. The shooting outside her apartment by the same man she had kicked. "In the end she saved my life, probably twice. She is a gutsy lady, and I'm sorry she got hurt over something I was involved with."

"Why did they shoot her, if they were after you?" asked Kirby.

Kirby wasn't quite as tall or muscular, but still was in shape, maybe lacking an inch and fifteen pounds on this brother. His short hair was darker, facial features to match his brother's, with only a few minor differences, like a mole on his cheek and sideburns. He was in jeans and T-shirt, with brown cowboy boots, to his brother's running shoes. He was calm, cool and settled, listening to every word. The diplomat of the siblings, it would seem.

"She embarrassed the man who she kicked in the nuts," I said. "He wanted to even the score, for he had been shamed in front of his partners, for having been felled by a woman. Pride pushed him to shoot her."

"And you let him?" stated Clay.

"Believe me when I say I wished I could have protected her better. I fault myself for not being more alert. I was a little distracted, which I shouldn't have been."

"Distracted by what?" asked Kirby.

I didn't want to say, so just shrugged.

"April distracted you. Are you two dating?" asked Clay.

"We went out to dinner. We are friends, is all."

Clay and Kirby looked at each other and smiled.

"We know our sister," said Kirby. "You may be friends, but she can be pretty aggressive. From your look I would say she made a pass at you."

"A simple suggestion to come in and have a drink."

"And see what happens," said Clay.

"A little lip-lock for emphasis," added Kirby. "Were you planning to go in?"

"Only to make sure she was safe in her apartment. I should have been worried about the outside as well."

"I guess we can't blame you," said Clay. "The question is what are you going to do about it? And what can we do to help?"

Having cops on my side was always a good thing, especially when I needed information that they could access more quickly than I could. Badges can provide leverage a private detective doesn't have. In the end, I liked to work alone unless bodyguards were required, or it was more than I could handle.

"If I may suggest, the most important thing you can do is be there for April. The man who shot her is dead, the two others who accosted me outside of Boone's are being sent to Cuba by the FBI. Right now, I have some leads on the murder of my client's husband I plan to track down. But if there is anything you can assist with, I won't hesitate to call you."

Each of them pulled out a business card and tossed it on the table.

"Please keep us informed," said Kirby. "We will help any way we can."

"What is her condition right now?" I asked. "Last I heard, she was going to be fine. Any long-term effects from the injury?"

"Too soon to say for certain," said Kirby. "They think she'll pull through fine. But it will be a long recovery. Several months before she can work again."

"She is strong and will work hard to get back as soon as possible," added Clay. "I'm betting it won't be a month before she is working again."

"She'll be making advances at you before you know it," said

Kirby.

That was good to hear. Guilt often tugged at me over moments like this. Enough people close to me had paid a big enough price recently. I didn't need to add to my burden list. It was plenty long enough.

"I'm sorry for roughing you up," said Clay. "But don't you dare break my sister's heart or I'll be back."

"I don't think that is possible," I replied. "She is too tough. Besides, her friendship means a great deal to me."

"She acts that way, but we know different. She is a wonderful sister and an even better person."

No argument from me. She might be the one woman whose heart I wouldn't want to break. Of course, I thought the same of Melissa and look how that turned out.

Chapter 23

My day was off to a slow start, thanks to my visitors. I moved quickly to shower, get dressed and stuff myself with whatever I could find in the fridge, which was juice, toast and jam, and some turkey sausage. Before eating, I retrieved the transcript of my conversation with Aleksi, which I had printed from the email Dezmond had sent me. I went over the details, refreshing my memory of what he had said. There were some holes but data enough to lead me in a fruitful direction.

The Platovs were out of the country when they got the call and immediately flew in on a private jet. Their job was to track me down, follow, and determine whom I was working for and why. They were told not to approach me at first, only to follow and observe. When I was seen at Mitch Crabtree's, the thinking was he might have hired me. Their following me led me to knifing their tire. This pissed them off, so they went to threaten Mitch, pushing him around and burning his car to scare him off. Still mad, they then approached me outside of Boone's with plans to beat out of me who did the hiring. When April intervened and had them arrested, their sources got Bristol & Bristol, namely Don Bristol, to bail them out. Who pulled those strings, Aleksi didn't know. Information was always relayed from another source. They then were told to back off for now and wait for further instructions. But Jasha couldn't and attacked us on his own.

Shortly after, the FBI had rounded up the remaining two, but not before he had called into a special number that they were in trouble. It was a Northern California cell number, tied to a burner phone, which no longer was active according to the note added to the transcript by Dezmond. It was in the general area of the WANN home office, so I was inclined to suspect someone there was orchestrating things. It made sense, but I needed to learn more. My best option now was to pay a visit to Bristol & Bristol to see what I could learn. A quick call revealed Don was in the office all afternoon today. I didn't make an appointment, as I planned to show up unannounced and aggressively query him for some answers.

I rode down on my motorcycle and was lucky enough to find

outside meter parking nearby. Feeding enough change to cover me, I was inside and at the front desk talking with the receptionist. She had been the one to tell Melissa to cut off my testicles if I'd ever cheated on her, so her reception wasn't warm. I had my senses tuned to any sharp, shiny metal objects she might be wielding.

"What the hell do you want?" stated Janet with some venom. "Melissa doesn't want to talk with you."

"Not here to see Melissa," I replied. "I need to speak with Don about something urgent."

She looked down at her phone, with its sidecar module, showing the status of all the phone lines in the office.

"He is on a call," she said. "He is too busy to speak with anyone today, especially you."

"That is all I needed to know."

Before she could speak or react I bolted down the hall and to the right. I knew right where his office was and went through the door, closing and locking it. He was talking on the phone and looked up seeing me. We had met a couple of times, only with a simple introduction, but he knew right away who I was and wasn't thrilled at my unannounced entrance. He cupped his hand over the mouthpiece, pointing and telling me to leave. I walked over and pressed on the phone switch to hang up his call, which got him even angrier.

"What the hell, Jarvis," he yelled. "Get out of my office right now before I call the police."

I grabbed the phone line and followed it to the wall and unplugged it. I then opened my leather bike jacket to show him my gun.

"Hand me your cell phone," I demanded.

"Who the hell do you think you are?"

"Do it now before this gets worse. We need to talk, and I want to make sure I have your undivided attention."

He thought about it for a minute and then handed me his oversized iPhone. I powered it down and tossed it on the sofa in his office. I took a seat in an expensive leather chair, on the front side of his desk. They probably spent more money on this chair than I spent on my entire living room set. I doubt they got their furnishings from neighborhood garage sales like I did.

"Don, are you OK in there?" said the voice of Janet, as she tried the door.

"Tell her you are fine," I whispered so only he could hear. "I promise this won't take long."

"Everything is good, Janet. Nothing to worry about. Jarvis just needs to speak with me privately."

"Are you certain?" she replied. "Should I call the police?"

"No, not at all. This won't take long."

We heard her heels walk away, and I turned my attention back to Don. He was dressed in clothes I could never afford or care to wear. His gray Armani jacket hung on his coat rack, his perfectly pressed white collared shirt and loose gray tie may have cost more than my entire personal wardrobe. He was younger than his brother and partner, Tony, by about five years. His perfectly combed black hair glistening from some type of gel, in contrast to his nicely tanned skin. When he smiled a gold-capped tooth, damaged when he was punched by a client, sparkled as if freshly shined each day. He leaned back into this black leather chair, placing his hands behind his head, his anger subsiding.

"Jarvis, what do you want?" he said calmly. "My time is valuable, and you are wasting precious minutes of it."

"You bailed out three Russian men a few days ago," I stated. "The Platov boys. I need to know who hired you to bail them out."

"I have no idea what you are referring to."

"Oh, cut the crap, Don. It's a matter of public record you got them out of jail."

"So what? A client calls and I get them out. Part of what I do."

"But I don't think they were clients of yours. Aleksi told me he didn't know you. I'm certain another paying customer of yours asked you to intervene. I need to know who that is."

"Come on, Jarvis. You know how this works. I can't tell you who it was. If I came to you asking the same question, you'd laugh at me."

"Don, I need to know what is going on. People are trying to kill me and almost killed a friend of mine. A cop, no less. And it all starts with those three you bailed out. Who hired you will lead me to who is calling the shots."

Don didn't flinch and didn't seem to care. I had heard he was the tough one of the two brothers and the one who brought in the questionable clients. Short of beating it out of him I probably wasn't going to get an answer. I stood up, went around his desk, pulled him out of his chair, and pushed him against the glass window behind him.

"Get your hands off me," he said, though with some fear in his eyes. "I can have you arrested or even better sue you."

"I couldn't care less right now," I replied. "When people shoot at me, I get a little angry. I want answers. Or should I go to Tony and inform him of the gangster clients you are working with? I'm sure he wouldn't be too thrilled either."

"Be my guest. Tony isn't going to tell you a damn thing and you know it."

I took my hand and slapped his face a couple of times. Not too hard, just enough to make sure he was aware I could hurt him. I then heard a key in the door and creak of it opening. I kept my attention on Don when someone spoke.

"Jarvis, please don't do this," said the voice of Melissa.

I turned my head and saw her standing there, beautiful as ever. Her tone was calming, so I released him, smoothing out his shirt.

"You are lucky, Don. I value what she thinks," I said. "Remember what we talked about, because I can always discuss this further with you when she is not around."

I walked away and past Melissa, stopping for a minute to look in her eyes. They were warm, and yet sad, at the same time. It broke my heart to see her. I then headed out and to the elevator. She was behind me and asked me to stop. I turned around to see her, dressed professionally in a dark blue pantsuit and black low heels. Her hair was shiny, bleached lighter from the sun, and longer, held back by her reading glasses she was wearing today. As always, she took my breath away. And it saddened me that I had lost her, thanks to my weakness for another woman.

"Jarvis, what are you doing here?" she asked.

My eyes moved down and then back up to her face, my stare caught in hers.

"I needed some answers from Don," I replied.

"So, you were going to beat them out of him?"

"It crossed my mind."

"For what reason was it worth going to jail over?"

"He has information that may help me find someone who tried to kill April and nearly succeeded. She is in the hospital with two bullet holes in her."

"What happened?"

"She stopped them from beating me up. Later, a man she disabled returned to kill her. I was there and couldn't stop him from shooting her. She killed him when he was about to kill me."

I could see the anguish in her eyes. She had been through this before with me and didn't care for it and the life I was leading.

"How is Don involved?"

"He bailed them out of jail. Someone, probably a client, asked him to do so. I believe it's related to a case I'm working on. The company is WANN Systems."

Her eyes lit up, as if she'd heard the name.

"You've heard of them," I said.

"You know I can't say anything. I'd lose my job."

"I know. I'm sorry. I don't want to get you in the middle of this. I'll leave and not bother Don again. I promise."

I walked towards the elevator and hit the down button.

"How is April?" Melissa asked.

"She'll make it, but has a long recovery ahead."

The door opened, and I stepped in, hitting the button for the first floor. Melissa stood watching, our eyes glued to each other.

"I'm sorry about April," she said. "I hope she gets well soon. I'll smooth things over with Don."

I saw her turn and walk away as the door closed. I so wanted to put my hand in the door and run after her and hug her tightly. But I let it shut and took the long ride down, feeling the loss of her as deeply as I ever had.

Chapter 24

I stood next to my bike, cursing silently. I needed something to hit, but nothing was around that wouldn't break bones in my hands. I was seething at myself for losing it and for the pain I'd caused Melissa. Getting over her was difficult. Forgiving myself even harder. I was getting nowhere when my cell phone rang. It was Mallard and he was angry.

"You need to get down here right now!" he growled. "You promised Internal Affairs a statement, and Montero is getting impatient. Been calling me asking where you were. I told him I'm not your mother but he didn't care. If you don't show soon he will be putting out an arrest warrant."

"How was your fishing trip? Catch anything good?"

"What are we, best buddies? You are a piece of work. Are you coming down here or not?"

With all that was going on I'd forgotten about going down. Some days I wondered if I could keep my schedule straight in my head. I wasn't in the best of mood to deal with IA, but I didn't care to spend the night in jail.

"Tell him I'm on my way," I said. "I'm downtown, so give me an hour."

"If you don't show, I'll be the one slapping the cuffs on."

He hung up before I could tell him "good luck with that." I strapped on my helmet and rode back towards my side of town, stopping for a late lunch at a sandwich shop before entering the police station. It was longer than an hour, but I didn't really care.

When I arrived, Luis Montero was sitting in his office, a perturbed look on his face. I'd dealt with him on the previous incident outside of Boone's, and he did seem like a reasonable person. Internal Affairs often got a bad rap in fiction, as being out to get cops at any cost. He didn't come across that way, though now that I'd angered him, maybe that would change.

"Jarvis, have a seat," he said, in a sour tone.

"Sorry I'm late. Case work went longer that I expected."

He grunted, as if to say he really didn't care. He took his drinking cup and swallowed down what appeared to be water. His deep brown eyes looked down at some paperwork. His tight curly hair was darker than his skin, and matched his neatly trimmed mustache. He was shorter than I was by a couple of inches, and slender in his black suit. He squinted at the printed words, not wanting to grab the reading glasses sitting to his left. I wasn't sure if it was vanity or laziness.

"Give me all the details of what happened last night?" he demanded. "I want to be very clear this is the second incident involving you and April. I need you to tell me everything that happened and leave nothing out."

"Have you gotten April's statement yet?" I asked.

"No. She is still under too much sedation to speak. That is why we need details now. A second instance of her pulling her gun, and this time killing someone, demands answers. The top brass wants a report ASAP."

"April and I pulled up to her place in my car," I said. "As we got out and approached her building, Jasha Platov stepped out and shot April…" I continued, giving him all the facts as I remembered then. He listened intently, making notes as he went along. I concluded with the point where April killed him, saving my life in the process.

"Why were April and you together?" he asked.

"We had gone out to dinner."

"Are you two dating or involved in any way?"

That was a tough question to answer. It was sort of a date, but we weren't dating per se.

"We are good friends. I was taking her to dinner to say thanks for saving my neck outside of Boone's."

"Were you planning on thanking in her in ways beyond buying her dinner?"

I didn't like the question, though there had been that possibility. But I wasn't going to give him the satisfaction.

"I bought her dinner and was walking her to her door to make sure she got in safely. Nothing else beyond that."

"Apparently the plan of getting her in safe didn't work."

"You are correct. I wasn't as alert as I should have been. I've been kicking myself about being sloppy."

"Maybe because your mind was on something else. Possibly something pleasurable on the horizon."

"I already answered that wasn't the case. Why are you pursuing this line of questioning?"

"A witness said they saw you walking arm in arm. Looking pretty chummy and close."

I didn't care to get into the "what could have happened" game with him.

"Look, Montero, this is getting you nowhere. April and I are close friends. What may have happened is irrelevant. She fired on a man who had shot her twice, killing him to keep him from killing me. She saved my life and I will be forever grateful."

"Where did she get the gun?" he asked, now going a different route. "Her service revolver was taken away from her in lieu of the investigation of the previous incident you two were involved with."

"I was concerned for her safety and she didn't have a personal weapon of her own. With the possible danger I loaned her one of mine."

He let out a low whistle.

"That could create a problem for her and you."

"She is a licensed police officer, with training on using a weapon. The gun is registered in my name with a clean history. I doubt there would be any issue here unless you care to make a federal case out of it."

He nodded his head, still taking notes. I wondered if any of this was being recorded in any way. Seemed odd if it wasn't, but he certainly would or should have told me this up front.

"Let's go over this again from the beginning..." Which we did two more times, each one the questioning took a similar path, though with some variations. Normal technique to catch me in a lie. But I never varied, and in the end, he had to be satisfied I was telling the truth.

"How many times are we going to go through this?" I asked.

"We are done. I've heard what I've needed to hear. I don't see there will be any issue for you or her, depending on what she says once we can talk. It sounds like a dire situation that neither of you could avoid."

I was grinning on the inside, but stoic on the outside. He dismissed me and as I walked towards the door, I turned around and made a statement.

"For the record, I want to say April is a hell of a cop. And her talents are wasted sitting behind a desk. When her wounds are healed, and she is physically able, she should be out on the streets where every good cop should be. I don't know if you have any say in the matter, but I wanted to make that clear."

Montero looked up from his notes after finishing whatever he was writing, a serious look on his face.

"I don't have much input, but I agree wholeheartedly. And I'll be certain to put that in my report."

I walked out of there feeling good about what I'd said. With little else to do, and the afternoon turning to evening I rode on down to Swedish Medical Center to check on April. When I arrived, I was told she was still in ICU and only family was allowed. I called Clay to see if he could get me in. He was with her and walked up to get me.

"She is still pretty doped up, but has been asking about you. Wanting to make sure you were safe."

When I got down there, she was lying down with all kinds of wires and tubes attached. Her eyes were closed when I touched her hand. She gave me a weak smile and closed her eyes again. I leaned down and gave her a soft peck on the forehead and then sat down in a chair next to her for about thirty minutes. I told her about what I'd been doing since the shooting and what my next steps were. Her head turned over to look at me from time to time, so I was pretty certain she could hear me. After I talked myself out I said goodbye, kissed her again and rode my bike back home, feeling good and bad at the same time, knowing she would be fine but it would be some time before her life became normal again.

As I got to the front door of my place, I found a sealed envelope tucked into the door frame. I looked around for some reason, wondering if someone was there watching me. I opened the door, walked in and tore open the letter. Inside on plain paper was handwritten, "Chief Security Officer Kyle Lambert hired Don." I looked at both sides and that was all that was written. Simple and to the point. But it was enough. And I recognized the handwriting.

"Thank you, Melissa," I said out loud, with a warmth in my heart I'd not experienced in some time.

Chapter 25

Being apprehensive and wanting to protect Melissa, I shredded the paper after memorizing the name. With a simple search of the Web using the term *Chief Security Officer Kyle Lambert*, I found out he was the company head of security for surprise, surprise: WANN Systems. He was based out of their main headquarters in the Silicon Valley, which was located in the southern portion of the San Francisco Bay Area, as were most of the world's high-tech corporations.

After consulting with my client, I found the cheapest flight I could find on short notice, and the next day was landing at Mineta San Jose International Airport. It was late morning and I was so happy to have my feet firmly on the ground, surviving jet travel, which I dreaded. With a small carry-on in hand, I got my rental car, a little Toyota Corolla, and was off on my day. Since I didn't know the city, I navigated by GPS on my phone to a sandwich shop to fill the void in my stomach from not eating before the flight, a necessity to keep me from getting airsick. San Jose was not too far from Sunnyvale, where their offices were located, and the hotel I booked was nearby. I didn't need much, a place to sleep and shower, so I went as cheap as I could find. But cheap in this area was over two-hundred dollars per night. Thankfully, my client was not hurting for money and floated me upfront cash to cover expenses.

I was able to check in early and unpacked. Testing the bed and finding it acceptable, I started plotting out my day. The plan was to stay for two nights and see what type of trouble I could stir up. I would call the WANN office and see if I could get a meeting. When I contacted their main number, I found out that their CSO was in today, but totally booked. Undeterred, I asked to talk with someone directly under Lambert and found that a Bronwen Pearson, Director of Security for the Western Region, would have some time at 3 p.m. to talk. When asked what I needed to meet with her for, I made up a story about possible breaches in credit card information for my small retail company, Smithfield Wearables, from using their security firewalls. Since I wasn't all that tech savvy, Mandy had provided technical information from a friend. This I needed to use to get in the front door, the handwritten notes I was referring to and attempting to memorize, so I'd get the tech slang correct. I was convincing enough to get on her schedule. Once inside I would play it by ear on what I would do.

Since I had some time I decided to take a quick nap, since sleep never came easy for me in a different bed. I set the alarm and nodded off briefly, long enough to dream about April getting shot. It was short and graphic, and I awoke not all that rested when the buzzer went off. But it did get me fired up to get inside of WANN and hopefully stir the drink.

Thanks to GPS technology I parked in a visitor space outside their shiny glass and chrome box-shaped headquarters. After entering and passing through security, I came to the main information desk, which directed me to the fifth floor, which was the Cyber Security level. There I was greeted by a gruff male receptionist, who eyed me closely when I gave him my information and why I was there. I was told to take a seat and someone would be with me shortly. I found a *Time* Magazine among all the tech periodicals, which had an article on WANN covering the two owners. I read through the piece learning nothing I'd not already known, beyond the self-promotion and *we are changing the world* self-rhetoric. I'd stomached enough and was about to open a copy of *Wired* when a slim, short Asian woman came forward, putting out her hand.

"Mr. Smithfield," she said. "So nice to meet you. I'm Ms. Pearson's assistant, Suki Nagano. She wanted me to come and get you, and bring you to her meeting room. She is on a call but should be finished soon."

We walked side by side, as she made chit-chat about the weather. She brought me to a small conference room, with an oval table and six chairs, while offering me something to drink. I answered water, and she pulled a Perrier out of the small refrigerator, removed the twist-off cap, and sat it on a coaster on the shiny dark wood table before leaving me, saying if I needed anything, to dial 8222 on the nearby phone and she'd be there to assist.

After leaving me alone I looked around the room. Being a detective, snooping was part of my MO. But there wasn't much to snoop for. Table, chairs, fridge, TV and video conference, and a view of the neighboring buildings out the Mecco Shade–covered window. There were a couple of paintings on the walls of beaches and boats. Unless there were hidden safes behind the pictures, the room held out little hope of clues.

After ten minutes and half a glass bottle of Perrier, in walked Bronwen Pearson. She was a tall lady, with broad shoulders, round face with a ruddy complexion, short dark hair and caterpillar eyebrows. When she stuck out her thick-fingered hand, she shook mine like a man would, firm and strong. Her slacks were black, polo top red, shoes flat, black and extremely plain. If it weren't for her large bosom, I'd swear she was a man. If she'd not been in the military at one time or another I would have been surprised. She looked firm, strong and stout, and I'd hate to have met her in a dark alley.

"Mr. Smithfield," she said with the handshake that blocked blood flow. "I understand you had some concerns about our equipment and its security. How can I help you on this matter?"

Thanks to the information Mandy's friend had sent over, I had rehearsed over and over again so I would sound like I knew what I was talking about. The details were good, and explanation provided made me sound knowledgeable enough. But I decided to throw it all out and play myself to see what type of information I could pry out of her.

"I have to admit, I'm not who I claimed I was when making the appointment," I said with a wry smile.

She did not look happy with my first words, always a bad sign.

"Who exactly would you be?" she stated with a hint of anger.

"My name is Jarvis Mann. I'm a private detective."

She didn't seem surprised. She had heard the name before.

"I'm aware of you. It has been spoken in some of our meetings."

"Happy to know I'm famous!" I said with a chuckle.

She didn't think I was funny.

"Hardly. More of an annoyance."

I smiled even wider.

"That is my motto. Annoy and pester until the truth is discovered."

"What truth are you searching for?"

"Who killed Aaron Bailey?"

"Who has hired you to bring clarity to this situation?"

She sounded almost poetic. I tried to match her words.

"The answer to that query is to remain a mystery of the ages."

Not quite Kipling, but not bad.

"I believe the police have determined it to be a random robbery."

"The police are not infallible in their deductions. I have reason to fathom there is more to the story."

"What have you deduced?"

"That someone in your company may have had him killed."

She leaned back in her chair, the vein in her neck bulging out ever so slightly. I don't think she cared for my accusation.

"Those are damning words. Words which could get you sued."

I leaned back as well, crossing my arms, flexing my muscles, trying to look tough. Next to her, though, I wasn't as brutish.

"I've only made them to you, yet you seem uncomfortable with me saying them. Which leads me to believe there may be some truth to them, that you would prefer not be uncovered."

"There is nothing to reveal. The death of the young man had nothing to do with us. Spreading rumors as such will only lead to us taking action against you."

"I believe you already have. Three Russian men paid me a visit, which did not go well. Leading to your company having local lawyers in Denver bailing them out."

"You have no proof of this."

"I know your boss, Kyle Lambert, made a call to Bristol & Bristol, who promptly got them released."

The vein in her neck tightened even more. Her fisted right hand began to turn red, as her fingers squeezed tighter and tighter. She rocked back, then forward in her chair, her eyes boring into me.

"I'm not sure where you got your information from, but it means nothing and can't be proven."

"I would like to speak to Mr. Lambert and get his thoughts."

"He isn't available nor has time to talk with someone as insignificant as yourself. And neither do I. Take your claims and walk away now, before I call security up here and have them throw you out."

"Mighty testy for someone with nothing to hide. You can have your goons come up and drag me out, but it won't change my investigation one iota. I will get answers and if it leads to someone within your corporation, they will be brought to justice."

She got out of her chair and went to the phone, dialing for Suki. I could only hear parts of what she said, but it encompassed a few expletives.

"Do you know what happened to Aaron's notebook computer?" I asked.

"I'm done listening and talking to you."

I really didn't care if she said another word. I was working her for even the slightest reaction.

"There is no mention of his computer at the crime scene. From what I understand, he took it everywhere with him. Why wasn't it recovered from the scene?"

She did her best not to look at me.

"Not even a mention or concern it was missing from WANN."

Pestering her was making her nervous.

"Stolen, like everything else," she finally said. "It was a robbery, plain and simple."

"I don't think so. My working theory is, those in your company who were involved retrieved and wiped it clean, then passed it onto another employee. Did you put in a claim with your insurance it was lost? Or maybe you didn't care, since nothing was lost and you found what you wanted!"

She didn't answer and was pacing, waiting for her assistant. In a few minutes Suki hustled into the room.

"We are done here. See that Mr. Mann leaves the building. If he doesn't, have someone from our security team drag him out!"

Suki looked surprised.

"Who am I supposed to see leaves?"

"Mr. Mann here."

"I thought he was Mr. Smithfield?"

"So did I. Make sure of it, Ms. Nagano, or else."

Before she walked out, Pearson walked over to where I stood, staring at me eye to eye, trying her best to intimidate me. I was probably too dumb to be scared and just grinned at her. After she left Suki came over and seemed apologetic.

"I'm so sorry, but you must leave now. Please don't force me to call someone."

I wanted to tell her it would take more than one, but I resisted.

"No worries. I will happily walk out with you. Please lead the way."

I had no reason to make life hard for Suki, so I went peacefully and even chit-chatted on the way down. As we reached the ground floor on the elevator, she left me with two security people who made sure I exited, likely blacklisting me from the building. As I left and reached my car, the sense of being followed was palpable. Once I was out on the street, I confirmed that a dark SUV was tailing me. A good sign I'd stirred up things within WANN. I had accomplished what I'd hoped for. The question was, who was going to take a run at me now.

Chapter 26

During our ride down the elevator, Suki had given me a nearby restaurant and bar to visit for some tasty food. It was only a half-mile away, so I stopped in and took a seat at the bar, with an unobstructed view of the entryway. I ordered a beer and chicken sandwich, one eye watching anyone coming in.

The place was quiet, with a couple other people sitting at the bar, and a few in the dining area. It still was a little early for the dinnertime crowd, so it would be easy to spot anyone coming in who might be following me. While I waited for my food sipping my beer, I got a call on my cell phone from a number I didn't recognize.

"Is this Jarvis Mann?" said the male voice on the other end.

"It is."

"I may have some information that will benefit you. I wonder if we can meet."

"Information about what?"

"I'd prefer not to say over the phone. But it is related to a technical issue you are having."

I wasn't sure I liked the coyness of the conversation.

"Not having any technical issues at the moment. You'll have to do better."

"Do you know what a Black Hat is?"

I'm glad it had been explained to me recently, or I might have thought he was talking about a magician.

"I do."

"I can help with a hack which may have led to violence."

It would appear he was speaking of the Aaron Bailey case.

"When would you like to meet?"

"Anytime you can make yourself available."

"Where are you located?"

"Denver."

"I'm out of town right now. It would be a day or two before I can meet."

"I will call you again in two days."

The call ended, leaving me curious. As with anything, I was leery of being lured into a situation that might get me killed.

Cryptic dealings like this often could be traps. It would be interesting learning whom it was on the other end. I would have to wait a couple of days to find out.

My sandwich arrived, along with some salt-free fries. For bar food it was not too bad. A few patrons strolled in, a couple of attractive ladies in jeans so tight it looked like they were painted on. A Hispanic couple holding hands, who joined another couple in a back booth. Mostly a later-twenties and early-thirties crowd was filling the place. I decided on a second beer, when the eighth person I saw coming into the bar caught my eye. He was by himself and sat at the other end of the bar, trying his best not to look at me. He was a shorter Asian man, dressed in jeans and a T-shirt, which strained against the muscles in his chest and arms. Various tattoos adorned his skin, with a prominent one of a dragon etched on his neck. He ordered a beer, his eyes glued on the Giants game on the TV behind the bar. He looked over for a split second but then was back to the TV. I might have been wrong, but I had a suspicion he was there to keep an eye on me. I called the bartender over.

"Do you know that guy at the end of the bar?" I asked.

"Not one of the regulars," he replied. "But neither are you."

"No, I'm from out of town. I have feeling he is as well. I was going to pay for his beer and maybe strike up a conversation. Who knows, we might become best pals."

"You may be in the Bay Area, but we are not that type of bar."

I smiled.

"I'm not trying to get a date. But I think he may be following me."

He looked back at him.

"He's a small guy but looks awful tough. You can pay for his beer but don't start anything. We recently remodeled and I don't care to start over."

"Not my style," I replied in a lie. "If you can let him know, I'd appreciate it."

The bartender nodded and headed to the other end. He spoke to him, but he didn't seem to completely understand. The bartender pointed my way and I held my beer up. He looked over and then was back staring at the game. Though he appeared not to be watching me I sensed the whole time his attention was in my direction.

Now, prudent people would say leave it alone, but I was rarely called prudent. I thought it over for a couple of minutes and got up from my seat and sat right next to him, bringing my beer and plate with me. His head never turned my way, still doing his best not to acknowledge me.

"Giants aren't doing as well this year," I said to him. "The Mets seem to be putting the lumber to their pitching staff in this game."

Again, no recognition he understood me. I wondered if he spoke English. If I had to guess I would say he was Chinese. Not that it did me any good, as I couldn't speak his language either short of saying "Sayonara." *Or was that Japanese?*

"Food isn't too bad here," I said, while pointing to my remaining sandwich. "You look famished."

"Beer," he said in broken English, after finishing his first mug.

"Or maybe a veggie burger. Though looking at you, I'd say you devoured protein to supplement your muscle mass."

Nothing. I thought I'd throw out some names and see his reaction.

"Kyle Lambert," I said at first.

He heard the words, but didn't seem to react much.

"Bronwen Pearson."

A slight reaction, though hard to say for certain.

"Suki Nagano," I said out loud.

His head twitched and then back to the TV. He definitely knew the name.

"Friend of yours?" I asked. "From WANN Systems. Maybe told you where I was going for dinner, since it was her suggestion."

He turned around and looked me square in the eye this time, speaking something in his native tongue of which I had no idea what it meant. He pointed at me and then gave me the thumbs-up "you are out of here" gesture, like an umpire when kicking someone out of the game. I wasn't sure if he wanted me to leave him alone, leave the bar or leave the state. Probably a little of all three.

"I have to finish my dinner and beer," I said with a smile. "I hate to waste food."

I took my time, taking the last few bites, his eyes still fixed on me. The fries weren't all that good. Ketchup couldn't even save them, so I left a few behind. I washed down the last of it with my beer, wiping my face with a paper napkin.

"Wow, that was good," I said while patting my stomach. "You really should eat something. A small guy like you needs to balance his food and beer intake."

We exchanged more stares, when I pointed at the TV and said, "Home run Giants." He and the bartender both looked at the game, and I cold-cocked him with a solid punch that put his lights out, his head hitting the bar with a thud. I put his arms on either side of his head, as if he was asleep.

"What the hell happened to him?" asked the bartender.

"I guess he can't hold his beer," I replied, throwing money on the counter. "I told him he should eat something. This should cover his tab and mine. And gee, we were getting along so well."

I walked out of the joint, flexing my hand, as it tingled from the contact. Once in my car I drove away, watching the SUV in the rearview mirror sitting there, waiting for its man inside to come out. It would be a long wait, for he likely would be sleeping for some time.

Chapter 27

Since they were no longer following me I was free to go back to my hotel. Since they might know where I was staying, I checked out early and found another room at a competing chain a couple of miles away. I didn't care to have them charging in on me in the middle of the night. I didn't have a gun, and though my fighting skills were good, not knowing who I was up against, it wasn't worth chancing it. Besides the man I cold-cocked might be inching to get even over my cheap shot. With a good night of sleep, well, as least as good as I could get in a new bed, I was off and running the next day.

My plan was to talk with the ex-wife of Logan Albers. Divorced women could often be quite candid about their former mates. There was something about their divorce, from what I read, which didn't sit right with me. She lived in the western part of the region in Los Altos Hills, one of the wealthiest towns in the San Francisco Bay area. Average price of homes was over two million dollars. So being divorced from a wealthy tech genius had its privileges. As my GPS guided me, the hilly and highly wooded area was much different than the Silicon Valley, and more like the foothill region west of Denver. The view from an aerial map showed many of the homes huge in size, with built-in outdoor pools and tennis courts. Money made for luxury and comfort, but not always a better life.

When I arrived at her house, I found it was not one of the larger ones in the area. When I say not larger, though, it was still huge in size, just not a mansion as many of the others were. I would probably get lost inside without a guide. I parked in front of the garage, next to a black BMW. Walking up the steps, I rang the doorbell and waited, when a forty-something Mexican woman, who appeared to be a maid, answered the door. She allowed me in and had me wait in the lobby, outside of an expansive living area, with vaulted ceilings and a winding staircase reaching to the upper floor. The maid returned and walked me through the living area, past a kitchen larger than my entire home office and out sliding glass doors to a deck overlooking a crystal-clear pool. Laying in the sun in her white bikini on a chaise lounge was a striking woman. Though I knew her approximate age of forty-five, if I hadn't known I'd have guessed no older than mid-thirties. She stood up, put on a robe and motioned for me to sit in a soft chair at a table, the sun filtered by the open umbrella above. She held out her hand, which I took, finding it soft and warm. She removed her sunglasses when sitting, crossing her tanned long legs. I did my best not to stare too much, but I was a full-blooded male, so I enjoyed the view, while trying not to drool on my cotton polo.

"You would be Jarvis Mann," she said, while sipping her tea she had carried over with her. "I'm Lyndi Albers. You said you wanted to talk about something related to WANN Systems and my ex-husband."

"Yes, I'm investigating a murder back in Colorado of an employee of WANN Systems."

"You are a police officer?"

"No, a private detective."

"May I see some ID?"

I showed her my license, the picture hardly flattering. They wouldn't let me take it with my shirt off and me flexing my biceps, so it was plain and boring. Those in the Colorado government were always killjoys.

"What does the death of this employee have to do with Logan?"

"Part of the job of a detective is learning all I can about those involved. When researching WANN Systems, I learned of your divorce and found the circumstances unusual. I was wondering if you would clarify the reasons why you are no longer married."

"Explaining to you those reasons would be a violation of the settlement."

"There is only us here, and no one will ever know you told me anything. I'm quite good at keeping secrets."

She sized me up before responding.

"Well, you do have an attractive and honest face. I can see what you want to know and decide from there."

I glowed with a smile. It was fun to flirt again, even if it was only to get information and not physical pleasure. Though it would be difficult to turn down such a sensual person.

"You met Logan in college?" I asked.

"Yes. A mutual friend set us up."

"What attracted him to you?"

"Mostly his ambition. He was a good-looking guy, but there

were many good-looking men to choose from, and to climb into bed with. I felt he was going to be successful and, to put it bluntly, wealthy. That was as much a turn-on as any physical aspect of him. I could wrap my legs around any man and get pleasure. But to live like this is truly what I wanted."

"Yet, it took many years to achieve his successes?"

"It did. But I was patient. And even in his tough times we had money. We were hardly starving."

"Where did the money come from in those tough times?"

"Family, friends and investors, for all I knew. I didn't know or care. So long as I could slap down the credit card and buy what I wanted, was all that mattered."

Lyndi grabbed her cell phone and typed out a quick message. It wasn't too long before the maid arrived.

"Maria, please get Jarvis here something to drink. He looks parched and could use something to calm his nerves."

"Yes, ma'am. What can I get you?"

If I was nervous, I didn't feel that way. Of course, maybe I was twitching, tapping my fingers and or feet without knowing it. Normally in the presence of beauty I remained calm, but she was showcasing sex without even trying.

"I'll take a beer, if you have one."

"Normally we don't keep beer on hand," said Lyndi. "Maria, give him something a little stronger. I'd say rum and Coke would be more his speed. I'll take some red wine."

Maria wandered off and I looked deep into Lyndi's eyes. If she was trying to get me drunk, she wasn't shy about it.

"I figured a private eye needs to have a strong drink from time to time. Keep the heart racing."

"It is racing plenty at the moment."

"Good. I like a man feeling excited. Besides, to answer all your questions may require payment on your part."

Maria returned with my drink and her wine. I took a short sip on the tall glass and found it was mostly rum and very little Coke. I needed to pace myself.

"From what I understand you divorced after thirteen years. I read it was because of your infidelity. Yet you received a large check as settlement and of course live in this multi-million-dollar home."

She took a quick sip of the wine, thinking over her answer.

"Though it might not be in my best interest to say, I believe you will keep this in confidence. It was all a crock, to make sure he looked good to the shareholders. I took the bullet for him and in return was well taken care of."

"Including this home?"

"Yes. And a trust fund for our daughter Nycole to pay for her Stanford education. And money enough for me to live the lifestyle I was used to."

"Was it his indiscretions or his gambling that ended the marriage?"

"I see you've done your research," she stated with a smile. "Little of both, though they were connected. He loved to fly to Vegas and play the poker, slots, blackjack, whatever else he could get the thrill off of. And of course, he'd hook up there."

"He had a taste for the ladies while gambling?"

"Yes, and young ones too. And young men as well. He liked to play both sides of the fence and both at the same time."

This was news not reported in the searches I'd done.

"How young of men?"

"They were of age, or so they said. You seem surprised."

"Sort of. Surprised it was kept quiet. It would seem someone would have reported on this. Tabloids and Internet gossip."

"With enough money secrets can be kept."

"How did you find out?"

"How else? Someone sent me pictures and videos."

"Were you shocked?"

"Not completely. I'd wondered about his desire for me. It was waning, and only confirmed what I suspected."

"Had you been unfaithful?"

"No. At least not until after I received the news. Found some hot stud about ten years younger and did him every way I could. It was fulfilling but still empty. Logan and I discussed how best to handle the situation. For a while we stayed married, with separate bedrooms and lives, but soon rumors started to fly and we needed to do something. Since his company was starting to take off again with a huge infusion of money, it was decided to put the blame on me so as not to freak out the shareholders. Make him out to be the good guy who took the high road. He would take care of me financially and I'd take the hit in the press. Made him a martyr. It was a fair trade, even though I was crucified at first. But that only lasted a brief time, as the press grows tired of the same old crap and finds someone new to ruin. I stayed out of the limelight, which was fine by me. I had what I wanted which was the house and enough money to live how I wanted to live."

"And you never remarried?"

"No. If I did I'd lose the fortune. Unless there was another man with deep pockets, I played the field to tend to my physical needs. When I felt like it I could bed whomever I wanted, when it pleased me to do so."

"Is today one of those days?"

She smiled, opening her robe up to show her bikini-covered body.

"Would that be so bad? For a woman my age, would you say I have a body for sin?"

"Most definitely. And if time wasn't an issue, I'd take you up on that offer. But I feel I must decline, for I'd need sufficient time to explore your sinful curves."

"A shame. Maybe you can return some day when you have more time. I might even be willing to pay for your flight?"

I had been elevated to gigolo status.

"An offer to ponder."

I took another drink of the rum. I'd have many sexy dreams about Lyndi to screw up my sleep patterns. For now, I needed to stay away from one-night stands, no matter how tempting.

"There were a couple of moments when WANN Systems was about to go under. The last one, when they were bailed out, seemed to coincide around the same time you learned of Logan's partying way of life. Did it ever occur to you that they might be related?"

"Never crossed my mind. I really didn't care about his work, so long as I had money to spend. What are you thinking?"

"I'm curious about where the pictures and videos came from. Did you ever learn the source?"

"No. The email accounts were always different and deleted, making them untraceable."

"Did anyone ever call and talk to you? Tell you verbally about his cheating?"

"Yes, a couple of times. Though the phone numbers were

always different and didn't work if I tried to call back."

"Do you remember the voice?"

She finished her wine, taking the carafe and filled her glass with more.

"It has been some time now, but yes, I do remember it was a male voice, with an accent if I recall correctly."

"What type of accent?"

She leaned back in her chair, throwing her chest out at me. It was full and certainly eye catching. She noticed my watching and took her hands, adjusting her top so her breasts moved.

"If I would hazard a guess, I would say Eastern European. Russian or some other Eastern Bloc country. Does that tell you something?"

I wanted to yell out "bingo" but resisted. But this certainly qualified as a clue.

"It could. I've had some dealings with some men in this case with links to your ex-husband's company, who are from that part of the world. I don't believe in coincidences, so I will have to look into this further. What about men of Asian descent? Were there any of them around as well?"

"One of the videos had a young Asian man and girl in them. The disgusting pig was enjoying them both in rather vulgar ways."

"Any business dealings with Russia or China you know of?"

Sighing, Lyndi drank the rest of her wine, then reached out her hand to touch my leg, her eyes boring into me.

"You realize all this talk of my ex is tiring and hardly arousing. You don't need to give me an afternoon. Thirty minutes of passion will suffice. Are you sure you wouldn't like to walk upstairs with me and help me out of my suit?"

The pressure was there, the desire filling me. She stood up letting the robe hit the ground, grabbing my hand and pulling me to her. Her lips brushed mine, tantalizingly, the smell of suntan lotion and chlorine filling my nose. She kissed me with full lips and tongue, guiding my hand to her rear end. I pulled away and smiled, taking my business card and sliding it into her cleavage.

"If you are ever in Denver, call me," I said while walking away. "I'll give you the full head-to-toe Jarvis Mann treatment."

When I reached the car, I took several deep breaths to ease the desire and stiffness I was feeling, and then drove away, happy I had learned something, unhappy I had not acted on her advances. But also knowing I was not ready to go back to that freewheeling life just yet, no matter how much I was tempted. *And oh, how I was tempted!*

Chapter 28

After a restless night of sexy thoughts of Lyndi and concerns at every sound outside my door that could be someone coming to get me, I was off to the airport at 5 a.m. Since it was a short plane ride, I headed to San Diego. I wanted to talk with Aaron's parents, who lived down there. Grieving family was never pleasant to deal with, but from what Mandy had told me this was hardly the case, which seemed odd. But it never hurt to get additional insight about the victim.

I landed at San Diego International Airport and then took an expensive cab ride to Chula Vista, a suburb of San Diego south and east, the second largest city in the metro area. I had talked with Aaron's mother and she said I could stop by, but that they had afternoon plans. I arrived at about 11 a.m., the cab dropping me at their expansive house, whose backyard faced a large golf country club. When I rang the doorbell, the mother answered, letting me in after I showed ID. I entered the living area with large vaulted ceilings and was led to the back patio, where her husband was enjoying a drink. Each was dressed in tennis clothing, as Aaron's mom had explained they had a match at 12:30. I was offered a seat and sat down on one of the more comfortable outdoor chairs I'd ever had the pleasure of placing my butt in.

"Can I get you something to drink?" she asked.

"Orange juice or iced water would be great, Mrs. Bailey."

"Oh, please call me June. And he is Darren."

I smiled, stood again and shook Darren's hand. It was firm, the skin soft and brown, with sunspots on his arms from a life in the sun and warmth.

"Good to meet you," said Darren with a raspy voice. "What can we help you with?"

"Oh, please wait, Darren. Let me get him his drink."

June hustled out and was back quickly with a bottle of OJ, the top removed, a glass with ice for me to pour into.

"I'm not sure if June told you, Darren, but I'm a private detective looking into your son's murder. I know it can be difficult to discuss, so I'm sorry to put you through it. I wanted to learn a little more about him. A parent's perspective."

"We were shocked when we heard the news," stated June. "So sad to hear."

She said it like it was a friend's or neighbor's son that was killed, with little emotion.

"What was Aaron like growing up?"

"He was an energetic boy," said Darren. "Loved the outdoors. Couldn't get him inside even in the snow."

"This is not the home he grew up in?"

"No, not at all," said June. "Lived in Colorado until about eight years ago. Wanted to live somewhere warmer. We love to be outdoors and enjoy the warm, moist air."

"Did Aaron move with you?"

June frowned.

"No. He was on his own by that time. Going to college. Shacking up with Mandy."

"You say that as if it was a dreadful thing," I said. "Did you not care for Mandy?"

Both of them looked at each other, as if to see who would answer. Finally, Darren did.

"No, we did not care for her. He had a better life ahead of him being something more than a computer geek. But love makes you do stupid things, no matter what your parents want for you."

"What were your hopes for him?"

"Day trading. Investment banking. The type of work I did and was successful at."

"How you were able to afford this expensive home."

"Exactly. I made in a couple of months what he made in a year. But we couldn't convince him. She blinded him, wrapping him around her finger."

"And you felt the same, June?"

"Yes. Really after she came into his life he had no time for us. It was as if he was already dead."

"Is that why you didn't go to the funeral?"

I assumed I'd hit a nerve with that statement, but both remained calm.

"She wouldn't have wanted us there," said June. "We were sad but dealt with it in our own way."

"No thoughts on why someone would kill him?" I asked.

"No, not at all," replied Darren. "One would not think a

computer nerd would ever have something like that happen to him. Besides, we were told it was random. A robbery."

"I'm not so certain. I believe there was more to it. He may have stumbled upon something going on in the company he worked for."

"WANN Systems?" asked Darren.

I nodded.

"I've bought and sold their stocks through the years. Been up and down, though mostly up recently. What have you discovered about them? If it's bad, I might be inclined to sell while it's still high."

I wanted to yell out at him, for all they seemed to care about was the money and not why their son was killed. Though I doubted it would make any difference.

"I can't reveal anything yet. Still early, but if I get anything I'll let you know."

Darren grabbed his phone and started typing out a text.

"Dear, that is rude," said June. "You know I hate it when you pull out your phone and tune out a guest or me."

He ignored her, and tapped away.

"It's alright, June. I'm used to it. Anything else you can tell me about Aaron or even Mandy?"

"Aaron loved his sports. Tennis, golf and baseball. Might have been good enough to go pro. But once the computer bug and that bitch Mandy rewrote his DNA, he was never the same man. Certainly not the same man we raised."

"Do you have other kids, June?"

"No, Aaron was the only one."

I wanted to say good to know, but resisted.

"It was a difficult birth and I nearly died. Doctors told me never to have kids again."

"And she took the only one you had away from you?"

"Exactly."

"She mentioned he was a computer nerd when they met."

"Not at all," said Darren, now done with his phone. "He was a jock all the way. Oh, he used a computer, but not like he did afterwards. Coding, hacking, whatever the hell he did. She introduced him to that world. Whatever dream we had of him being a pro athlete or making money in my line of business was out the window."

"Maybe his dreams didn't align with yours," I said.

I'd probably said too much, as they both looked at their watches.

"We must be going now," said Darren. "We have to drive to our match. If there is anything else we can help with, let us know."

I pulled out a business card and left it on the table, and was led out the door. I'm sure the only time it was handled by them was to place it in the trash.

Chapter 29

Landing in Denver, I was happy as always to have my feet firmly planted on the ground again. When I arrived late afternoon, and turned on my phone I received a couple of text messages and pictures of Lyndi, leading to more temptation. I'd never done any sexting before, even with Melissa, but now I had someone to flirt with via SMS. After retrieving my car from the expansive DIA parking lot, I headed back to town, my first call to my client, who had left me a more routine message on voicemail while on my flight, urgently asking me to contact her.

"You are back in town?" asked Mandy.

"Yep, I landed at DIA a short while ago. I was able to come up with some information that may be helpful."

"Good, I'm glad you're back."

She sound concerned.

"Is something wrong?"

"Yes, that creepy detective Adam King called a couple more times. I thought you were going to talk with him."

Crap, I'd completely forgotten about him with all going on.

"Sorry. I didn't pay him a visit."

"Can you please? I'm tired of hearing from him."

"Next time he calls tell him you'll meet him somewhere. Pick some place open like a park. I'll show up instead and convince him to bother someone else."

"Anywhere in particular?"

I chose a location and details of what to say.

"I will do that. What did you learn in California?"

I gave her the highlights of the trip. I'm not sure she was convinced it meant much.

"I don't see what any of that means in relation to Aaron's murder."

"So far I've had Russian and Chinese thugs come after me. One of the founders and principal owners of WANN likes to gamble and sleep with younger men and women. It is possible they are using that against him to have access to his business. An Internet business where lots of money is made. From what I understand, Russian and China are two of the largest Internet hacking countries in the world, stealing mountains of personal data and people's finances. A lot of that information runs across WANN's switches and routers. If Aaron did find evidence of this, it could be a motive to kill him."

"Sounds like it's mostly circumstantial."

"It is. But I'm making them nervous. And nervous people do stupid things which can expose them."

"Like trying to hurt you!"

"I will do my best not to let that happen. And we'll need to be careful with you as well. Though they don't know you hired me, it's just a matter of time before they start putting a connection together. So be on the lookout for anything suspicious, and let me know no matter how trivial it seems."

There was a long pause, and I sensed worry on the other end of the call.

"It will be alright. But stay put for now and don't venture out too much. Your place is relatively secure. No reasons to take any chances, though."

Still silence. I figured now was as good a time as any to bring up my visit to San Diego.

"I went and talked with Aaron's parents."

The silence remained, though I heard breathing and it seemed like rapid inhaling caused by anger.

"Why did you talk with them?" she asked. "They fucking don't care at all about him or why he was killed."

The expletive seemed surprising to hear from her.

"I discovered that. Please understand it is part of the process." I had to stop to compose myself. "I need to learn as much as I can from all who knew him."

"They don't know a damn thing about him."

"Told me he was a jock before meeting you."

"Bullshit. He enjoyed sports, but was never going to be anything more than a journeyman."

"They say you convinced him computers were the way to go."

"It was his own choice. He was tired of being in their shadow, doing what they wanted him to do. All I did was tell him to be what he wanted to be."

She didn't seem thrilled talking about this, so I then told her about the odd call I got in California, asking if she might know who it could have been. She answered me quickly. Almost too quickly.

"I haven't a clue. Sorry. I need to go. I have something cooking on the stove. I'll contact you when the creep calls me back."

The line abruptly went dead. The tingle on the back of my neck told me she might know more than she was letting on. Or maybe she was just mad at me for visiting the Baileys. For now, I'd let it slide. I was home soon and tired, but needed to workout. I changed quickly and hit the gym, running the indoor track, doing several laps, using free weights to work my arms, chest, abs and legs, before cooling down with a slow walk around the track. Once done I smiled widely at the pretty redhead behind the counter and made some small talk. I noticed no ring and considered asking her out for a drink, but decided to wait for now. My friskiness from my time with Lyndi made me brave again around women, but I knew hopping in bed with anyone right now wasn't the best idea. I said my goodbyes and strolled out to my car when my cell phone rang. It was my mystery caller again.

"Hello, Mr. Mann. Have you returned to town?" he asked.

"I have indeed."

"Do you have time to meet in the next few hours?"

I checked the clock on my dash, and though I was tired, and hungry, I was curious about what information he could provide me.

"Where and when?"

"What about we meet at 6 p.m. at Bible Park. Do you know where that is?"

"Yes. I probably can make that."

"Over by the tennis courts."

He then promptly hung up. It seemed risky, but I was a curious person and was prepared for whatever happened. I dropped by a Subway along the way to pick up a turkey sub, drove home and changed into jeans, a long short-sleeved shirt, which covered my hip holster and .38, and my good running shoes. The shoes were always important for a fast getaway. The gun, which I didn't care to carry all the time, was becoming necessary again for proper protection, as shown by what happened to April. Wishes for bulletproof Superman powers had never been granted, so I had to improvise. I doubt the turkey sub would enhance those powers, but I didn't care, as I was famished and wolfed it down quickly with some lemon iced tea and two moist chocolate chip cookies.

Bible Park is on the eastern side of Denver just short of the Aurora border, and I arrived just after six. It was a large green, grassy place, bordered with tall trees. It was normally a beehive of activity, with family picnics, baseball, football and soccer practices, and more cars than the large parking lot could handle, so they flowed out onto Yale Avenue. I found this true today, driving in, and luckily found a parking spot when someone was leaving. Once out, I made sure my gun was covered by my shirt tail, as I didn't want any panic among the families and children there. I strolled the park, not seeing the tennis courts and asked someone for help. They pointed to the east beyond a row of trees, which I followed across a walk bridge over a creek, along a path where the four lighted, fenced courts were located. I found a wrought-iron bench and took a seat, watching the full courts of tennis action. It wasn't the US Open, but the players looked pretty good and seemed to be having a fair amount of fun. I checked my phone and there was a text from the number I received the call from saying he was nearby. I answered back I was sitting on the bench and gave him a concise description of my shirt. Within about five minutes a tall man showed up and sat down next to me.

"Jarvis," he said while watching the action before us.

"Yes." I answered.

"Sorry for all the cloak and dagger stuff. I'm being cautious with good reason."

I wanted to say "paranoid," but resisted. With what I'd experience so far, maybe I was as well.

"Prudent to be safe. Though I'm uncertain right now what you are in fear of."

"WANN Systems."

"And why?"

"Because I don't want to end up like Aaron: dead!"

"You believe they killed him?"

"I know they did."

"Can you prove it?"

"Possibly, with your help. What do you know so far?"

"I would prefer to hold off on telling you much, since I don't know who you are. For all I know you could be working for them. My way of being cautious too."

He continued to stare forward. He was probably close to my age, with long in back and short in front blond hair. He was tall and slender, probably 6' 2" and 170 pounds. His skin was pale, as if he was rarely in the sun, with long beige khakis and a long-sleeved T-shirt with the term "Code Until You Drop!" on it. A shoulder bag sat next to him, which he dug into, pulling out some paper, which he handed to me. At the top showed a business name of Colorado Cyber Border Security and the name Wilmar Boylan.

"Is this you?" I asked.

He gave a short nod.

"Are you a private company?"

Again, a slight nod.

"You could still be working for WANN. Maybe as a contractor."

"Believe me, I'm not. They are an evil company, stealing from those who use their products."

"What are they stealing?"

"Information and identities."

"How do you know this?"

Stopping to think over what to say, he turned his head and looked me in the eye.

"Because Aaron and I were working on it together. He was passing on the things he was learning and sharing them with me."

"For how long?"

"Nearly a year now."

"Did WANN know you were working together?"

"I don't think so."

"You haven't been threatened?"

"No. But still I'm cautious. He gave me backdoor access to their network. But since he was killed, that was closed off. I was careful not to leave any traces of a digital fingerprint that would lead them to me. Anytime I'd access them I would do it bouncing off several different IP addresses, spoofing my identity, making it hard to trace."

A lot of this tech talk didn't mean much to me, but I nodded my head as if I completely understood.

"Do you trust me now?" asked Wilmar.

"More so now than before."

"I've told you some things. How about sharing what you

know?"

I figured I could give up some information without exposing myself too much.

"There appears to be some unsavory Russian and Chinese figures involved. I've had run-ins with both. The Russian confrontation turned deadly."

"You are certain it's related to Aaron's killing?"

"Most definitely. They wanted to know what I knew and who hired me. They planned to beat the information out of me before a friend intervened."

"But you didn't tell them anything?"

"No."

"You mentioned you were out of the state when I first called. Was that part of the investigation as well?"

"I was in California trying to speak to some higher-ups at WANN. They didn't receive me with open arms. Shortly after I talked with the Director of West Coast Security, a car with Chinese men started following me."

"China is the world leader in cyber theft. I'm almost certain they have their hooks into WANN. Probably funding them. They should have gone under a few years back, but were bailed out. I believe it was money from outside sources that saved them. I'm sure Russian mobsters may have also stepped in. Could be they are rivals competing for their share, or working together. Though that seems a little far-fetched, as both sides would likely not be willing to split the profits."

"Any ideas on the name of the Chinese organization? I do have some contacts in the FBI who might be able to provide some assistance if they know who they are?"

"Not certain. I've heard various names. They change pretty frequently. Breaking up and reforming into various splitter groups. Some even are backed by the Chinese government, or at least those on the military side of the government."

The warm day was cooling now, as dark clouds were coming in, which was normal for the afternoon and evening in the summer months. I pulled off my sunglasses, which were no longer needed. I wasn't sure where we were headed in our conversation, but needed to come to some conclusion.

"We have a lot of information, but nothing solid we can take to the police or the Feds," I stated. "So where do we go from here?"

"Since I'm locked out, I'm not sure I can help much more. I can give you all I have."

"You can't hack your way in and find more out?"

He hesitated, seeming nervous at the question.

"Certainly, you can get in," I added. "No system is unbreakable."

"I really don't want to be involved anymore. I'm afraid of what happened to Aaron will happen to me."

"He was your friend. Don't you want to catch his killer?"

"I'm not sure I'm brave enough to continue."

"What about for his wife? I'm assuming you know her. She could be in danger as well."

He looked away and didn't answer right off.

"I don't know her that well. We only met a couple of times."

If I had to guess, I think he was lying, and knew her better than that. No reason to push too hard.

"Look, I don't have the skills to make a dent in their firewalls. I can work on them from the investigation side, but I need motive to prove intent, and I can't get that without understanding what they are doing on the technical side. I need someone like you to find that smoking gun. Otherwise they likely are going to get away with killing Aaron. And I'm certain you don't want that,"

He sighed, as I could see his hands shaking.

"Do what you do best," I said. "Poke around, but be careful like before and bounce off as many IPs as you need to be safe." I threw out the tech jargon as if it would calm him. "And I will do what I do best, which is pester the hell out of them until they do something stupid. We can bring them down by the balls or whatever the digital equivalent of balls would be."

I think I made him smile, though not enough to stop the hand tremors. Another fifteen minutes of convincing and he was onboard, and would see what else he could dig up. While I needed to go back and get more acquainted with tech-speak so I knew what the hell he was doing.

Chapter 30

The next day I decided to use one of my contacts to understand more about what Wilmar was talking about. I could have gleaned more from him, but he seemed too scared and paranoid to speak much more. I needed to make sense of the documentation he gave me. Since it seemed many tech geeks were of the younger generation, I turned to a young friend who might steer me in the correct direction. When in doubt, go back to high school.

Dennis Gash was enjoying his summer vacation, like most young men with their senior year on the horizon, employed to save for college and working out to get ready for the coming football season. He'd remained the same young man I remembered, though maybe an inch taller now and strong enough to plow through any defensive line like a running back should. He'd shaved most of his hair off, only short stubs remaining on his dark skull. He was getting off work at the local King Soopers grocery store when I called and agreed to meet me at the Burger King on Evans and Broadway. We had bonded a couple years back over a lost Ernie Banks trading card and had kept in touch since. He was wise for his age, and had a bright future no matter the course life directed him in. When I pulled up he was outside waiting and gave me a thumbs up when he saw the Harley. We shook hands and had a quick embrace before grabbing a drink and fries while finding an open booth of hard, brightly painted plastic that fast food joints deemed as worldly decoration.

"Looking good, Dennis," I said. "I'd hate to be the one who had to tackle you."

He grinned.

"Maybe you should try it someday," he replied. "Could suit up and see what you can do. I might go easy on you, at least for a play or two."

"No thanks. I think I'd rather dodge a bullet than the Gash locomotive. How do you think the team will do this year?"

"We have most everyone back. Lots of seniors and juniors with skills. We could be pretty good. The schedule is daunting. Though to be the best, you must beat the best. I'm looking forward to the season."

"Any thoughts on college?"

"Sure. Would love to go up north and play. CSU or UNC. Would love to be a teammate with Ray. I've seen him around and he is looking good. We'd be a helluva one-two punch. But for now, I'm just looking forward to my last year. Want to go out with a bang."

Ray Malone was the son of Bill, my Denver Police contact, and the one I'd helped out of a jam last year. He was a prototype tight end, playing for the UNC Bears, with NFL caliber skills.

"I plan on going to as many games as possible," I said. "I always enjoy watching the way you play. I hope to go up and see Ray compete as well."

"Bring Melissa along to watch us play. We could double after the game with my new girlfriend and grab a bite. Would love for you to meet her."

"Sorry, son. Melissa and I are no longer."

His face showed surprise, as I'd not talked to him since returning from Iowa.

"Gee, I'm sorry to hear that. What happened?"

"My usual mistake. Failed to be faithful to her."

Dennis shook his head.

"Seems to be a pattern, from what you've told me of your past relationships. Habits are hard to break."

"Don't fall into the same trap I've gotten myself into. You find a good woman, hold onto her."

"Gezelle is a good one. Whether she is the right one, it's too soon to tell. Only been together a few months. But we are having fun right now, which is alright with me and her."

We chatted a few more minutes, as he challenged me to come workout with him and his other football teammates. They had a brutal routine for getting in shape for the coming season, which included running up and down the bleacher steps with ankle weights strapped on. He thought I was looking a little soft. Compared to his physique, that was probably true. A little martial arts and football training and I could best all the bad guys.

"I wonder if you know much about cyber security," I asked. "If your school has a cyber security teacher. I know many of the schools do these days. I need to pick someone's brain for a case I'm working."

"I don't believe so. We do have STEM classes: science, technology, engineering and math, as I've been taking them since middle school. One of the teachers there is pretty cool and makes science fun. He might be able to direct you to someone. I can text him and see how he answers."

Dennis pulled out his Android phone and started typing away. It didn't take long before he got a response.

"He says one of the best programs in the city is at Rangeview High School in Aurora. The teacher there knows his stuff and is an old friend. School starts in early August, so he is likely around getting ready for the new school year. He said he could contact him and see if he'd be willing to meet you."

"That would be great. Give him my number and tell him to reach out. I'd buy him lunch."

Dennis typed out the message faster than I could speak the words.

"He said 'LOL.' Seems the teacher can eat you into the poor house. He says it may be better to make a donation to the club to help pay for their competitions, and not add any inches to his waistline."

"Works for me. I can expense it as research."

"And lunch today?"

"That too, since it's related to my client's case. Why?"

Apparently, a chiseled football physique required calories, as Dennis got up and ordered a double-whopper value meal and I had my answer.

Chapter 31

As I got outside my cell phone rang. It was Kate, owner of the beauty salon above my home office.

"Something odd just happened," she said.

The street traffic was loud, so it was hard to hear her. I went back inside.

"What is going on?" I asked.

"Two men came in asking about you," replied Kate. "Was wondering if I knew you and knew where you were. Said they were looking for a detective to hire."

"What did you say?"

"I told them I did know you, since you lived below, but had no idea where you were. Something about them didn't register right with me."

Kate had good instincts. If something seemed wrong, I was all ears.

"One of the men seemed very slick, wearing fancy clothes, and a fedora you often don't see these days. Tall and classy-looking."

"So, not my normal clientele, I'm gathering."

"Not normally. But that wasn't all, the other man with him was shorter, not dressed as nicely: basic plain slacks and short-sleeved polo, but strong looking, with tattoos all over. One on his neck appeared to be a dragon, from what I could see. Looked a little like Jet Li, the martial arts movie star. Didn't say a word, but his eyes were cold and scary."

"They were of Asian descent, then?" I asked.

"Yes. Do you know them?"

"I know the shorter of the two. I got the best of him a couple days ago. They may be back to even the score."

"Well, they went out and got into a dark blue Cadillac. Pulled around back and are parked there. I saw them go down the stairs to your place out my back window. Didn't see them come out. Who are they?"

"Not for certain, but likely tied to my latest case. I intend on finding out."

"Do you purposely attract this type of bad guys?"

"Goes with the job sometimes. I think I'd rather be dealing with cheating spouses, but even those don't always go as planned."

It was a reference to a previous case I'd helped Kate on that turned into a messy one.

"Try not to mess up your place, please. We just got it fixed from the fire and I'd rather not have to do any further repairs. I love you, Jarvis, but if this keeps up I may need to increase your rent or look for a new tenant."

"I'll do my best to keep from chipping the paint with any bullets."

I heard her laugh and then hang up the phone. She'd miss my jokes if I was gone, but would probably feel safer. I went back outside and climbed on my bike, thinking what I would do. Since they were either searching my place or waiting for me, I decided the direct approach made the most sense, though might not have been the smartest. I pulled down the alley and parked my bike next to the dumpster. I rested all my gear on the bike and pulled out my .38, holding it at my side, walking across the small parking area to my stairwell. I was cautious in case of an ambush, reaching the rail looking down the stairs, seeing my front door standing wide open. I slowly moved down the steps, back to the wall, gun at the ready. As I reached the door, I peered around the opening to see them both inside, the slick one sitting on my sofa, the other standing behind him. Neither appeared to be armed, as I pulled my head back, thinking on what to do.

"Please come in," said a voice, in nearly perfect English. "We are not armed. We only wish to talk."

Thinking for a minute, the odds certainly had to be in my favor. I stepped in, my gun at my side ready if needed. My eyes watching for any slight sign of danger.

"You are letting in all the flies and mosquitoes by leaving my door open," I stated, closing it behind me. "It is a bitch to get them out of here once they get inside."

"My apologies, Mr. Mann. We wanted to make sure you knew we were here and of no threat."

If he wasn't a threat, I wasn't convinced. I slowly tapped my gun on my thigh.

"I am at a disadvantage since you know my name, but I don't know yours."

"My name is Cong Niu," he said. "I hope we can discuss

matters peacefully."

I looked at the man behind him. His eyes looked cold and peaceful at the same time. There was a calm, yet a lingering danger as if it would spring out at any second.

"Well, Mr. Niu, it would seem you have broken into my place. Grounds to get arrested."

"No evidence that was the case. If you check the lock it wasn't forced. The door was open, so we came in and patiently sat until your return, making sure a stray person didn't steal anything."

I stepped back to look, all components appearing as if brand-new. Not a scrape or sign of wear or damage anywhere. They had expertly opened my lock without leaving a trace, as I knew for certain it had been secured when I left.

"Impressive, Mr. Niu. Is that your work or your associate's?"

"Can we dispense with the formalities? Please call me Cong. May I call you Jarvis?"

I nodded.

"And can we put away the gun. There is no need for it."

"I'll hold onto it for now. My apologies for not trusting your word, as I've had others like you attack me looking for information."

His grin turned into a short chuckle, his hands waving, as if being dismissive.

"We are hardly like the Platov boys. They are animals, while we are reasonable men when dealing with reasonable people. Jarvis, can you be reasoned with?"

"I'm willing to listen to what you have to say."

"I'm so happy you are open to what I have to offer."

"Listening and accepting are two different things. But please explain your terms."

Cong sat there with a pleasant smile, his legs crossed. He was dressed in beige slacks and a mahogany brown tailored suit, with freshly polished, expensive loafers. The beige wool fedora sat on the sofa next to him, a gray feather accenting the black lace band; his well-mannered disposition had taught him to remove it when inside. His black hair was short and neatly combed, the hat never disturbing a follicle. He reached slowly into his coat pocket and I raised my gun. His smile grew wider as he pulled out an envelope and handed it to the man behind him.

"Not to worry, Jarvis. May my associate Lok bring this to you?"

I waived my gun, and he walked over slowly, handing it to me, then stepping back a couple of feet. I motioned him to move back further, which he did. I looked down quickly with one eye, while the other was alert for any action. I pulled the contents out with my left hand and saw it was cash. A lot of cash, all in hundreds. I whistled out loud, wondering how much was there.

"Ten thousand dollars," said Cong.

"What did I do to earn this?"

"Simply walk away. Tell those that hired you that the police were correct, and Aaron Bailey was killed during a robbery. You get a nice payday and we go back to our business, never to bother you again."

"And that business would be?"

"Commerce."

"Legal or illegal?"

"Does it matter? Free enterprise, whether legal or not, creates jobs for those who need them. Hell, we even pay taxes like you do. Capitalism at its finest."

"Will I need to pay taxes on this windfall?"

"That is truly between you and your accountant. The money will not show up on our ledger in any way."

I stood there for a moment, staring at the wad of bills, thinking of all the things I could do with it. Money didn't always come easy to me, and it would put me on easy street for a while. It was so tempting, yet something inside said taking this money, selling my soul, would come back to haunt me, as had some of the many other bad decisions I had made through the years. I tossed the thick envelope on my kitchen table, motioning for Lok to take it back.

"Though it is a grand gesture, I must decline. I've made a promise to my client to find out who killed Aaron. And I generally keep my promises, or at least try to. I must ask you to leave and allow me to do what I do best, which is find a killer. Whoever that may be. Hopefully it wasn't you or Lok here."

"You are certain of this, Jarvis," said Cong. "It is a one-time offer. A most generous one that won't be repeated."

"I am a man of my word when it comes to my clients. Without it I would not be in business very long. Surely you can understand this, as you appear to be a businessman yourself."

"I am. May I say I respect and even admire your integrity, even if it is ill-advised. I often attempt to take the high road to avoid the unpleasantness I so dislike. Is there a higher amount to persuade you to reconsider? An agreeable number for both of us."

"I'm sorry, no."

"You realize then I must take the next step, a step that won't be pleasant for you or me."

Even with his cool exterior I doubted he would dislike whatever action he took any more than I would.

"You can try, as have others. So far I'm still in business and still standing."

"Yes, we have checked you out. Know what you've faced. You are formidable, though not infallible. Your brother was killed because of his recklessness. It can happen to you as well."

"Is that a threat?"

Cong stood up from the sofa, straightening his slacks and buttoning his coat. My attention on him allowed his associate to move closer with hardly a sound. My gun hand tensed and pointed back at Lok. His body was loose and relaxed, no sign of fear on his face.

"I will shoot you if I have to," I said forcefully.

"A shame we must do this the hard way," stated Cong. "Take him, Lok."

The words surprised me, as my gun was pointed right at him. But he sprung like a tightly wound coil, and moved in a blur. His motion was swift and elusive; as I pulled the trigger a foot kicked up, the gun firing, the bullet hitting the ceiling. I felt another kick to the head, so fast that even as I raised my left arm in defense, I couldn't block it. My knees buckled and soon I was face down, my left arm pulled upward and held by the wrist, so I couldn't move, a knee on my back. It happened so quickly I swore only a split second had passed. I was completely helpless.

"Lok here has been hoping for a rematch," said Cong, whom I could hear moving across my kitchen floor where I was pinned. "You sucker punched him, so he hoped to show you what you are truly up against."

I could feel the pressure increasing on my arm. Much more, and it would be broken at the elbow. I tried to relax, though wanting deep down to somehow come up with a magic move to free myself. But fighting his position on me would only lead to more pain.

"I, though, am a patient, civilized man. I wanted to try and buy you first. Since this didn't work, I often would give you some time to decide before my next action. But you seemed confident that you couldn't be persuaded with money. So now we take the next step."

I heard him speak some dialogue to Lok. It might have been Chinese or Mandarin, or some other language from that region of the world. It really didn't matter, for I had no idea what he said, until Lok acted. He took the two smallest fingers on my left hand, and bent them completely backwards until they snapped. The pain was brutal, certainly as bad as I'd ever felt. He released my arm, both fingers still pointing upwardly. I gritted my teeth as long as I could before yelling. Though why we yell is uncertain, as it doesn't help with the pain any and often makes it worse since our bodies tense up so much. I heard them both walking towards the door, a faint sound of sirens in the background.

"Lok wanted to kill you," said Cong calmly. "But I'm a civil man, as I said. Take this as a warning. The next time will be a shoulder, or a knee or your heart cut from your chest. Think on it long and hard as the paramedics straighten out your dislocated fingers. Good day, Mr. Mann."

With that they left the room, leaving the door wide open. I tried to fight off the pain, and even rolled over carefully and righted myself, all without further injuring my twisted hand. Deep within the agony, a humorous thought crept into my head, knowing I'd not kept my promise to Kate of not chipping the paint with a bullet. I would have laughed at my joke if I weren't about to cry when I saw my mangled fingers.

Chapter 32

My place became a beehive of activity. Kate was the first to arrive, daring the danger. She saw my hand, took a deep breath and helped me to my feet, moving me over to my kitchen chair. She stood next to me, a hand on my shoulder.

"I won't ask the stupid question 'does it hurt,'" she said.

I gave a weak smile and took some deep breaths to control the pain. A minute later a Denver cop, one I knew, though not well, came through the door, gun at the ready. He saw us both and then my hand, holstering his weapon. He spoke into his shoulder-mounted microphone, saying he needed paramedics ASAP.

"What the hell happened?" he asked, while walking the room.

I explained as best as I could, as talking was difficult. Soon two paramedics came in, examined my hand, and concluded the next course of action. With a quick yank, they had both fingers pointing the correct way. It didn't hurt as much as when Lok snapped them out of joint, but it was close. At least they were now at the correct angle. They pulled out some tape and ice packs, and went to work.

"You'll need a trip to the ER for some x-rays," one of them said.

"I'd rather not."

I didn't care for hospitals or doctors. Especially when I was the patient.

"No choice. They did a pretty good job with the dislocation. I don't think anything was fractured, but you still need to make sure. Substantial difference in treatment for the injury."

I wasn't happy but went on down. Kate said she'd lock up after the crime scene people were done, which would be a while. The officer on scene called in to have a detective meet me at Swedish to get a full statement. My .38 would be held for evidence, since it had been fired. I needed to have a rotating group of guns, one for use and one the police held after every firing event. While the supply was running low, the danger remained high.

I went through the ER process, one that is no more thrilling than getting teeth pulled, without the Novocain. There was a wait, and since I wasn't bleeding or my bones weren't sticking through skin, it was maybe an hour before they got to me. Another hour for x-rays and developing, and I was about done with the whole mess to the point of walking out. A Denver detective did arrive to take my statement, and it was Dan Cummings, who despised me for some reason. I think I'd rather have my fingers dislocated again, instead of talking with him. But I did my best to rise above his disdain for me.

"Give me the details of what happened," he said, pulling out his notepad. "And don't leave anything out, for I have no patience for you like Mallard does."

Normally I'd push his buttons and get under his skin, but I had no energy for it. My hand was throbbing despite the pain pills, wrapping, and ice pack. I gave him all the details, including the names they used, model of the car, license number, and what it was in relation to. Cummings listened to every word without interruption, which was rare for him.

"This was related to the Aaron Bailey murder?" he asked.

"Yes. They tried to buy me off. I said no and that is when this man, Lok, attacked."

"Why not just shoot you?" he asked. "Seems like they had you cold. Would be what I'd have done, if in their shoes."

I think I saw a coy smirk on his face, as if he was the funny one for once. It was a rare show of humor on his part.

"Puts unwanted focus on them. For now, scaring me off is their plan. Thinking I'm small time and won't keep pushing."

"You are small time."

"Maybe. But with a big heart. I've been through enough the last couple of years to ride through this."

"In the end, though, they will be coming to put you down permanently. My advice is to walk away. Even I wouldn't have faulted you for taking the money."

"Not my nature to walk away from a fight or accept a bribe."

Cummings shook his head. "I'll be sure to send flowers to your funeral."

I'm sure they would be dead ones!

Once he was done and gone, I finally got the prognosis. No broken bones, just stretched tendons and ligaments, which would be sore for some time. Fingers taped, rest, ice and anti-inflammatory medicine. Nearly four hours of my life lost, once I was done with all the paperwork and paid the bill. While I was here I decided to check on April. It was getting late, but not quite past visiting hours. She had been moved to a private room and was now out of ICU. After some assistance on location I found her a few floors up. When I arrived she had a visitor, a male I'd not met yet. He was reaching for his gun when April told him who I was. I soon learned it was brother number three.

"This is Neil," said April. "He finally was able to break away and see me."

We shook hands. He was tall, slim and as scruffy looking as you'd expect a Vice-undercover cop to be.

"I'm sorry to intrude," I said. "Good to meet you."

"April and I were just catching up. We hadn't seen each other in some time. She was explaining what happened. She has always been a tough girl, even when we were growing up. Though I never imagined her being the first one of us to get shot."

"I will leave you two alone so you can talk," I said.

"No, please stay," said Neil. "I have to go. Still working a case and must get back to it."

He leaned over and kissed his sister, while squeezing her hand.

"Take care, Neil," said April. "I should be going home in a few days, with any luck. Stop by when you can."

Neil walked out, and she and I were alone. She noticed my hand.

"Do I need to ask?" she said.

"Another battle wound. Compared to yours, it's minor."

"More issues with our Eastern Bloc friends?"

"This time it's Chinese bad guys."

"Same case?"

"Yes. Apparently, they have a stake in this as well."

"Don't get dead."

"Not planning to. Though I may need some backup and you appear to be still recovering, so I'll have to go to plan B."

She started to laugh and then stopped, for it was painful.

"No belly laughs. Can't be popping stitches. My other two brothers offered."

"I know. But being cops, they must be careful about getting into any type of personal fight. I'll keep them in mind. But I have a few other sources I'll check into. People who don't have to necessarily follow the law."

"You always are teetering on that fine line."

"Part of the PI credo. Well, visiting hours are almost over. I wanted to stop and see how you were. You look to be doing well. Let me know when you are back home, and maybe I can pick up some dinner and we can eat together."

"I'd love that."

I grabbed her hand and leaned over to kiss her on the cheek, but she turned her face, so her lips met mine, kissing me softly.

"Sorry about my breath," she said. "Hard to brush regularly when hooked up to so many wires."

I didn't mind and kissed her again, hearing the pulse rate on the monitor by her bed rising.

Chapter 33

It was obvious I was in need of backup. After a restless night, with my Beretta on the nightstand, I was awake the next morning feeling sore, not only from my hand but other areas that had been thrown around by the martial arts expert. After hitting the gym, and soaking in the hot tub to ease some of my pain, I showered, ate some breakfast and started making calls. The first was to Brandon Sparks, though I only was able to reach his assistant, Sue. She was tough, hard-nosed and liked to be in charge.

"Mr. Sparks is away on business," she said. "He can't be disturbed and will be gone for several more weeks."

"So, no way for me to get in contact with him," I asked.

"I believe I already said as much."

"Even for your good old buddy Jarvis?"

She swore at me. Apparently, we weren't as close as I thought.

"What about Rocky?"

"I have no connection to his outside associates."

"Thought you knew everyone Brandon knew."

"Hardly. Certain matters he handles himself, so as not to involve me."

"You have no way of contacting Rocky?"

"No. At least if it's the man I believe you are referring to."

Rocky wasn't his real name. What it was, I likely would never know, since he lived in the shadows of a dangerous past.

"How is your love life?" I asked.

"None of your business. Is there anything else I can do for you, Mr. Mann?"

"I'd ask you to lunch, but I think I know the answer."

"I believe you do, but I'll spell it out for you…" With a graphic four-letter word, she abruptly ended the call.

I next called Max Groves. He was the second in command of the Toro crime family, though now likely first in command, as he helped me put his boss in the ground. A boss who had killed my brother. The wife now ruled the empire, but let Max do the day to day. When I tracked him down he was less than thrilled to hear from me.

"I'm busy. What do you want?"

"Crime never sleeps," I replied.

"Yes. And it pays the bills. But not by talking with you."

"I need someone to watch my back and possibly my client."

"Well, normally I have people on standby just for helping you, but you caught me in my busy season, so no."

"Any ideas on getting ahold of Rocky?"

"He is your friend. Why would I know?"

"Not really a friend and I don't have him on speed dial. Seems as if he'd done work in the past for The Bull. Thought maybe you might have an avenue to reach out."

"Sorry, no. He is a lone wolf. Only takes jobs he cares to take. I wouldn't have the foggiest idea on how to find him, or would want to. Now can I get back to work?"

"How are Kellie and her son?"

"Doing great. Kid now has a normal life. Might even grow up to be something decent. Would you like me to give you a financial report of our earnings, or can I hang up now?"

"Well, if you insist, but only the highlights."

He swore at me too, before hanging up. It appeared most of my resources didn't care to bail me out. I still had April's brothers but wanted to hold them only as a last resort. As I mulled over my next option, my phone rang. It was Mandy Bailey.

"That detective called again," she said.

"Adam King?"

"Yes. I did like you told me to do. Said I'd meet with him to discuss the possibility of hiring him. Washington Park in about two hours. Is that enough time?"

"Perfect. I'll be sure to surprise him and make it clear he is not to bother you anymore."

"Good. I was nervous talking with him. He seems kind of creepy."

"Understatement. How are you doing?"

"I'm hanging in there. Though still hoping to get some answers about Aaron. Are you making any progress?"

I didn't want to worry her about my latest encounter. There was no reason to think they knew she hired me or have reason to go after her. Still no need to put thoughts in her head.

"Yes, I've been ruffling feathers and making them nervous. Someone or a group of someone's is involved. Right now, trying to narrow down suspects, as the list keeps growing."

"I'm trying to stay patient, but it's getting difficult."

"Perfectly understandable. We'll get there." I wanted to give her something positive to hold onto. "Remember that odd call I got, from the person who said he had some inside information."

There was a pause.

"Vaguely. What was it about?"

"He was a friend of Aaron's. A Wilmar Boylan. Has his own cyber security firm. I'm sure you recognize the name."

"No, not really."

"No matter. He said he only met you a couple of times in passing. But he was working with Aaron and knows about what is going on. Possibly what got him killed. He has agreed to help look into it further. Gave me some information. Most of it I don't understand, but will with some help."

"That is great news."

She said it like she didn't mean it.

"Really it is. Something with some meat to work with. Once I know more I'll let you know."

I'm not sure if I convinced her or not, but I knew it was only a matter of time before all the pieces fit and I would know for certain what I was up against. We said our goodbyes and I went to change.

Since it was a nice summer day, I dressed in running shorts, a long tank top and my best jogging shoes. I lathered on some sunscreen, hopped in my car and headed to the park. Washington Park was 165 acres of grass, tall majestic trees, tennis courts, trails, flower gardens, a busy recreation center, and two lakes. It had been around since 1899 and had hundreds of thousands of visitors every year. Today was no different with people running, playing and resting. Mandy had told King to meet her at the north end of the park, south of Smith Lake near the boat house. I planned on getting there early and jogging the area until I found him. I wore dark sunglasses and a skull cap, to make for a simple disguise. Even though I was essentially one-handed, I figured I could handle him. After lightly jogging for about twenty minutes I saw him off the trail waiting by some trees. I passed him and then circled around coming up behind. He never sensed me, as I snuck up and tapped his shoulder. When he turned around I popped him once in the jaw dropping him backward into the grass. Once his eyes cleared, I removed my sunglasses, so he could recognize me.

"Surprise," I said, with a cheer.

"What the fuck, Jarvis?" he bellowed. "What is the idea of the cheap shot?"

"I needed to get your attention."

He started rubbing his jaw. He would have a bruise pretty soon.

"Did it work? Are you going to listen to me?"

"Why should I?"

"Because it could be worse. I could have kicked you in the balls. Because it is ballsy you coming onto one of my clients after what happened the last time."

He looked around to see if anyone was coming to his rescue.

"I don't know what you are talking about. I was just waiting here for a client and you came up and attacked me."

"You mean my client, who you won't leave alone."

"She called me."

"No she didn't. Just like the last time. You can't find your own clients, so you come and try and steal mine. This is the last time I warn you nicely. The next time I pop you and then serve papers my lawyer will draw up, suing you. Leave Mandy Bailey alone, or else."

King picked himself up, looked around again and then pulled out his gun.

"I could shoot you right here and now, and nobody would fault me. I was defending myself from some maniac, and bang, I took him down. I was in fear for my life."

I laughed. Not sure why, since he held the gun, but I didn't really think he'd shoot.

"Put that damn thing away. You know you can't shoot me. You're just mad at yourself for getting caught again."

His anger was subsiding, and his gun went back into this holster. He turned and walked on, mumbling something, about this not being over. I couldn't tell for sure but didn't care, for I'd made my point again with him. Now all I had to do is prove to my client he wasn't right about me.

Chapter 34

After a decent night of sleep, I was ready to try and workout when I got a call from Bill.

"They found your two assailants and brought them in for questioning a short while ago. I thought you'd want to stop down and see the proceedings."

"Who is handling it?"

"Mallard, I believe."

"Do you think he'll mind?"

"Does it matter? You generally don't give a damn about what others think."

"So true. I'll be right there."

Changing course, I put on some jeans and shirt and drove to the precinct. Once there Bill got me signed in with a guest ID and escorted me back.

"Guess who just showed up to bail them out?"

"Don Bristol?"

"Yep. Probably still have an hour before the paperwork comes through. But hell, they didn't even make a call and he shows up."

"Nice to have friends in high places. And I'm pretty certain who that would be."

We reached the interrogation room. Mallard was standing outside next to Cummings. Both looked up and showed no joy in seeing me. Bill walked away before they could say anything to him. Not that it mattered, because, like me, he didn't give a damn what they thought.

"One of these days Malone and I are going to have a long chat about his friendship with you," said Mallard.

"Gee, I'm sure he would listen carefully to everything you said, and then flip you off and stroll away laughing. Why waste the energy. I'm here because those two attacked and threatened me." I held up my bandaged hand. "You need me here to identify them, so I'm here."

Mallard sighed and waved me to come into the adjoining room, with a view of where Cong was sitting and waiting. He was dapper as ever, dressed as if he was going to a fancy soiree. He still had his hat, with beige jacket and slacks, a silk shirt open to show some of his hairless chest. He seemed to be singing to himself while he waited. Something in his native language. He didn't look nervous or worried, for he knew he wouldn't be held long.

"That is Cong," I stated. "He is the man who made the threats against me. What do you know about him?"

"Not much so far," said Cummings. "Nothing in our system about him. But we figure he isn't from here. Has a California license. Last name Niu."

"I have some contacts at the FBI that may be able to help. What about Lok?"

"He is in the other room," said Cummings. "Also, a California license. Last name Feng. He has crazy eyes. Calm, but there is danger behind them."

"Yes, I know that look. He is the one that rearranged my fingers. Did he put up any resistance?"

"Not at all," said Mallard. "Officers pulled them over and they came quietly. There were three cars on the scene when they were cuffed, guns at the ready just in case."

"It may not have mattered," I said. "I had a gun on Lok and still couldn't stop him. I'm guessing they figured they had nothing to gain by confronting the cops. Have they said anything?"

"Not a word," said Mallard. "They are refusing to talk. Waiting on their lawyers. Don Bristol is hard at work springing them. We don't expect them to do anything but sit and wait to be released."

"Can I go in and talk with Cong?" I asked.

Mallard looked at Cummings and shook his head, which was no surprise.

"Look, I'm not going to do anything. I want to make sure Cong understands I'm not backing off this case."

"It would appear you are setting yourself up for them to make a run at you," said Mallard.

"My client deserves my best. Walking isn't my best. If you poke the hornets' nest sometimes it reveals something. Right now, I don't have all the answers and this might bring them to light. They are working for WANN Systems. And Aaron Bailey was killed in their parking lot. Someone in that company had him killed, and I plan on finding out who it was."

"Or die trying," said Mallard.

Cummings smiled, as if he would be happy with my death.

"Like I stated, my client deserves my best."

"You can have ten minutes."

"Damn, Stu," said Cummings. "Do you always give this gumshoe what he wants?"

It was the first time I'd heard Mallard's first name used. He shot a stern look at Cummings.

"Dan, I'm the senior detective and I decide. You don't like it, go running to the chief. Jarvis here might be a pain in the ass, but he does get results." He turned back my way. "Don't make me regret this. I'll be watching."

I stepped out of the room and walked into where Cong was sitting. He looked up at me with a smile as I sat down across from him. I stared for a couple minutes, contemplating what to say. He actually spoke first.

"Good to see you again, Mr. Mann. I hope you are doing well."

"Except for my left hand, I'm great."

I showed him the bandaged digits.

"Oh my, what happened?"

"You know the answer to that. Your man, Lok, was making a point with me that you wanted delivered."

"I'm sorry to say I don't know what you are referring to. I hope you aren't in much pain."

"He did an expert job. Oh, it hurts, but nothing permanent was damaged."

"Sounds as if you were fortunate, this time!"

"I was. And so were you. Next time I plan on turning the tables."

"Really. That sounds most courageous on your part. I hope you are up to the challenge. I'd hate for something worse to happen the next time."

"Oh, I will be. But let me tell you something for you to take back to your employers."

"You may say what you wish."

I learned forward and spoke softly this time, so the microphones in the room couldn't hear me.

"I won't be stopping my investigation. I'm kind of silly about things like that. I complete the job, one way or another. Send your best, but I will find out who killed Aaron Bailey."

Cong's expression never changed. I doubt I scared him, but I was pretty certain he'd pass on my words to those in charge. I leaned back in the chair and matched his smile, when Don Bristol walked in the room, followed by Mallard. He was not at all pleased to see me.

"What the hell is he doing here?" he said sternly. "He has no right to question my client without me present."

"Oh, don't worry any, Don," I said. "I wasn't questioning. Only talking with Cong. We had a pleasant and revealing discussion, didn't we? We needed to clear the air on a couple of matters."

"Jarvis was telling me about some, how do you put it, pie in the sky morals he has," added Cong. "Most interesting listening to his point of view."

"I don't care," bellowed Don. "No one talks with my clients without me present."

"Don, there is nothing to worry about here," I said. "And no client to defend. I plan on dropping the charges."

"What the hell, Jarvis," said Mallard.

"It was a simple misunderstanding between us. No harm, no foul. As far as I'm concerned, they are free to go, and Don, you can get back your bail money."

Mallard turned around and walked out of the room in disgust, as Don and Cong followed him. Once they retrieved Lok and the paperwork was processed, both walked out the front door, going to get their car, which had been impounded. As Don left I followed him too, and confronted him before he could get in, my hand holding the door closed.

"Don, I don't know what or why you are involved," I said. "But these are bad people here, who are trying to injure and even kill me. Whatever you are into, get out now, or else you can go down with them."

"I thought you said it was a misunderstanding?"

"They weren't going to spend a minute in jail. There was no shot of any charges ever sticking or of it going to court. They have better things to deal with. I know they will be coming after me again and this time I won't be the one to get hurt. I will make this clear to you. Walk away, because this is going to get messy."

He looked at me hard, but I knew he was stubborn. I stepped away from the door, and he climbed in and drove away. The seeds had been planted. Now it was a matter of seeing what grew out of them. My neck was going to get sore, for I would be looking over my shoulder a lot from now on.

Chapter 35

After reading though and not getting much more out of the pages of information the hacker Wilmar had provided me, I was sitting in one of the hundreds of Starbucks that seemed to be on every other corner in town. This one was in Aurora, a couple blocks from Rangeview High School. Across from me sat the cyber security teacher of the school, Phil Brand, going through the pages for a second time. In front of him was a flavored coffee, more like warm soda, and a cranberry orange scone. The second of two, the first he'd polished off before beginning to read. He was reading through the copy of the documents, the original locked away in my safe. He sat the pages down and took a long draw on his drink.

"Interesting reading," he said. "I'm guessing you aren't understanding what it all means."

"You are correct," I replied. "Too much geek-speak. I was hoping you could break it down to me in layman's terms. Something a simple-minded PI could understand."

"Certainly. I'm used to talking to school administrators. They don't understand binary all that well either."

I nodded, while drinking my own hot chocolate and taking a bite of a whole-grain muffin. Whole grain sounded healthier, though it likely wasn't. When Phil had first arrived, he didn't strike me as a school teacher, let alone a cyber expert. He was wearing long beige cargo shorts, a black and red Rangeview T-shirt and ball cap. He had white sneakers and socks, pulled up to nearly his knees. He had a round chubby face that matched his round belly. What hair I could see under his cap was white and he wore prescription glasses, dark in tint from being out on the sunny day. His handshake was solid and he didn't hesitate to order what he wanted when I offered to buy. The way he ate the first scone, in two bites, made me glad I'd not taken him to lunch, though Starbucks prices would mean it might still add up to a hefty bill.

"Let me first start off by saying that I'm only going by what I'm reading on the page," he said. "I have no way to know if any of this is true or not. It could all be an elaborate fabrication."

"You are saying it could be pure fiction?" I asked.

"Possibly. WANN Systems have been around for some time. And have certainly staked their claim to a decent chunk of the multi-billion-dollar networking business."

"Have you ever used their products or know of others who have?"

"Within the school system, no. We use Cisco products only. And in our cyber competition we only use Cisco, as they are a big supporter of us. But I know Cisco is highly aware of them as a competitor. And have even reacted by cutting some of their pricing to better match WANN's. Though they are still more expensive."

"What have you determined from reading this?" I said while tapping the pages on the table with my index finger.

"WANN makes routers, switches and firewalls, along with the operating systems that run them. They even have security software and appliances, intrusion and malware protection. Designed to detect breaches as they are about to happen while keeping companies safe from the bad guys on the Internet. From what I'm reading here, is that in their stealthiest, they are in reality a Trojan horse, gathering and stealing information as it crosses their gateways."

"What type of information?"

"Anything of value. Personal IDs, passwords, security questions, credit card numbers, birth dates and social security numbers. Whatever it deems worthy of retaining. It caches the information and then sends it off to various servers elsewhere in the world, where the data is mined."

"What can they do with it?"

"Pretty much anything. They can sell it to other cyber thieves. Identity theft, for stealing or ransoming users to free up their information. Cyber theft is a lucrative business."

"I'm hardly an expert. But I thought when much of that type of information is transmitted, I thought it was encrypted. Making it impossible to snoop."

Phil ate down his second scone, this time in one swallow, followed by more of this coffee. He grabbed a napkin and wiped his face, his appetite seemingly satisfied for now.

"When going to secure sites, banking, and when purchasing online like via Amazon, yes, you are running via HTTPS connections which are secure. But oftentimes people will transmit that information via email, or messaging services, which aren't secure. They can even be spoofed into thinking it is a real site, put in their personal information thinking it is secure, when it isn't. But here is where it gets interesting. From what they are saying here, when using WANN's native encryption, which some of their customers do via software they provide, it isn't secure at all. Though it claims to be 256-bit, it really isn't and can easily be decoded while in transit. And when you install their software, there is a key logger embedded caching everything you type, and sending it off to cyber space before encryption, for data mining." He took another long sip. "Again, I can only repeat what I'm reading, but if it's true, it is some pretty serious stuff."

"But wouldn't some regulatory agency catch this? Surely there are monitors in place checking for this type of crime or fraud."

"The Federal Trade Commission has some power. But like with most government agencies, they are underfunded and lack the technical brain power and equipment to keep up with the thieves. And with Net Neutrality being the big buzzword these days, where the Internet is free and open without limits, there is little they can do to stop it without solid proof. They are powerless. By the time someone has built any type of case, it's too late. Most companies who lose money to cyber theft just write it off as an expense of doing business."

"Doesn't the FBI have a cyber division?" I asked.

"Sure, they do. And again, they do what they can. But they and the NSA are mostly concerned with stopping terrorists before they blow themselves up or knock down another skyscraper with a jet. They snoop the information superhighway, using various keywords themselves. But stealing someone's credit card number and buying a bunch of merchandise is small potatoes in their eyes."

"In your opinion is all of this possible? Could it all be true?"

Phil stopped for a minute, adjusting his glasses, then rubbing his jaw of day-old gray whiskers.

"With all that goes on in this world, yeah, I believe it is possible. The Internet is a wonderful place, with information at your fingertips. It is also full of porn, violence and hatred. In an open society the good goes with the bad. You'd like to think people would respect each other, but we know that isn't the case. Companies are in the business of making money and some do it any way they can. Lie, cheat and steal is their mission statement."

A pretty twentysomething Hispanic girl strolled past the table making eye contact. Her tight spandex shorts and halter top were hard to ignore. I smiled and received one in return, before she reached the counter to order.

"Ever since I've been on this case, there have been those who have tried to run me off it by any means necessary. That in itself leads me to believe it is possible. Now the question is what I can do to stop it. In the end, I'm trying to solve a murder. But the two seem to be connected."

"Most of the cyber theft happens overseas. China, Russia and even North Korea. But they all, especially China and North Korea, are trying to infiltrate the US government and military networks. I don't know what equipment the government uses, but they have a history of going with the lowest bidder when it comes to contracts. Heaven help us if this is true about WANN and if any of their networking gear controls our government or military infrastructure."

His words weren't comforting, and gave me quite a chill. I looked over at him and decided refills were in order. Oh, and he wanted a couple of more scones, too. Apparently, his appetite wasn't affected by world-changing events.

Chapter 36

Once back home I sat down on the sofa, feeling exhausted. I understood more about technology now than I cared to, though it was important to understand. Still, it made my head hurt, and along with a still-throbbing left hand, I was spent. I should have crashed right there and fell asleep. But I didn't want to. I needed to go out and drink a few beers and maybe shoot the breeze with someone. Standing up, I piled back into my Mustang and headed to my favorite watering hole, Boone's, with many questions on my mind.

Why was it some people worked so hard to steal from others, when with the same effort they could make an honest living? Of course, why did people strap on bombs, walk into a crowded area and blow themselves up.

Trying to solve the perplexities of life would drive you insane. If I had answers to all of life's mysteries I could probably retire a rich man. It was why hard-working people went to places like Boone's, to forget their personal troubles and avoid the shocking news headlines, and just enjoy themselves, escaping to a sane environment, if for only a little while.

When I arrived, I found the place fairly quiet. It was the middle of the week, and students at Denver University weren't back in session yet, so it wasn't surprising. I found a spot at the bar waiting for Nick the bartender, who was always normally there. But instead it was Julie tonight tending bar, rather than waiting tables.

"Hi, Jarvis," she said with a smile. "A beer, I presume?"

"Hello, Julie. Yes on the beer, and some mild chicken wings. I don't think I've ever been here when Nick wasn't working the bar."

"Believe it or not he does take nights off and has a life. A wife and three kids, with another on the way."

"I didn't know that about him. We always talked sports. Funny, I never inquired about his personal life."

"He is a fairly private guy," Julie said while placing a cold mug of brew in front of me. "When tending bar, it's all about the customer. Let them blow off steam and forget about their day."

She must have been reading my mind. Bartenders were often amateur psychologists.

"True. But next time I will try not to be too self-absorbed and ask how he is doing. With him soon having four kids I'm sure he would have something to talk about."

Julie smiled and moved on to help another patron, and put in my order for the wings. I sipped my beer and looked around the room. There were a few people I knew and saluted with my mug to a couple of them. To the left of me in one of the booths was one of April's friends, Jessica, who was being wooed by a tall gentleman in jeans and T-shirt. She looked around him, straight at me, and gritted her teeth. It would seem she was not enjoying the company. I waved down Julie.

"Who is the guy with Jessica?" I asked.

"No one, really. He is always trying to make a move on her. She has shot him down so many times, but keeps coming back for more. Can't take no for an answer."

"Do you know what she is drinking?"

"I'll find out."

Julie waved over to the waitress handling that side of the room and found she was drinking a Cosmopolitan. I had her make another and I carried it over to her table.

"Jessica, so good to see you again," I said, while sitting down the drink next to her other one. "So glad you could meet me here. It's been a long time. We have so much to catch up on."

I leaned over and kissed her on the cheek, then turned and smiled at her hopeful suitor.

"Jessica and I have known each other for years. I'm Jarvis, and I hope I'm not interrupting anything."

"No, not at all," replied Jessica. "The gentleman was about to leave, weren't you?"

He was a little stunned, but turned and walked away. Jessica put her hand on my shoulder, with a big sigh of relief.

"Thanks for saving me, Jarvis. You are my hero. He really is persistent. Every time I come in here he tries the same move. Really not my type. Too full of himself. Always talking in the third person. Likes to tell me how much money he has and what he has spent it on recently. How he works out every day to keep in shape and goes to the tanning salon so he can have a bronze body. Oh my, he is so self-absorbed!"

"Glad to help. No worries on prattling on about finances from me. I don't have any money to spend, so nothing to brag about."

"No, but I know you can carry on a conversation that will include the person you are talking to. Something he knows nothing about." She started fondling the drink I brought her. "So, how have you been?"

"Busy. Been running all over town working a case. I needed to come in tonight and unwind. Hopefully not think about it. Have you talked with April recently?"

"Yes, I have," Jessica said after a sip of her drink. "Most every day since she has been in the hospital. She'll be coming home in a day or so. I told her I'd take a day or two off and help her out once she is home. Damn shame about her getting shot."

"Something I don't feel good about," I said. "Saved my life. She is a tough lady."

"Well, if it makes you feel any better, she says you saved hers as well. If you hadn't tended to her wounds and gotten her the help when you did, she probably would have died. I know she is a little smitten with you. Hard not to feel something for a good-looking private detective. I know you've caught my eye many times when you walk in."

She has certainly caught mine as well. Tonight, the thirtysomething woman wore pink capris and a dark blue halter top, braless from what I could tell, for the fabric barely contained her chest, nipples poking through. She had straight shoulder-length auburn hair she twirled between her fingers at times, with telling hazel eyes, with a few freckles on her cheeks. She was wearing flat shoes, but was still almost 5'10", with a good firm rear end and smooth tanned legs and skin. We had talked a few times before, but never alone. April had mentioned her pleasurable disposition towards me, but I had always remained distant. For some reason tonight, I was feeling amorous and wanting companionship. I needed a release and she might be able and willing to provide it.

"Jessica, I don't believe I know what you do for a living?" I asked.

"Executive assistant to some asshole CEO," she replied. "Got a bachelor's degree to bring him coffee, make his travel and hotel arrangements, do his personal shopping, pick up his dry cleaning and make sure his wife doesn't know about his mistress. It pays well but hardly challenges me. Every now and then I'm thrown a bone and actually do some real work."

The waitress brought me my chicken wings. I offered some to Jessica but she declined, for she had eaten earlier. I gnawed off the tender meat carefully, without making a total mess of myself. But there were plenty of napkins handy.

"Sounds hideous, if you don't mind me saying so."

"It is, most of the time. I hope not to do this forever. I have a profession on the side, that I hope someday will provide the income I need. What did you do to your hand?"

I held it up, the two last fingers on my left hand bandaged. The knuckles still swollen.

"I had someone try to point these two fingers towards the heavens by dislocating them. One of the hazards of my profession."

"Sounds painful."

"It was and still is. Though slowly healing."

"That speaks to my other profession. I sell essential oils. I have stuff which can help with the pain and healing."

I nodded my head. I was willing to try anything, if it helped at all. She reached for her purse and pulled out a black zipper pouch with small vials, removing one and showing it to me.

"This should help," she said.

Taking the liquid, and pouring some on her fingers, she gently rubbed it into my exposed knuckles, her skin soft and soothing when contacting mine. It smelled minty and a little warm to the skin. Maybe it was smoke and mirrors, but it seemed to help. I flexed my fingers and found the pain didn't seem as bad and I had more range of motion.

"Definitely helped."

"It's not magic. It won't heal your injured tissue and joints instantly. You'll need to apply each day, maybe several times. But it should help speed up the process."

"I'm sure that small bottle won't last long. Do you have more?"

"I have more out in my car."

"What does it cost?"

"One drink and running interference to protect me from a loser. In my book you've already paid. Care to escort me to my car?"

We both finished off our drinks while I finished off the wings, and I walked her out. On the way her body kept brushing up against me. She certainly wasn't tipsy, but was doing this to let me know she was interested. When we got to her car, she opened the trunk and found what she was looking for, placing it in my right hand, while squeezing it, her skin pleasurable to the touch.

"I could also provide a massage for you as well, if you want to come to my place. Deep tissue will rub those worries away. Once you are relaxed we could take a swim and sit in the hot tub at my townhouse and enjoy each other's company."

She still held my hand, as I looked into her eyes. I pulled her forward, took a minute and kissed her. I felt a surge in my body I'd not felt in a while. She didn't resist any, and squeezed in closely, her hands on my chest. Her heart rate was increasing, as was mine.

"Nice," she said after ending the kiss. "I'm guessing that is a yes to the massage."

I mouthed the positive answer and was ready to plunge in head first, when my cell phone rang. When I looked and saw the name, I knew I had to answer it.

"Sorry, I need to take this. Please wait here."

I stepped away and hit the answer button. The nervous voice on the other end, matched the name on my phone.

"I need to meet with you," said Wilmar Boylan. His timing couldn't have been worse.

"When?" I asked, hoping for something like tomorrow.

"Tonight. Right now, if you can. I have additional information about Aaron's death."

I could hear the quake in his voice. I wondered if he lived his whole life nervous.

"Can't it wait until tomorrow?"

There was a pause of silence, as if he muted his phone. Then I could hear his breathing, which was labored.

"No, right now. Come by my office. This is big news. And I can't give it over the phone."

Crap, I said to myself. I was primed for a little interaction with Jessica. But duty came first.

"OK. Give me about thirty minutes."

"You know where it is?"

"The same as the address on the document?"

"Yes. And come alone."

I looked at my phone and it showed after eight.

"How do I get in so late at night?"

"The front entrance isn't secured. Text me when you are in the parking lot. I'll text back and then you come on up to the third floor. Knock on my door and I'll let you in."

"This better be good."

Another long pause.

"It is." And he ended the call.

I turned and walked back to Jessica. I reached out my hand to grab hers.

"I'm sorry but I have to leave. Something related to the case I mentioned earlier, which I must deal with. It could be important."

She had a look of disappointment, but seemed to understand.

"If you finish up early, call me," she said. "I'll be up for a while. Here is my card." She wrote her home address on the back. "I'm not generally to bed until eleven or so. If I know you are coming over, then I can stay up as late as necessary. I can always call in sick if you decide to keep me active all night."

She leaned in and wrapped her arms around me, kissing me, her heated chest against mine. I paused as she drove away, cursing I had to wait, hoping the meeting wouldn't last long, as I headed towards his office, trying to concentrate on the task at hand and not on Jessica's body and mine entwined. I was in a daze of languor the whole way there.

Chapter 37

Back to where this all started, now I stood there with Adam King's gun pointed at me, uncertain what to do. Thoughts filled my head of why he was there again. He kept popping up into this case, like a bad disease. And now it looked as if he might have killed my cyber informant, who had inside information on WANN Systems that might solve a murder. I needed to stall for time.

"Adam, what are you doing here?" I asked.

"I was going to ask you the same thing," he said.

His hand was shaking some. I hoped the gun didn't have a hair-trigger. Mine still was at my side. If his went off all I could do was hope to move fast enough and shoot back. At this distance that was unlikely and I'd be dead before getting off a shot.

"I was called here to meet someone." I said.

"Who?"

I looked over his shoulder at the dead body of Wilmar, and pointed at him.

"The dead man over there. The one you shot."

"Me?"

"You have the gun."

"So do you."

On instinct I holstered mine, hoping he'd feel less threatened.

"Mine wasn't pointed, ready to fire."

Adam had a stunned look on his bruised face, from where I'd hit him. He finally lowered his gun.

"I didn't kill him, Jarvis. I reached this room shortly before you. Found him this way. I pulled my gun to make sure the killer didn't come back. When you stepped in, I was prepared to shoot whomever it was."

"Did you call the police?"

"Hell no. Didn't you hear me? I just got here. No time. I wanted to make sure they didn't circle around and take me out too."

"So, you didn't see anyone."

Adam looked as if he had an answer, but didn't say anything.

"Look, this man was about to feed me some essential information. You keep worming into my case like the parasite you are. If you know something, you better damn well tell me. Or I'm going to punch it out of you, gun or no gun, and then call the police."

He hesitated, trying to find an answer, his free hand feeling the welt on his cheek.

"Not here. Not now. We need to get out of here before the cops show up and think we did it."

"Leaving the scene of the crime is a criminal offense."

"I don't care. If you don't leave, then I will. And you can't stop me."

"Let me smell your gun?"

He looked at me as if I was crazy. I offered my gun to him, handle first.

"Here, check mine and you'll see it's not been used. I need to make sure it wasn't you. Let me check the gun to see if it had been fired."

He handed it over to me. Not wanting to put my fingerprints on it, I pulled out my handkerchief and held it. A quick whiff confirmed what he said was true.

"Did you touch anything?"

"No. I saw the door open, pulled my gun and pushed it open with my elbow. Believe it or not, I'm not a complete idiot."

I wanted to counter, but figured now was not the time.

"OK, there is a fifties diner on the east side of Arapahoe and I-25. Let's meet there and talk. I will call into the police."

We got outside and once in my car I called into the Denver dispatch that I was worried about a phone call I'd gotten earlier from a lead and could they send a unit over to check on him. Then I sent a text to Jessica, telling her things had gotten even more complicated and I would be up very late tonight and couldn't come over. Though I hoped to take her up on the offer at a later date. Her frowny-face response didn't improve my mood any. After that I arrived at Gunther Toody's and found Adam King sitting in one of the nostalgic fifties-style booths, with built-in jukebox, though the music likely was digital. I was hungry and ordered a burger, fries and chocolate shake. He didn't want anything and just ordered a soda, after which the waitress reminded us they'd be closing soon. As I sat there I wondered how best to approach what had taken place. Something was going on I wasn't seeing. King was a pest, but even more so on this case. There had to be a reason beyond his normal predatory behavior.

"Something is going on here, King, I'm not aware of. It's time to 'fess up."

He thought over his response before replying.

"I'm on a case myself," he said. "I was supposed to keep an eye on two Asian men."

This couldn't be a coincidence.

"Let me guess. Were their names Cong and Lok?"

"Yes."

"Who hired you?"

"Come on, you know I can't tell you that."

"You don't have that many clients, so I'd be willing to guess Bristol & Bristol."

His face revealed I was correct. The question is who at the law firm would arrange this. For it seemed unlikely Don Bristol would have done it. He was too carefree with his clients and only worried about making money. His brother was a different story.

"My guess would be Tony. He is having you watch them to make sure his brother isn't into something?"

I'd heard Adam wasn't good at keeping his mouth shut. It didn't surprise me when he opened up once I nailed whom it was. He looked around to make sure no one else was listening, which was funny, as we were the only two in the place besides the waitress and whoever was running the grill.

"In a way, yes, for he made the final approval. But your girlfriend, Melissa, is the one who called and gave me the details of what the job involved. All my findings, I report to her. Tony thinks fondly of her. Hopes she'll be a partner someday. Once she is through with school."

I was surprised by the words, but upon further contemplation I wasn't. Melissa was a good woman. I know she often worried about me. Even though we weren't together she would still worry. It was her nature. Her note about who hired Bristol & Bristol to bail out the Platov brothers was proof of that.

"Ex-girlfriend," I said.

"Sorry to hear. It would seem she still holds a torch. Or doesn't want you dead. Either way she talked Tony into bringing me in and start digging around."

"And you kept bugging my client for business?"

"As I told you, she called me. Said she had hired you and even gave you a retainer, but hadn't heard back. Was exploring her options."

"She was going to hire you?"

"No, she didn't. I never heard back, so I called her a couple times to follow-up."

"Then badmouth me in the process."

His eyes couldn't meet mine and he didn't argue the point.

"You have no class, Adam," I stated.

"I needed the work. I do what it takes."

I could call him some other names, but it wouldn't matter, so I saved my breath. The waitress brought our drinks. The shake was cold and thick, but lacking in chocolate flavor, a no-no for a chocolate shake.

"I go back to what I asked you at the scene. Didn't you see anyone? By your reaction when I first asked, it appeared you may have. And how did you end up at his office?"

"I was following the two Asian guys, Cong and Lok. Been tailing them when I can. Not much going on, until they pick up this passenger on the street corner. A thick guy, maybe six foot and two hundred pounds or so. Wearing a hat and a long coat, which seemed odd for August, being it was still warm this evening. I figure trying to hide who he was. They drove down to the building there in the Tech Center and dropped the person off. Now I have a choice: either continue to follow the two men or see what this person is up to. Seemed a little suspicious, so I decided to follow him up. When he hits the elevator, I watch the indicator above the door and see it stops on the third floor. I decide to take the stairs. This building is so open you can pretty much go anywhere. I hit the third floor and start reading the nameplates on the doors. Nothing really stands out, so I wait. After about twenty minutes or so, I hear a noise. Sounds like two people fighting and then a gunshot. The person then runs out a door down the hall, so I yell at them to stop. They hit the stairs on the other side in a flash. I could chase after them, but he moved quickly for a large person, so I thought I should see if I could help who had been shot. Once I get in there I see the body and can tell right away they were dead. He'd been shot in the head. A couple minutes later you show up and I nearly shoot you."

The waitress arrived with my burger and fries, reminding us once again the place would be closing soon. They were in a rush, as the burger was barely cooked, bloody red inside and the fries were lukewarm. *I hated medium-rare beef.* I should have sent it back, but I forced down the sandwich, lots of ketchup and mustard making it bearable.

"Can you identify the person you saw?" I asked.

"No. Like I said, six-foot-tall and a bit chunky. Looked like dark short hair under the hat. But I never saw the face."

"The security in the building is crap, so I doubt there are any cameras to look at. We need to go back there and tell the police what you know."

"Hell no. I'm not getting involved in this. I want no part of it."

"You have an obligation to do this. You are a licensed private detective, and that license says you need to report any crimes you witness."

"But I didn't witness it. All I saw was someone leaving. I can't say for certain they killed the guy. For all I know, he may have killed himself."

I wanted to take the rest of my food and throw it at it him, for that was all it was worth. King was an ass, and I wondered why he was in the business. Or how he even survived and made a living. My phone was ringing, the number showing it was the Denver police calling me back.

"The cops are calling me now and are going to want to talk with me. You need to 'fess up or I'll tell them to come see you."

"I can't, Jarvis." He stopped and lowered his head. "I screwed up a couple months back and I can't afford another mistake. You've got to help me here! I'm begging you. I don't have much other than this job and I'm barely getting by as it is. If I lose my license and my business, I'm out on the street working lowly security jobs."

I didn't care for the guy, so why did I feel sorry for him? Sometimes I was too much of a pushover.

"OK. On one condition."

"You name it."

"You keep following Cong and Lok, but you will report to me what you find, as well as to Melissa. And I mean regular updates, without holding back any information. Then if I need your help with anything, you will be there to assist. This is getting messy, and I might need some protection for my client. You are about all I have right now."

"At my regular rates?"

I frowned.

"Bristol & Bristol is paying you. I'm not. I'm doing you a favor here. You don't like it, then we talk with the police."

He looked around and nodded his head. Lights started getting turned off in the building, as they were pushing us to leave. I finished my shake, leaving half the sandwich and nearly all the fries behind. I paid the bill and left a paltry tip. *That will show them!* We parted ways, but I made him promise to call me each day. Then I drove back to the scene of the crime, ready to face the Denver police with whatever story I could come up with.

Chapter 38

Arriving on the scene, there were several police cars, an ambulance with paramedics and a tech van. I was greeted by an officer on the scene, where I showed him my ID and told him I was summoned. After a short talk on his radio, I was escorted to the third floor where a buzz of activity filled the halls and the office. I was taken to the man on the scene, who was Detective Mallard. Buildings often didn't run their cooling systems at night, to save on costs, so the office was hot and he showed it by the sweat on his forehead. This late evening was still toasty, with the temps still in the eighties, all the bodies coming and going not helping any. The heat didn't seem to calm Mallard's mood any, as his gruff and growl was in full-on direct mode when he first saw me.

"Are you going to make this difficult for me, as usual?" was his first question. "Because I'm really not in the mood."

"Wow, Detective, I just got here. Ask me some questions first before accusing me of anything."

"Well, you called in, worried about this guy, and we find him dead. With your history, this leads me to believe there is more to it than that."

"He was providing me leads to a case. He called and sounded worried. I couldn't immediately get here, so I called you guys when he wouldn't answer my callbacks."

"What case?"

"Aaron Bailey."

"I figured as much, but had to ask. From the sign on the door he appeared to be a tech geek."

"Yes, a security expert. He had been working with Aaron before he was killed."

"And now he is dead?"

"Exactly. I believe a pattern is appearing. There is little doubt in my mind that Aaron wasn't killed in a random robbery. And neither was Wilmar."

"Crap! I was hoping for a quiet night."

"Working the late shift these days?"

"A double. Been going for twelve straight, with hardly a break.

Vacation season will do that. I get back from a sabbatical and already need another. And a vacation from you."

"Not my intention to make your life miserable. Just lucky, I guess."

I smiled, but Mallard didn't, letting out some air in disgust. He pulled off his coat and tossed it to one of the uniforms to hold. He led me back to the office where the body lay. A fifty-something man was kneeling next to Wilmar, doing a quick exam. I'd seen him around before and only knew him as Floyd.

"Any further conclusions?" asked Mallard.

"Not been dead long. Bullet to the head likely the kill shot. But he was also shot in the stomach, it would appear. Need more time on the order of the wounds, but I imagine stomach first, and then to the head to finish him off."

"Appears there was a struggle," said Mallard. "Chair knocked over, papers and a few wall-framed pictures on the floor. Any signs he fought back?"

"Possibly. Some scratches on his hands and arms. They appear to be fresh, with a little bit of blood. Is this the man who called it in? Looks familiar to me."

"I've seen you around too, Floyd. Private Detective Jarvis Mann."

"Oh, yes. The gumshoe who drives our good detectives crazy. Why did you call in?"

"We were supposed to meet. He didn't call me back and when I called I got no answer."

"Do you suspect foul play?" asked Floyd.

"Yes."

"Jarvis was investigating the killing of Aaron Bailey," said Mallard. "He believes they are tied together."

Floyd rubbed at his stubble of gray hair, coaxing a memory from his noggin.

"Computer tech from WANN systems, killed in their parking lot a few months back. What is the connection?"

"He was a friend who was working on something with Aaron. They believed something illegal was going on inside WANN. Software-related hacking or theft. They were working on putting the pieces together when Aaron was killed. Wilmar contacted me but was afraid to dig in too deep. I talked him into working with me to find more evidence."

"No sign of a computer," said Mallard. "There is a docking station, monitor and keyboard. But no notebook."

"Have to have been taken by the killer," I said. "I doubt a cyber security person would go anywhere without a computer."

"Could have been killed for the computer," said Mallard. "Could have been a robbery."

"I doubt it and so do you. Computers aren't five grand these days. Hell, I can do amazing things on my phone and it didn't cost me much. Nobody kills over a notebook computer, unless it has something important on it the killer wanted."

"Floyd, get him on the table as quickly as possible," stated Mallard. "We need to fast-track this and have some answers. I'm afraid Jarvis here is correct. This certainly looks like a murder. And if it's in any way tied to Aaron's killing, that case needs to be reopened."

"I will work through the night," said Floyd. "I will say by the size of the holes in the wound, the caliber of the weapon appears to be smaller. As I recall they were 9mm in the Bailey case. If this were 9mm, one or both likely would have exited from the other side. In this case both are still inside of the body. We'll know for sure once they are removed and examined."

We walked out of the room, which was fine with me. I'd seen a few dead bodies, though I handled the sight of them as well as one could. The carnage and blood a bullet could do, viewing a crime scene to this day was still unnerving. Memories of Flynn's body still crept into my dreams. And there had been enough dead ones over the last few years that I'd not been able to completely shake them from my thoughts. I wondered if I ever would.

"Jarvis," said Mallard, once we'd hit the hallway. "I've dealt with you now on enough of these, to know you are holding out on me. For once, tell me the whole truth. There is more to this than you are revealing."

"You are so cynical, officer."

"I prefer the term experienced. My time spent wrangling with you."

"I've given you all I know for certain," I said, though it was a lie. "But my gut tells me Cong and Lok are involved. It wouldn't hurt to bring them back in."

"I doubt your gut is enough to bring them down for questioning. Besides, you were the one that dropped the charges and had them released."

He had a point.

"There has to be more," stated Mallard.

"I wish there was. All I have is mostly circumstantial. But I'm close and it has to do with WANN. And they are getting nervous. Someone at the top is directing this to cover up something. When I have it, I'll let you know."

"Sure you will. I'm certain you have me number one on your speed dial. This whole situation is leaving a nagging twinge on the back of my neck. You are correct something isn't right here. And it will now get our full attention. If I find out you are holding back, which I'd bet my right nut you are, there will be hell to pay. Now get out of here and don't come back down to the station to bother us unless you provide me something worth the drive."

I walked out of the room, knowing he'd figure things out eventually. Once he started checking phone and text records he would know I wasn't on the up and up. I headed home, hoping some new plan would pop in my head while I was sleeping. But I'd not gotten any smarter over the last twenty-four hours, so it wasn't likely.

Chapter 39

The next day no real answers were coming to me. I'd gone over everything again and again. There were too many mysteries. And like Mallard, I figured someone might be holding out on me. And the best place to start was my client. After checking and double-checking I wasn't being followed, I stopped by her house for a visit. I was tired and grumpy, for I'd not gotten a lot of sleep. The first words out of my mouth were down right cold and straight to the point. But I wanted to read her reaction.

"Mandy, Wilmar Boylan was murdered last night," I stated.

She was standing when I said it. She immediately sat down, stunned by the statement, her hands covering her mouth. She tried to hold back the tears, but her eyes were moist. She grabbed a tissue from the coffee table and dabbed at her eyes.

"You knew him," I asked.

She hesitated for a moment before nodding her head.

"How?"

"He was my friend."

It was a different answer than she had given me before. I was angry, but did my best to hold it back.

"Why didn't you tell me?"

She didn't answer and couldn't look me in the eye.

"I can't help you if you don't tell me the truth. Clients who have lied to me have led to cases that didn't end well. For me or for them."

Still no response. She could have been in shock, but I persisted.

"Dammit, Mandy, say something. Give me what is really going on here. You know more than you are telling. And now your friend is dead because of it. I'm walking away from this before anyone else gets hurt, unless you 'fess up."

Turning, I started for the door. I'd laid the blame on her fully and it broke her down. She started crying, her face in her hands. The sobs were genuine; this I could tell immediately. Never had a crying woman ever made me joyful. I hated it and would rather have bamboo shoots put up my fingernails. Stopping, I walked back towards the sofa and sat down, putting my arm around her, cautious of being lured into any type of physical emotional response. She wasn't Emily White, a client I'd forever remember and regret my sexual encounter with. Though it was pleasurable up until the point where Emily shot me to exact her revenge for me shooting her. Mandy, though, was different. She wasn't going to jump my bones at the slightest contact, even pulling away at my touch. Her game and deceit was something very different. I just needed to discover what it was. After a few minutes and several more tissues, she found her composure and walked out of the room. A few minutes later she returned with an oversized notebook computer, placing in on the dining room table, and then waving me to come over and sit next to her. The first thought that overcame me was her earlier statement she didn't own a computer. But I kept it to myself. The real question was what did this mean.

"I was afraid to say anything," Mandy said. "Fear took control of me. I was scared of someone finding out the truth. Most wouldn't believe me anyway without proof. Women in the computer field, especially hackers, are still considered second-class in many circles. So, we created a charade. A good one, too. But it ended up getting the man I loved killed. And now a good friend."

"What charade did you create?" I asked.

"Aaron had computer skills, but not to the level of a master hacker. Neither did Wilmar. I'm the hacking prodigy. I'm the one who helped Aaron get his job, rising quickly in the ranks at WANN. Walking him through areas he needed help with. I was Wilmar's partner, a silent one, within Colorado Cyber Border Security. I'm the white or black hat, depending on your perspective, who breaks into networks, exploiting and fixing the security holes depending on the job at hand."

"You weren't an administrative assistant. Why lie about it?"

"Look at me. Would you take me seriously as a computer engineer? All anyone would see was a pretty face with an empty brain. I've interviewed for jobs in the past and they wouldn't even call me back. Most think all I'm good for is getting coffee, printing expense reports, translating handwritten memos into Word documents, and filling out a pretty dress to flaunt my body."

I understood what she meant. With her looks I'd have never suspected a computer hacker lurking inside. Maybe with her hair up and big thick-framed glasses, the stereotypical female nerd look. I guess I, too, had a preconceived notion about beautiful women.

"Hard to disagree."

"They also pay men more money and promote them faster," Mandy said. "Women just aren't looked upon as computer experts. Much like many other fields out there where women are discriminated against. The Old Boys network is hard to crack through. We did this and made it work. Aaron was promoted several times at WANN. Probably wouldn't have happened if it wasn't for me."

"So why not be up front and tell me?" I asked.

"Hard to say. I do have trust issues at times, especially with men I hardly know. Though you came highly recommended I felt it wasn't important for you to know to do your job. I wanted to make sure I didn't fall victim and be killed."

"No, instead your friend is now dead."

I think I stunned her again and got an unpleasant stare from her.

"Sorry," I said. "I didn't get much sleep last night."

"You don't need to spell it out for me. I understand what I've done and who has paid the price."

"We don't know before he was killed, if Wilmar talked. It's possible they know you are the true hacker and person they must shut up. The question is, what do you know now? He called me saying he had additional information."

"We really didn't have much new. Since Aaron's death they shut off our access and tightened up security significantly. We've been attempting to get in. Haven't had a lot of luck. Been trying a lot of different avenues."

The killer must have convinced Wilmar to call me, as a trap, but was killed trying to get away before I got there. He had fought back, it would appear, said Floyd at the scene. A frightened man would often grow courage in the face of death.

"Whose access would be the best to have to get into WANN's network?" I asked.

"Anyone on the security team, security engineers. Though they likely change their passwords frequently and use complex ones that are hard to break."

"What about those in upper management?"

"Good question. But they often use easier ones to guess. Family names, and birthdates. And likely don't change them as frequently. They generally complain if they must remember something complicated. Often will use the same ones repeatedly."

"I may have an avenue to a possible password for one of the higher-ups. I will have to get back to you on this. For now, we need to think about your safety. I don't need a dead client on my resume. Do you have somewhere else to stay for now? A friend or family member?"

She stopped to think for a second. You could tell she wasn't overjoyed with moving out.

"No, not really. No family in town. And I'm not thrilled about leaving this house. Can't you stay here and protect me?"

"I can't detect and watch you at the same time. Nights, yes, but during the day I'd need someone else. And it will cost you more. Twenty-four-hour protection isn't cheap."

"Money is no object. Besides I can work from here and still see if I can get more dirt on WANN."

I thought over my options. If I got Rocky, there'd be no issue. I knew I could trust him and she'd be safe. But I had no idea where he was or how to get ahold of him. And most of my other contacts seemed to be uninterested in helping me. I had a stupid thought, one I might regret later. Since he was already involved, maybe Adam King would be an option. Yes, he was creepy, but I had him in my pocket right now on Wilmar's murder. The question was, could he do the job properly. I'd heard he was a pretty good shot with a gun. And if he could act like a human being, it might work, if no other possibilities were forthcoming.

"I will check around for some options and get back to you. For now, please lay low and stay home. If you need to run an errand, tell me now and I will take you there. Don't do any more hacking until I call you. I will have someone by the end of the day."

"I'm fine staying home for now?"

"If anything suspicious happens, call 911 and then call me. I don't care how trivial, make the call if you think something is out of the ordinary. If someone calls, don't answer unless it's me. Anyone knocking at the door, ignore it. Keep all your windows, blinds and curtains closed. Doors always double-locked. I will do a walk-through to verify before I leave."

"Do you think you'll find someone capable of protecting me?"

I said "yes" as I started my walk-through, trying not to snicker. *Capable* probably wasn't the word I'd use to describe King, so Mister Creepy might have to do.

Chapter 40

I didn't have a lot of luck finding anyone else. I reached out to Bill to see if he wanted to make some extra money, but he couldn't take time off because of the vacation season leaving the Denver PD shorthanded. Calls out to my other contacts got me nothing but static. I checked with April's brothers, at least the two I could get ahold of, but they couldn't commit to watching every day since I didn't know for how long I'd need them. For now, only one person seemed to be around or available. It looked more and more like King would be my only option. Since he was working for Tony Bristol, I needed to talk with him first. I owed him at least that much. I called and arranged a late lunch with him in downtown Denver.

I arrived at the Rock Bottom Brewery at around one, and strode in to find Tony already seated. He was dressed dapperly as always, expensive dark blue suit and tie, the jacket hanging over the back of his chair. He stood up to shake my hand, his 6' 2" height taller than me, though thinner. His dark hair was showing grayer these days, his gold Rolex and massive diamond ring still adorning his left arm and finger. We had a decent relationship, though a businesslike one. Much better than I had with his younger brother Don. He had ordered me a beer, while he drank some wine. The waiter brought out some ball-park pretzels he had ordered. We both sat, and I grabbed a menu to see what sounded good today.

"Jarvis, you are looking fit these days," stated Tony. "Good to see after all you've gone through these last couple of years."

"Been busy, which is good," I replied. "Some of the results were not ideal, but I'm still standing and making a living."

"Sorry to hear about you and Melissa," he said. "She is a great lady. Too bad you screwed that up."

Straight and to the point.

"Not ideal either, what happened. A mistake I will live with the rest of my life."

"It would seem she still cares for you. Though trust is no longer there. Once you lose that, it is hard to reclaim."

The waiter returned and we each ordered. Tony had the chopped BBQ chicken salad, while I ordered a hickory bacon chicken sandwich. I handed over the menu and rested my arms on the table, like mother taught me not to do. I planned to be direct with Tony as well.

"Enough of the small talk," I said. "I need a favor. One that may prevent the death of my client."

"I'm listening."

"Our paths have been crossing on my current case. You've been bailing out your clients, who were trying to injure and even kill me."

"Not our clients. But our clients asked our assistance to get them released. And the term is 'allegedly' tried to injure or kill you."

"Nothing alleged about it. I was there, I know what happened."

"The lawyer in me must spell that out."

I made a face and decided against using one of the many lawyer jokes out there as a response.

"Because of the current situation my client is at risk and needs protection. And I can't protect and detect at the same time. I'm asking for assistance."

"Surely you have other avenues to obtain help."

"All my previous helpers are unavailable. I'm scraping the bottom of the barrel. I want to use Adam King."

"He is currently employed by me at this time."

"I'm aware of this, and is tracking Cong and Lok. You need to pull him off this and allow me to hire him."

"Why should I agree to this?"

"Because we have a good business relationship that is in our best interests to maintain. I can tell you what Cong and Lok are up to. They are trying to prevent me from solving this murder, which now has turned into murder number two. They dropped off the possible murderer at the scene."

"You know this how?"

"Adam King. I found him at the scene. He told me how he got there and what he saw. I'm now covering for him. The police don't know this, but that can change."

Tony sipped on his wine and took several bites of pretzel, dipping it in hot mustard. Somehow, he could avoid getting any on his shirt. Must be his upbringing that taught him the secret.

"This sounds like a threat."

"Not at all. We can work together. I have no need to make it any messier than it is. All I need is his help making sure my client lives through this."

"So, you think King is capable enough to provide protection?"

"I certainly hope so. Right now, I have little choice. If someone better is available to you, then by all means give me a name."

"You've tried Brandon Sparks?"

"Appears to be out of the state and not taking my calls."

The waiter returned with our lunch. I took a bite and found it delicious. Tony took several mouthfuls and asked for a refill on his wine. I'd only drank a little of my beer, but another frosty mug was placed beside it.

"I'm willing to agree to this, on one condition. Stay out of my brother's business."

"If his doesn't cross over into mine, that won't be a problem."

"He is a decent litigator, but an excellent salesman who brings in a fair amount of business for us. Our success is much of his doing."

"Even if the clients are of the shady kind?"

"Oh please, Jarvis. You've worked with some as well. There would be no work for any of us if it weren't for the criminal element."

"There are criminals, and then there are those who kill in the name of profit only. It is hard to side with them, in my book."

Tony poked at a couple of large pieces of chicken and swallowed them down, followed by more wine. He took the cloth napkin and patted his face. More learned behavior from high-end breeding.

"You can play the high moral ground. I like you, Jarvis, but in the end, I will choose my brother over you every time. I'm sure you understand this after what happened with your brother. Leave Don alone, or else we will come down hard on you."

"Even if Melissa asks you not to?"

He laughed after two more bites of his salad.

"Melissa is like a daughter to me. She will be a great litigator who will join our firm one day as a lawyer, once her schooling is done. Maybe even get her name on the outside door as a partner. Even so, Don is blood and helps our profit margin with his work, allowing me a lifestyle my wife and I relish. Melissa knows this and would never put me in a position to choose."

I saw where he was coming from, and the defiant one in me wanted to tell him to go fuck himself. But I wasn't in a position to argue. I needed his help, and for now was willing to agree to the stipulations.

"I agree to your terms."

I put out my hand and he shook it. Our food was finished and the check arrived. Tony picked it up and, after reading it, put down his credit card.

"Do you have any say in the matter on keeping Cong and Lok off my back," I asked.

"No. Simply doing a favor for our client."

"WANN Systems?"

"You know I can't divulge that information."

I nodded.

"Besides, you must have some strings of your own to pull," stated Tony. "You made the Russian brothers disappear, or so it would seem."

"Their cousin nearly killed a friend of mine, before she killed him."

"Do you know where they are? I might be able to sweeten the pot some with a little hint of their location."

"They are being detained."

"Illegally, I presume, without being given their civil rights for counsel."

I gave him a wicked smile before responding.

"Allegedly!"

Chapter 41

We finished up our conversation, and Tony was tasked with letting King know of our new arrangement, while I would deal with Mandy. She did not like King at all, from his hounding her previously, so I needed to break it to her gently. Since I'd take the night shift I decided I'd cover the rest of the day with her and let her know over dinner. But first off, I needed to call Dezmond Price and see what he knew about Cong and Lok. When he answered the phone, he was a joy to talk with.

"Do you have a target on your back, stating you want nasty people to accost you?" he said.

"I'm naturally gifted at attracting attention. What do you know about them?"

Hearing a few taps on his keyboard, it appeared he was retrieving the information on his computer.

"We are pretty sure they work for the Chinese government. High up in their cyber division."

"I doubt Lok has ever even used a computer."

"No, he is an enforcer. Came from one of the many Chinese gangs, though not sure which. But he is deadly with his hands. Never touches a gun, from what I'm reading. May use other martial arts weapons, but never a gun. Doesn't feel he needs one."

"Yeah, I learned that the hard way. I won't make that mistake again. And what about Cong? He dresses and talks like a businessman. Very classy and professional, yet doesn't seem like he would hesitate to order Lok to rip out your heart if necessary."

"Not a lot on him. Seems to have climbed up the ranks quickly. Likely for the reasons you just stated. Moves around a lot, going from place to place. Goes where he needs to go and scare people, I'm guessing."

"That seems to be his mission with me as well. Any connections to WANN Systems?"

"No obvious ones. But again, the rumors were of an influx of cash that saved them, coming from overseas. Could have been China as well. Hell, they own the US government with all the loans to cover our debt, why not the corporations as well. Do you have anything new for me?"

"Someone killed a computer tech who was feeding me information on WANN. Cong and Lok may have dropped off the killer at the building where the murder happened."

"It wasn't them that did the killing?"

"I don't think so. Though they could have farmed it out to someone else so as not to risk getting caught."

"Their connections are deep. Am I going to need to bring them in as well?"

"For now, I'd say no. I'd like to see what they do next. Maybe this time I can fend them off."

"If not, I'll be sure to send flowers to your funeral."

At least I'd know there'd be lots of flowers at my burial!

"What about the Platov brothers? Where are they at now?"

"Out of my hands. Off to Miami. From there they will be sent on. Left here a couple nights ago on a military cargo plane out of Buckley. They will be processed and sent on from there within a few days. Why, do you miss them?"

I chuckled. "Hardly. Just making sure you were following through and they didn't fall through the Bureau red-tape cracks."

"Fuck you!" he said before hanging up.

It was good having such close friends in the FBI.

Next, I wanted to check in with April. Should have been home by now, so I wanted to see how her recovery was going. I called her cell phone and she answered right away. There was joy in her voice.

"Jarvis! When are you coming by to see me?"

"Are you home?"

"Yes. So happy to be in my own bed."

"Well, I will try and stop by. But I'm pulling double shifts right now. I have to protect my client, so I'll be watching her at night, staying at her place. Then sleuthing during the day."

"Hard to sleep on the couch?"

"I've done it before. Nothing new. Better than my client ending up dead."

"It's gotten that bad?"

"Yes. To the point where I had to bring in someone I don't care for to protect her during the day. But I had no other choice."

"Can you trust him?"

"I think so. I have something over him, so he must toe the line."

"My brothers would be willing to assist. All you have to do is call."

"I did, but they couldn't commit to taking a shift every day. But could help out to cover a night shift here and there if I needed a break. Right now, this should work. How are you feeling?"

"Better each day. Still hurt, but at least I was able to cut back on the pain meds. I don't like taking pills if I don't have to."

"Is Jessica there helping you?"

"Yes, she is. I'm so thrilled she is helping me get around. Just simply sitting on the toilet still is an adventure. She mentioned you helped her out the other night. Very gallant of you. Says she almost seduced you if you hadn't had work interfere. I guess I should be happy that happened."

I really didn't want to comment on the situation with her friend. Yes, I probably would have slept with her, had it not been for the murder. One would never know. Maybe it was a convenient excuse.

"I think it was probably for the best, no matter how tempting. It likely would have only been a fleeting moment of pleasure."

"That would be Jessica. It would have been quite fun for both of you, but nothing permanent. I'd like to think there is more out there for you."

"Anyone you have in mind?"

"I might have a better answer once I'm healed. But yes, I think there is someone you are more suited for."

"Let's hope so. Picking up a woman in a bar is fun, but not the life I want when I'm old and gray."

We talked for a few more minutes before hanging up. There was certainly a spark between us, but only time would tell. I'd felt many a spark through the years and always seemed to douse them with the water of infidelity or the brisk breath of cold feet.

The day was winding down and I needed food. I picked up some dinner at a local BBQ and brought it over to Mandy's. She was there working away on her computer, it appeared. With a couple of bags in hand I placed them on the dining room table, while she grabbed plates, silverware and glasses. I had chicken, ribs, mashed potatoes, mac and cheese, and even some apple pie for dessert. I dished up a plate for her before filling mine. She was having ice water, so I had some as well. As we ate, the quietness bothered me. After I savored the tender pork off the bone, I spoke.

"I'm so sorry about Wilmar," I said. "Was he married?"

"No, not anymore," she replied, after finishing off a drumstick. "Once was, but divorced for many years now. No kids either. He lived for his work."

"He was good at what he did?"

"He was sharp at finding security holes in business networks. Had some good tools he'd developed. Leaned on me for some of the tougher tasks."

"How did you meet?"

"At a security seminar here in Denver. He was doing a speech on intrusion protection. Afterwards Aaron and I both went up to talk with him. Really hit it off. Went out for drinks and have been friends ever since. He was the first to call me after Aaron was killed. Came right over and offered whatever help he could provide.""

"Which included continuing the work you were doing trying to expose WANN?"

"Yes. What ultimately got them both killed. All my fault."

I wanted to argue it wasn't, but I couldn't make a solid case. If she had been upfront with me, maybe Wilmar's death could have been prevented. Rubbing it in was not prudent. For now, I needed to make sure she lived through it.

"We will find out who is involved and they will go to jail," I said. "It's a matter of putting all the pieces together."

"I know it's them. Someone at WANN is orchestrating this. And it all starts at the top."

"No argument from me. But we need something more solid. Getting inside their network again would be helpful."

"I've been trying, but with little luck. They must have discovered the backdoors we were using and closed them. The only way in is via someone's login. And someone high up that will give me unfettered access."

"Would one of the founders of the company have the access you need?"

"Absolutely. Do you think you can get it?"

"Yes. Or at least a good idea of what it could be. Though I may have to hand over my virtue and provide services to get it."

"Who?"

"Ex-wife."

"Users are creatures of habits. They often use the same passwords or variations. She could give you a clue of what it might be."

I thought so as well. And if I had to provide pleasure to get the information, I was willing to sacrifice myself physically. One minute I was talking about trying to get away from casual sexual encounters, and the next I was willing to do so to advance my case. It was all part of the job and one I might not mind all that much. I smiled as I enjoyed some more pork, my happy thoughts on the nicely tanned bathing suit body, what lay underneath and how best to explore it. At times I really was an enigma that I didn't truly understand.

Chapter 42

I had done a thorough job of going over the house inch by inch last evening, learning all about it, its weaknesses, blind spots and vulnerable entry locations to try and minimize attack points. But I was doing it again, now with Adam King, making sure he understood it as well as I did. I don't think he cared to be told things, since like me he was used to working alone. But he endured and soon knew everything about the house I did.

When Mandy learned who was going to be guarding her during the daytime, she was not thrilled. But I guaranteed her she'd be alright and that King would act nothing but professional while around her—something I'd spelled out to him in no uncertain terms. If there was even a whiff of anything from him that was beyond the job at hand, sexual innuendo, comments about me, or slacking on the job in any way, I would be knocking him on his ass and finding someone else. Afterwards, turning him into the police for leaving the scene of a murder. I knew he needed the job and couldn't afford any issues with the cops. He agreed, and I felt pretty good he would do the job needed.

I wanted Mandy to have the ability to protect herself, as a last resort. I'd finally gotten back both my .38 revolvers. One from the Cong and Lok incident, since I'd dropped the charges; the other from the April shooting, since the case had been cleared as being self-defense. I showed it to Mandy, but she wasn't thrilled about using it.

"I hate guns," she said defiantly.

"I'm not a huge fan myself," I answered. "Especially when they are pointed at me. But when they are I'd prefer to have one to even the odds. It will only be as a last resort. But you need to understand how to use it."

She huffed and puffed, but finally gave in. I went over all the basics: how to hold it, how to aim, and how to fire, all with an empty gun. We spent twenty minutes until she was at least marginally comfortable, before I loaded it.

"Do I need to know how to load it as well?" she asked.

"No. If you need more than the six bullets inside, then it probably won't matter. If you shoot, don't hesitate if in danger.

I've done that enough to know it won't end up well for you. Point, aim center mass, and squeeze the trigger. Make the shot count. Of course, be aware of what you are shooting at. King and I would prefer not to be shot, if at all possible, by you accidentally."

She presented a rare and brief smile of comprehension. I left the gun in a safe place where she could get it. During the day it would be left downstairs, and at night she would take it upstairs in her bedroom. We would cover using the gun again each day we were there until this was over.

"She's all yours, King," I said, preparing to leave. "You have my number. Don't hesitate to call if I'm needed. Call 911 if you sense any danger."

"I brought some books to read to pass the time," he said, pointing to his backpack. "Spare gun and ammo, too."

"Hopefully you won't need it. I'll be back at six."

It had been a rocky night of sleep, but that was fine, so I went back home with a few BBQ leftovers, and took a quick shower. Once I knew it was not too early in California, I sent a text to see what type of response I would get. It wasn't long before I had an answer and Lyndi asked if we could do a Skype call. Not being a total tech illiterate, I understood what that meant, got her ID and connected with her via webcam. She was sitting in what would appear to be the same location where we first met, at her outside table next to the pool. She was wearing something soft around her shoulders, showing chest skin, the bathing suit top covering enough to want more. Lyndi Albers leaned back into her chair, giving me more of her to look at, a view I certainly was admiring.

"Jarvis Mann," she said, almost out of breath. "I didn't think I'd hear from you again. To what do I owe the pleasure?"

"I wanted to say hi and see how you are doing," I said. "So good to see you in all your digital glory."

As was usual with the Internet the picture and sound would be good one minute and bad the next. So far it was holding up, though not the same as being up close and personal.

"I must say you look good too. Though I'd prefer you sitting in the chair next to me, but this is a start."

"Once this case is over, and the check is cashed, I will see what flights and hotels are available to come see you."

"Oh, you probably can skip the hotel. I'm sure we can find you a bed to sleep in here."

Her right hand slid down her front and disappeared from the camera, doing who knows what. But her eyes closed and her mouth opened, as her tongue rolled around her lips.

"Easy now," I stated. "Don't get yourself too riled up. I'm not sure I'm into virtual sex. Save yourself for when I come to visit."

"Well, I'd much rather have your hands where mine are now, but a lady has to tend to her needs."

"Tend to them later. I have a question to ask, and I need your undivided attention."

Her eyes opened and her mouth closed. She seemed a little put off, but I'd make it up to her someday, maybe.

"You are no fun. But go ahead, ask away. I'm listening."

"It's about your ex-husband, Logan. How much do you know about him these days? You mentioned his trips to Vegas and his taste in younger women and men. What about his computer habits? Does he fall into patterns?"

Lyndi thought for a minute before responding.

"I would say yes, he does. What are you hoping to find out?"

"Well, we need to gather some information, and get inside WANN's network. We, that is one of my sources, had a backdoor, but it's been closed off to them. We need to find another way in. I was wondering if maybe Logan uses the same passwords, even when accessing his own network."

"And what is in it for me?"

"A night of carnal, animal pleasure with me."

"How do I know you'll come through?"

"Because my word is gold. And how could a full-blooded male like me turn down a beauty like yourself."

"A few have through the years. I'm not sure what to believe."

"Let me tell you what I'd do to you once I got there…"

I went into a long detailed, graphic description of several sexual acts I would perform on her and would allow her to perform on me. It felt odd, yet rather exciting reciting the words across the Internet. When I finished I noticed her hand had disappeared again, and her face was flush with excitement.

"Oh my, Jarvis, that was hot. I may have to wrap my legs around the pool man now once he arrives so I can relieve this burning desire you've instilled in me."

"I'm sure he'd be more than willing. You believe me and will help?"

"Oh my, yes. But if you don't come to me, I will come to you and take you right where I find you."

"Deal."

Her hand returned and she grabbed a glass from the table that looked like some type of fruit smoothie and sipped from her straw.

"One other promise you have to make," Lyndi said. "Don't damage him too much. He needs to still pay me my monthly check from our settlement. I'd rather not have to get a job. I prefer lounging around, working out to keep my bod of sin in shape, and then use it on studs like yourself."

I wasn't sure I could make that promise, but I took my index finger and made an X on my chest and held up three fingers, as if I was a boy scout.

"Logan loves sports. His favorite teams are always part of his password. He is a huge Giants, 49ers and Warriors fan. Something like *Sanfrangiants* or *Sanfranniners,* I know he used a lot."

"Did he substitute numbers for some of the letters? Use special characters? Capitalize some of them?"

"Sure he did. I know they wouldn't let him reuse his password right away. I believe five changes or more before he could use it again. He'd change little things here and there. And he almost always capitalized the first letter. He was a bright man but he hated trying to remember passwords. He made it as simple as possible."

Most users did. I often would take shortcuts on my passwords as well. After this case I would have to go through and change them all, trying to find better ones to use. Of course, I'd see if I'd actually do it.

"Thank you. That will be most helpful."

"Thank me by following through on your promise. It pains me to have my ex getting more action on his twice monthly, long weekend trips to Vegas. The man is a sex addict, if you ask me."

I was beginning to think she was as well. Maybe what had brought them together in the first place, other than the money.

"So how many days a month is he in Vegas?"

"Anywhere from six to ten, from what I've heard. And he'll have anywhere from two to four women or men, in combos, on those trips with him. Gambling and screwing his brains out. He lives a decadent life, if you ask me."

It was something else for me to keep in mind. Something I might be able to use against him. Who knows, maybe I'd dial up a trip to Vegas myself and check on him.

"Do you know when he is out of town?"

"Yes, my daughter tells me. She lives with him part of the time. When he is gone, she gets free rein of his house. Normally throws a party with her college friends. Why?"

"Let me know the next time he is in Vegas. I might have to pay him a visit."

"Only if you promise to take me with you. Otherwise, no deal."

"OK, I can do that. Though I will be working, so I don't know how much time I'll get to spend with you."

"Oh, you'll be working all right and it will be all over my body, from head to toe, as you described earlier. Once you've satisfied me, then you can go chasing after him."

"I guess I'll need to schedule an extra day."

"At least!" Lyndi replied.

How could I refuse such an offer.

"Then we have a deal. I would shake your hand, but it's hard to do via Skype, and who knows where it's been."

"Oh, I can tell you where…!"

She then proceeded to heat up the Internet with her own explicit description.

Chapter 43

I was on my way down to Denver Police headquarters to talk with Mallard. I'd been working out, relieving the stress after my call with Lyndi, when he called in a huff, wanting me down there ASAP. It didn't appear to be good news, so I called my lawyer Barry Anders to see if he was available. He agreed to meet me down there just in case, though he was on the other side of town and it would take some time. When I arrived, I was sent to Mallard's office. I felt like a student in trouble with the principal.

"We've reopened the Aaron Bailey case," he said after I'd taken a seat. "Thought you'd like to know."

"Glad to hear. I'd lay 100-to-1 odds it wasn't a robbery."

"We will be digging in deeper, talking with parties at WANN. See what we can come up with. Though I doubt we'll scare them any."

"I'm sure you didn't call me all the way down here just to tell me that," I replied.

Mallard had a clipboard in hand and flipped through several of the pages.

"No. We've done some digging into phone records. Found Wilmar texted you to come on up. As if you were outside waiting."

"I was supposed to be, but got hung up. That is why I tried to call him, but got no answer."

He looked down at the sheet again, then at another.

"No record of it."

I looked him square in the eye. I'd gotten good at lying.

"Must be a technical mistake. Can't trust these computers running these phone companies."

"Can't trust pain in the ass gumshoes, is what I'd say. Come on Jarvis, tell the truth for once. I know there is more to this."

"I'm working with Adam King now. He is helping protect my client. That is new, though I doubt it's important for you to know."

"King the PI? I thought you hated him?"

"All I could get on short notice. Beggars can't be choosers."

"Is she in danger?"

The chair was uncomfortable. Probably that way on purpose to make who was being questioned squirm.

"Yes. She actually was Wilmar's partner in their business."

"This is something new that you hadn't told me."

"Just found out myself. My clients like to withhold facts."

"You figure you can withhold as well."

"Been busy. I would have told you eventually."

He shook his head and let out a long sigh, while leaning back in his chair. His chair you could probably fall asleep in. No reason he should squirm.

"I've let you slide too long. Cummings keeps going to the Captain telling him I do you favors, which is a load of crap. But I do give you more leeway than I should at times. I have no choice but to lock you up for withholding evidence."

"Are you serious?" I said.

"Yes. Give me your gun and ID."

He picked up the phone and made a call, asking for someone to come down and process me. As he hung up, in the door walked Barry.

"Shit!" said Mallard.

"Good to see you too, Detective."

Mallard looked over at me and I shrugged.

"So, you knew?"

"Suspected," I replied. "When you called the tone didn't sound positive. I wanted to be prepared."

"Do I need to post bail?" asked Barry.

"Soon."

"What are the charges?"

"Withholding evidence in a murder investigation."

"A murder I believe he pointed you in the direction of."

I had informed Barry on my earlier call of the circumstances.

"And that they now are reopening thanks to me," I added.

"Yes. But you haven't been forthcoming about how you came about this information."

"Much of which I can claim as client privilege."

All Mallard could do was sigh.

"Let's walk down and get this taken care of," said Barry. "Of course, you are wasting valuable time and money, as you know this charge has no merit. But hey, I don't care. I'm paid by the hour."

I laughed as I got out of my chair, holding out my hands, as if I needed to be cuffed. Mallard swore at me for the gesture and soon I was escorted by another officer to be processed. It took around ninety minutes, but I was out the door with Barry, his nose buried in his phone already logging his bill to me.

"Easy money," he commented. "I suspect they will drop the charges in a day or so. This will never make it to a judge."

"I agree. Mallard said he needed to prove a point to his captain. I guess I'm not as popular as I once was."

"Oh my. Sometimes you are a hoot," said Barry. "When have you ever been popular? Hell, I can barely stand you, yet I'm always there to save your ass. Which is odd because you always are slow to pay my bill."

"You certainly aren't slow to send it."

My cell phone chimed, for the incoming email likely from Barry. Shortly it was followed by the tone of someone calling. It was King.

"Someone just stopped by and served Mandy some legal papers."

"From whom?"

"WANN systems. It came from Bristol & Bristol."

It was my turn to curse.

"Did you know about this?" I asked.

"Hell no. Do you think they run their law cases through me? I'm just a lowly gumshoe like you."

"Do you know what they are for?"

"Not yet. Mandy wanted to wait until you came by. May need a lawyer to read it, though. You know how these legalese documents go. Can't make heads or tails of half of it."

"Lucky for me, I have a lawyer present. Barry, do you feel like taking a drive?"

He pulled out his phone and went to work.

"You bet. More easy money. Let me start the clock again."

Good thing my client could afford it, because Barry's meter wasn't cheap.

Chapter 44

When we arrived at Mandy's, I let King take off for the day, since his shift was almost over. I called for pizza to be delivered, while Barry grabbed the papers and went to the kitchen table to read them over. It was several pages and, like King said, was probably written to confuse the layman. The time it took him to go over every word was the time it took for the pizza to arrive. I sat the two boxes down, while Mandy grabbed some drinks. Barry had a slice before talking.

"Jarvis, can I talk with you privately for a minute," he said while standing.

"Sure," I replied. I stood as well, grabbing a piece to take with me.

"Pardon us, Mandy. This will only take a minute."

Barry led me out into the living area. He spoke softly so Mandy couldn't hear him.

"Were you aware of some type of agreement Mandy had with WANN that involved payment?"

"She mentioned to me they offered to pay a year's salary as a benefit because of his death."

"Did she mention any stipulations in the agreement?"

"No. I figured it was hush money, but never asked if there was some type of contract involved."

"Well you should have, because there was. I would say from what I read it was more than a year's salary. Unless computer engineers make a whole lot more than I'm aware of. The payment was for five hundred thousand."

I wanted to yell out. I looked over at Mandy who was slowly eating, trying to act like she wasn't interested in our conversation. But now I suspected otherwise. I took a bite of my pizza, which wasn't too bad. Even the worst pizza was normally edible.

"She did tell me money was not an issue. Now I know why. Did they pay it all up front?"

"No. Fifty thousand a month over a ten-month period. Do you want to know the stipulation?"

"Let me guess. Payment in lieu of not pursuing any legal charges against WANN for wrongful death?"

"Exactly. So long as she leaves them alone she gets paid."

"So, this is a cease and desist order?"

"Yes. And they are using her hiring you as being an act of defying the agreement. That your job is to find fault with the company."

"I can't argue that. At least finding fault with who killed Aaron, which certainly seems to be someone at WANN. So they have a strong case, then?"

"I would say so."

"How much have they paid her so far?"

"Four months. She is due a payment next week. But they are withholding it and wanting the other money returned if she continues to hire you to find her husband's killer. And of course, legal fees on top of that."

I took two more bites. The pepperoni had some kick to it, so I required a drink and needed to talk with Mandy. We both walked over and sat down, and I tried to cool my palate with some iced 7-Up.

"Mandy, it appears you've neglected to tell me something again," I said.

Her eyes averted downward. She appeared to know what was coming.

"These papers here are saying we must stop searching for your husband's killer," I said.

"We can't. We are getting close to finding who did it."

"You signed a paper saying you wouldn't go after WANN," said Barry.

"No, I didn't. All I signed was papers paying me his salary."

"He made five hundred grand a year?" I asked.

"They added a bonus."

"Yes, they did. Not to pursue WANN."

"It didn't say that."

"Did you read it?" asked Barry. "Or have a lawyer read it?"

"No. But they promised."

"They lied. They included a copy. It specifically says that you are not to implicate WANN in any wrongdoing in Aaron's death."

"But we haven't."

"Not yet," I said. "But we are digging into their business. Looking for a killer that likely works there, at the very least. At the most, possibly a conspiracy high up in the company. This document is to protect themselves from what we are pursuing."

"That is not what they told me."

"It may not matter," said Barry. "We would have to prove they manipulated you in an emotional state, to try and buy you off. But that is hard to convince a judge or a jury of."

"We can't stop now; we are so close."

"They will drag you into court and try to take back the money they paid you, along with court and legal fees."

"How much time do we have?" I said.

"Knowing the court system, and how backed up it is, probably several weeks," replied Barry. "But you won't be receiving any more checks from them."

"I have plenty of money. We need to finish this."

"Even at the cost of them suing you?"

"Yes. Can you help me? I don't have a lawyer."

Barry looked at me and I nodded.

"Sure. I will need a retainer from you. I can stall for time, possibly get it pushed back some. But Bristol & Bristol have a lot of pull in this town with the court system. They can get things done few others can. I figure four to six weeks before we go in front of a judge. But they could have us there in two."

"I need to see this through. I need both of you and will pay what it takes. If we prove them complicit in his death, it could be worth more than five hundred thousand. Wouldn't you agree?"

Barry looked at me and smiled. I could see the dollar signs in his eyes. The question was, if we continued would we live to collect?

Chapter 45

Barry left a happy man, with a big check in his wallet and several pieces of pizza in his stomach. Law, food, and money were his passions. For me the pizza was filling, but I wasn't as thrilled. More issues to deal with on another messy case. Life was not boring, but I was missing boredom, if even only for a lazy Sunday. It seemed in the distant past when I had a solemn afternoon with nothing to do but relax.

Mandy went back to work on cracking into the WANN network, with the information I'd provided her from Lyndi. So far, she had not made it in, and had to take her time, since too many wrong attempts, ten within thirty minutes she told me, would lock out the account for an hour. If this happened too many times it was a red flag to the WANN security. She had to take her time. She showed determination working away, noting each password she tried, the time it was tried and the number of failed attempts during the time frame. She was patient, never trying to do too much, too quickly. It was like being on a stakeout waiting for something to happen. If she could learn to shoot and fight, she might consider the occupation of detective as a second job.

As darkness and fatigue set in, the clock nearing ten, we called it a night. Even with exhaustion consuming me, I didn't sleep too well, as my mind went over the whole case, piece by piece. From the first day Mandy and I met, to today with Barry and learning something else she had kept from me. She lied to me, and I lied to the police. It was a string I wished I could break, but likely wouldn't. Working in the shadows of deception sometimes was necessary. But it made for acid reflux and hair-trigger responses. I sat between a slow and painful, or sudden and bloody, death each and every day. I had to adapt, but was finding it challenging. My professional and personal lives seemed to always be in a state of flux.

When I woke up, it was still dark, the digital red numbers showing 2:17 a.m. I went to take a pee, drink some water and got back to the sofa, finding a return to slumber hard. Women now occupied my brain. Those early in life, up to the present. Each had their good and bad traits. I still could name them all. Well, at least the important ones that shaped my life. There had been a few one-night flings, where the names would escape me. Many of the women had brought pleasure to my life. Only a couple being quite bad. Balance had been good, but not enough to fulfill me to mend my eye-wandering ways.

Three had captured my attention this time. Lyndi, who seemed to strictly be looking for a physical encounter. Jessica, who was much the same. Both had been frank, maybe Lyndi more so, about what each wanted from me. And April, who could talk and act dirty, yet seemed to be looking for maybe a little bit more than sex, though was never shy about enjoying it. All had provided temptation. But still I felt the longing for the one I'd lost because of my indiscretions. She filled my waking thoughts and sleeping dreams. The faint hope that somehow, she could see her way back to me. Even awake, the dream seemed unrealistic that I'd be one with Melissa, ever again.

Time passed, sleep came and I sensed someone moving around me. It was light but I didn't want to wake up, even though I'd grown tired of the couch. I smelled coffee, which I hated, and fried bacon that I loved. I heard the front door open and I jumped up to my feet in one motion. It was Adam King walking in, time for his shift, the digital numbers reading just after eight.

"Hopefully I didn't wake you from a pleasurable dream," he said.

My head hurt from the sudden rush of adrenaline from my quick arising. I rubbed the sleep from my eyes, or what little I'd experienced.

"No dream. It was a void of darkness before you came in."

"You look terrible," said King. "Not that you were a day at the beach before. Still, if I were you, I'd go home and take a nap."

"Need to sleep in my own bed for a night or two."

"Or a bed in general. Preferably with someone naked lying next to you."

King was showing a little humor. Not something I'd often seen in him.

"Do you think you can cover a night shift or two?"

His smile turned to a frown.

"I'm already pulling enough time on this. Sitting doing nothing, short of catching up on my reading. Besides, I can't sleep on a sofa, and I doubt our client will allow me in her bed."

"Not in a million years!" yelled Mandy from the first-floor office.

I needed a break. I would work on finding someone to stay the night. April's brothers looked like my best option.

"There is a familiar car out front," said King. "Looks like Cong and Lok's car."

I went over to the window to check. Sure enough, it was sitting outside about a house or two down.

"Who was inside?" I asked.

"Couldn't tell. Those tinted windows are impossible to see through from a distance. Hard to tell even up close."

I was tired and feeling a bit cranky. Being confrontational was not a smart idea, but I didn't care. The mood I was in didn't matter. I got dressed, went to the bathroom and grabbed some of the remaining bacon, with a glass of OJ. With shoes on and .38 tucked in my back belt I headed outside in the warm morning sun, walked right up to the window and knocked on it. It slowly eased down and it was Lok sitting there, looking as if he'd eaten glass for breakfast. A glance in the back showed he was alone.

"Good morning, Lok," I said. "Mind telling me what you are doing here?"

He didn't return the greeting, only looking at me with cold eyes that had frozen many a victim. Since he didn't speak much, if any, English, I knew it would be a one-way conversation. It didn't matter, as I liked to hear myself talk and there would be no point-counter-point debate.

"If you are here to try and scare us off, it's not going to work. I'm sure a busy guy like you has better things to do than sit out here in the hot sun all day long. Go and karate chop some three-quarter-inch planks."

His eyes seemed to recognize some of what I was saying. He answered me back in Chinese, but I didn't have a clue what he said. The gist of it was, he didn't give a flying fuck what I thought.

"Fuck you too!" I said.

He flipped me off, the F-word one expression he recognized, and I walked back to the house. I'd had all I could take. I told Adam I'd be back tonight, hopefully with someone to cover the night shift. I then went and talked with Mandy.

"Any luck?" I asked.

"Nothing yet. I've been through a lot of combinations for the 49ers. May need to move onto the Giants."

"Try Golden State," I suggested. "They won a championship recently. Since they are the hot team in town, it might make sense. Team nickname is the Warriors."

"Sure, I can go with them after I've exhausted my 49er options. I will break through eventually. Only a matter of time."

"I may have someone else take the night shift. I need to get some better sleep."

"Not King, I hope!"

She still didn't think much of him.

"No. If it's anyone, it would be a cop I know. You'll be safe. If I can't find someone I will be back."

"There is a spare bedroom upstairs."

"I know. But being down here is better for hearing anyone breaking in. Upstairs I wouldn't know until they are inside. And I don't want that to happen."

She understood and I said my goodbyes. No reason to tell her about Lok. I didn't think he'd try anything and was only there to intimidate. As I headed home, the wind blowing in my face, the open helmet shield letting in the breeze, I decided I needed company, either for lunch or dinner. When I walked in the door I pulled out my cell phone, looking at the number several times, uncertain what the outcome would be. But I wanted to be bold. I dialed the number and heard the familiar voice, getting an answer, I'd hoped for.

Chapter 46

I needed rest before my late lunch. I always had a tough time sleeping during the day and made my bedroom as dark as I could. Still, I was only able to truly get about an hour before waking up, my mind a jumble of activity that I couldn't bring myself to focus on. I went to work out, which often got my mind back on the right track. After that a long shower and I was dressed ready to go shortly after one.

We were meeting up at Ted's Montana Grill on West Alameda Avenue. I arrived early, before two, and got a table. I was nervous but happy she'd agreed to have lunch with me this Sunday afternoon. For now, I ordered iced water, waiting. At about five minutes after two, she walked in. I stood up to greet her, giving her a gentle hug that she didn't shy away from. She was dressed in light colored shorts and tank top, with flip-flops on her feet. Her hair was longer and somewhat bleached looking, her skin tanned from the sun. She seemed to be out a lot enjoying the rays and heat of the summer. Melissa sat down, with a nice smile, appearing happy to see me. I certainly was happy as well.

"You look great," I said. "It appears you've been basking in the sun a lot this summer."

"I have been staying as busy as I can. Riding my bike, going for walks, lounging some on my deck. A lot of me time, which I needed."

"I'm glad."

The waitress arrived and we both ordered drinks. She wanted iced tea, which I decided to have as well. When asked about an appetizer, we decided on the Bison Nachos.

"I'd like to say you look good too," stated Melissa. "When you called you sounded tired, which is how you look as well."

"Been sleeping on a couch, providing protection for my client. Not at all comfortable, to say the least."

"Then working during the day?"

"Yes. Except for today. I needed a break. Something where I wasn't looking over my shoulder, wondering what might be coming my way."

Our drinks and nachos arrived. Melissa had asked for some

extra lemons, and was squeezing them into the tea, then stirring and tasting until she got it right. I enjoyed a couple of nachos, finding the sodium content on extra high. We weren't ready to order just yet, so the waitress said she'd check back shortly.

"You called me," said Melissa.

"Yes. I was glad you agreed."

"I almost didn't. I'm still hurting from what happened. Seeing you is difficult, but it was such a sudden break…" She stopped, trying to find the words. "I missed seeing you every day. The feelings are still there, both of love and of anger. I hope to find a middle ground."

"I understand. Going cold turkey without seeing you is painful for me as well. All I can do is blame myself for messing up and say I wished it never happened. But time travel isn't possible. I'm trudging on, hoping to do better."

Melissa looked at me, her eyes moist. She grabbed a napkin and dabbed at them.

"Someday I may be able to forgive you," she said. "For now, it hurts. But I do want to stay in contact. Hopefully be friendly, if not friends."

"Someday I hope to forgive myself. Yes, I would like for us to remain friends. I don't have many, so I need all of them I can come by."

Melissa reached out her hand and touched mine. Healing was beginning, that I was happy for. I'm sure she'd still hold mistrust in her heart at my ability to commit to a faithful relationship. Hell, I mistrusted myself as well.

"What else have you been doing this summer?" I asked.

"Working and what I already told you. I will be starting back to school in a few weeks. I've decided to cut back my hours at Bristol & Bristol and try to finish up this year and be ready to take the bar exam by next summer. Tony has been supportive of my decision. Even willing to pay me nearly at my normal rate, though I would be working ten to fifteen hours less per week."

I smiled, for I was happy she was getting what she wanted. She'd make a good lawyer, though deep down I hoped she wouldn't stay with Bristol & Bristol. The waitress returned and we each ordered. Melissa wanted Caesar grilled chicken salad, while I ordered Ted's Beef Filet, well done, and garlic mashed potatoes.

"How about you?" Melissa asked. "I'd query more about this case, but it sounds like you would prefer to distance yourself from it today."

"No, I'm able to discuss it. At least with you no one is shooting at me."

"Well, at least not yet. Though we have experienced it together."

"Not one of our better days."

"No, but we lived through it. Though I still have nightmares about it."

"So do I."

It was a fatal moment in time I'd regret her having to live through. Caught in the mitts of two bad men and their crew of enforcers, all of whom ended up dying violently, along with another innocent young woman, all before Melissa's eyes. It was a bloody, horrible scene that still played out in my head, awake or asleep.

"Still, because you work for Bristol & Bristol, and they are involved, it is probably best I not give you any details. Prudent to protect you, so you don't have to choose sides."

"It was scary seeing you acting as you were, with Don."

"I know and I'm sorry. But I needed answers, and sometimes emotions overtake logic. In my line of business, you have to push hard to get results."

Our meals were delivered and our drinks were topped off. Cutting into the filet I found it perfect, with no red, but still juicy. I savored a bite, along with the garlic potatoes. They were delicious as well. Melissa seemed happy with her salad, having two large forkfuls, eating faster than I recall her ever eating. I looked at her in surprise.

"Sorry, I'm hungry. I didn't have any breakfast this morning, and took a long bike ride. I needed some calories. What else shall we talk about?"

"I appreciate you talking with Tony about keeping an eye on things."

"All I told him is make sure nothing happens to you, in relation to anything Don was doing. Tony is a good man. He knows I'd be crushed if you were killed, which sounds like was a real possibility."

"It was and still could be. I've not gotten to the bottom of things, but we are getting close. Hopefully no one else dies before I get it solved."

"If anyone can, you can. Have you found backup? Is Rocky lending support?"

"No, he isn't available. Sorry to say he doesn't have a website where I can track him down. Thugs and protection for hire dot com."

Melissa laughed, which was good to hear.

"No, I have a resource thanks to an agreement with Tony. Adam King."

Melissa almost choked on her iced tea.

"You've got to be kidding. I thought you hated him?"

"Hate might be too strong, but certainly not one of my favorite people. Still he was all I could get on short notice. So far he has done what he said he'd do."

"I'm surprised Tony agreed."

"He was reluctant. But I convinced him and gave him a little icing on the cake."

"What was that?"

"Best you not know. Just say it helped out a client of his."

"I've often told Tony he should hire you instead of King. He is a little creepy."

She would get no argument from me, as I finished up my meal. Melissa had slowed down and was still a couple of bites from finishing. I wiped my face and looked at her, amazed at her beauty. But heaping praise on her now wasn't the right time.

"Yes, Tony could benefit from my skills. But Don would never go for it. He even is putting the screws to my client right now, filing a suit against her."

"Really. I don't work with Don, so I wasn't aware. How did he find out who your client is? I doubt you told him."

"No, I didn't. I think it was a couple of enforcers from the Chinese government, who are working for WANN. Don seems to represent them too. As he did the three Russians."

"What is he suing her for?"

"Breach of contract. They got her to sign something, stating they'd pay her a hefty sum of money to not pursue action against them for the murder of her husband."

"You are right. Maybe I shouldn't be hearing this."

Melissa excused herself and went to the restroom. I paid the check, remembering a time when she did the same and came back panty-less for a round of pleasure at Lookout Mountain. Those were moments I'd never forget. I knew that would not be the case this time.

She met me up front and I walked her to her car. We were silent, no words, just the sounds of the cars passing on West Alameda and the clicking of her remote locks before I opened her door. She turned to me, grabbing my hand.

"Thank you for lunch," she said. "I'm glad I got to see you. Things are going to start getting busy for me soon, with school, so I won't have a lot of time going forward. But I hope we can get together once a month or so and talk, as friends."

I had hoped for more, but couldn't realistically expect it.

"I'd like that."

She gave me a quick sisterly hug, got in her car and drove off. It felt good to have seen her again, though it was sad I would only see her sparingly over the next year. But still she was in my life, which was a good thing. And I needed as much good as I could get.

As I reached my car, my cell phone rang. It was Mandy and she was yelling.

"Jarvis! Oh god, please no. I need your help now. Where are you?"

She was in a panic. I jumped in my car and started heading her direction. Though I was probably fifteen minutes away.

"Mandy, slow down and tell me what is wrong."

There was a long pause, but I could hear breathing. She was trying to gather herself.

"Adam and I went shopping. I needed to get some food and other essentials. When we returned someone was in the house waiting for us. He had gone in first and I was outside still when I heard some shots and him yelling for me to run away. I took off down the street and I'm still running. I don't know if they are after me or not."

"Where are you?"

"I took off south from my house. I was in a panic, so I'm not sure where I am. I think I'm almost to Hampden."

"Did you call the police?"

"No. I just ran and called you when I could get my phone out of my purse."

"Call them now and then call me right back. And then get somewhere public and stay inside. A store, a restaurant, anything but being out on the street. I'm headed your way."

She hung up as I raced as fast as I could without getting in an accident. It seemed my hope for a calm day had gone out the window.

Chapter 47

I tried not to panic, but still I was driving aggressively when Mandy called me back with her location, though she still hadn't called the police. I cursed and made a call to Bill at the station house. Even though it was Sunday, he was working. I gave him the details and told him to send a car and paramedics to Mandy's house. I wasn't sure what they'd find, but I had a feeling it wouldn't be good.

It took me about twenty minutes before I arrived at a pawn shop at the corner of Hampden and Federal. She was standing outside, nervously pacing.

"Why didn't you go inside?" I asked.

"I did. They told me I was making them nervous and to go stand outside. When I told them someone was trying to kill me, he just laughed and said 'so what!'."

"Get in my car. You will be safe there. We will head back to your place. The police should be there by now."

"What are we going to find?"

"I don't know."

When we arrived, there were marked and unmarked police cars, and a paramedics unit. I was happy to see no Coroner vehicle, at least not yet. One of the uniforms on the scene was Officer Bale, who had been at Aaron's murder site. He recognized me and waved us to come past the crime scene tape. I was starting to think I needed my own personalized tape, since I seemed to be connected to many of them over the last couple of years. Branded crime scene tape, probably nothing to be proud of.

"Jarvis," said Bale. "I'm hearing you are involved in this. Cummings said when you arrived to let you through."

"I'm touched he was thinking of me."

"Actually, his exact words were 'when that PI asshole shows, escort him straight to me.'"

"Sounds more like the Cummings I've grown to know and bear. This is Mandy Bailey, the wife of Aaron Bailey."

"I'm sorry for your loss, ma'am."

Mandy softly answered back. She appeared to be in shock. Bale led us to the front door. We walked inside and there was blood all over the carpet. On a gurney was King, as the paramedics were working on him. It didn't look good

"Took one to the chest," said Cummings, who had seen us arrive. "Looks like he got off a round of his own. Not sure if he hit the intruder or not."

"Did he see who did it?" I asked.

"Was out of it when we arrived and wasn't talking. They are trying to stabilize him and will rush him to the ER here shortly."

"Do they think he will make it?" asked Mandy.

"Too soon to tell. And you are?"

"She is the person King was protecting. My client, Mandy Bailey."

"The widow of Aaron. The murder you are investigating."

I nodded.

"More bodies dropping all around you, Mann. Are you paid by the amount of blood spilled?"

I mouthed, "Fuck you!"

Cummings could certainly push my buttons.

"Did you see the culprit, ma'am?" asked Cummings.

"No, I didn't see them."

"One. More than one. A car outside waiting. Anything?"

Mandy just shook her head. "I'm sorry, no. All I heard were what sounded like two shots and then Adam telling me to run. Nothing else."

"Lok was outside earlier. He was one of the Chinese men who accosted me before."

"Oh, the ones you let go. Are you saying it was him?"

"Someone to check with. He doesn't use a gun, though, so I doubt it was him. And it wouldn't be Cong either. But they could have led someone here to do the job."

"What leads you to that conclusion?"

I couldn't tell him about them dropping off the killer of Wilmar, since they didn't know all those facts, since I was protecting King.

"A hunch."

"Sure it is. Like all your other ones. Mrs. Bailey, this will be a crime scene for a while now. And we'll need to take your statements. Likely you'll need to stay somewhere else tonight."

"Did they take anything?" asked Mandy.

"Don't know yet. Still piecing things together. What would they want?"

Mandy pushed past him and ran into her office. Cummings and I followed her, Dan yelling at her to stop. When he got into the room she was clutching onto her computer and a big pile of papers.

"I wished you hadn't touched that. It could be evidence."

"I need all of this. It's how I'm going to find who killed Aaron."

Cummings looked at me and I nodded.

"Long story, but yes, it's important for her to have her computer and the papers."

"Can I see them, Mandy?" Cummings asked.

She looked at me and I told her to go ahead. He looked through them all and handed them back. Not sure if he knew what he was reading.

"Looked Greek to me. Was it some type of code on those sheets?"

"Best you not know all the details. What she is doing might be considered illegal."

Cummings didn't like the sound of that.

"You never can give me us a straight answer."

"I'm hacking into WANN to find out if they killed Aaron," said Mandy. "It's the only way, since the police haven't been able to solve it. Jarvis and I need to see this through."

"Wonderful." Cummings shook his head. He normally never let anything slide, but this time he showed some compassion. "I never saw anything. Take it with you. But first, statements."

"Thank you," said Mandy.

"Go in the kitchen and sit down. We will get to you shortly."

"Gee, Dan, it would seem there is a human being under that cheap suit after all. Thanks."

"Don't you dare tell Mallard! He'd think I was going soft."

"My lips are sealed. Where is he anyway?"

"Family reunion and picnic. Things were quiet until this. Of course, it had to be something involving you."

I went and sat next to Mandy, waiting to be questioned, holding in reserve my idea of the personalized crime scene tape. My genius was often lost upon his narrow thinking. The paramedics had taken away King. I wondered if he would survive. Though I didn't care for the man, I still didn't wish to see him dead. Another to haunt my dreams. As I sat there my cell phone chirped. It was Lyndi.

"Hello, Lyndi," I said. "Probably not the best time to talk. I'm dealing with a police matter."

"You are such a sweet talker," she replied. "Logan is heading to Vegas on Thursday. Staying at Caesar's Palace. He generally gets in around noon. They let him check-in early. Should be meeting up with his guy and gal pals. Leaving Sunday afternoon."

"I will check into flights and a hotel room to see what is available."

"Let me know. As I said, I want your attention first before you go off and pester my ex."

"I'm all yours. I will call you back once I know when I'm getting in."

I put my phone down and spoke to Mandy.

"Looks like Logan Albers will be in Vegas for a long weekend. It would be good if we had something to bargain with before I reason with him."

"I'm doing my best. Still have a couple of days to crack. The question is, where are we staying tonight?"

I didn't have an answer for her and wouldn't for a while, as she was taken away for questioning, allowing me time to search for Vegas options and contemplate which part of Lyndi's body I'd start on first.

Chapter 48

Once all was done, they let Mandy grab a duffle bag of some clothes and personal items, and we were off. I wasn't sure where to put her up for the night. My place was not ideal, since Cong and Lok had been there before, and had no trouble getting inside. A hotel could be an option, and would at least provide me a bed to sleep in, but seemed too confining. I decided on taking a chance and called up April. Though she was still recovering, she was willing to help. When we arrived, one of her brothers, Neil, was there. It appeared his undercover case had finished and was taking some time off.

"Jarvis," he said, while walking over to shake my hand.

"Thanks for helping out," I replied. "I'm worried my place isn't safe."

"We have pretty good building security here," said April. "She will be protected by us."

Mandy took a seat on the sofa opening her computer, placing the papers next to it.

"Do you have Wi-Fi I can connect to?" she asked. "I need to get working again. I've lost a lot of time today."

April gave her the passkey.

"Don't worry, they won't be able to trace me back to your home router. I have lots of mirrored sites I bounce off of."

"Do you know what she is talking about?" asked Neil of me.

"Not really. I know she is trying to hack into the network of the company we suspect had her husband killed. We are trying to find a smoking gun to work with."

"Computer espionage," replied Neil. "Too hi-tech for me. I'm lucky I'm able to use my smartphone properly"

"I can use mine," I said. "But what she is doing is way over my head. I'm more about fists and guns."

"Computers ruin, damage and kill almost as many human lives, these days, as humans do with their loaded toys," said Mandy. "Of course, there are humans driving those computers."

Mandy was typing away, then writing on her papers, which seemed so analog when I thought about it. April grabbed me by the arm and pulled me into the kitchen.

"She is a looker," said April. "Even with her hair up and those big glasses. Hard to believe she is a computer nerd."

"Kept it quiet all this time. Says the old boys' network is as bad in the computer world as in most other businesses. One look at her and they can't believe she can code."

"I find it hard to believe too. So where are you staying tonight?"

"I doubt I could stand another night on the couch, since Mandy will be in your spare room. I was hoping to go back to my place. Though I will have a gun handy."

"There is always room in my bed. It's a king. Not that I can do much. We could just snuggle together."

I smiled and hugged her.

"In time, little lady. But I need my sleep and next to you I doubt I'd sleep at all. But I appreciate the offer. How long can Neil stay?"

"He is off this week. He doesn't have to be to work until next Monday. He was planning on helping me. But he is happy to help protect her as well."

"Good. I need to take a trip to Vegas. Flying out Thursday morning."

"What for?"

"To check up on one of the founders of WANN. He has the taste of gambling and screwing when in Sin City. My information is he will be there Thursday noon for one of his weekend trysts."

"And what are you going to do?"

"Appeal to his better judgment."

"You plan on knocking him around some."

"Maybe. He has an entourage I plan on talking to. Could tell me more about the man. Then I might knock him around some. If Mandy can come up with some additional dirt on him or WANN, I can use that as leverage."

April laughed. "I wish I could go with you."

"Oh, you wouldn't have any fun. All work for this boy."

No need to explain to April that it wouldn't be all work, since Lyndi planned on boffing my brains out shortly after I arrived, as part of the deal for giving me her ex-husband's plans. Sometimes work required me to go the extra mile. In this case the mile would be up and down a beautiful woman's body.

"Neil, don't you have a cop friend in Vegas?" said April, after going back into the living area.

"I do. Why?"

"Jarvis is heading there on a lead for his case. Figured it wouldn't hurt to have a friend in high places in case of trouble."

"Do you plan on getting in trouble, Jarvis?" Neil asked.

"Not if I can avoid it. But with all going on I may need to up the pressure, which may require physical persuasion."

"Let me send you his contact info. If I can figure out how on this nightmare of a phone."

He struggled with it for a few minutes before Mandy took it from him and did what he couldn't do in five seconds and then handed him back his phone. I think I saw her lips whisper "amateurs" before going back to her computer.

"He is a good guy. Owes me a couple of favors. So be sure to mention my name."

It was getting late, so I said my goodbyes and got a short kiss from April. Once at home I crashed, with gun handy. It wasn't the best night of sleep I ever had, but at least it was in my own bed, senses tuned to any possible trouble coming my way.

Chapter 49

I was slowly waking up when I heard pounding on my door. The last time, it was April's brothers coming to roust me. I wondered if it was some of King's family coming for paybacks. I put on some pants, with gun in hand, and saw who it was. I let Mallard in, cardboard coffee container in his hand, noticeable sweat on his brow, from another hot August day, even though it was only around nine.

"How can you drink that hot shit in this weather?" I asked.

"Need the caffeine to get me moving."

"Don't they have iced coffees too?"

"I hate that crap. If I want cold, I'll drink a soda. Mind if I sit?"

I pointed to my kitchen chairs, where he sat down. I put my gun on the kitchen counter and grabbed some juice from my nearly empty fridge. I needed to grocery shop, but as usual there hadn't been any time.

"Expecting trouble?" Mallard said, while motioning to my gun.

"Seems like a daily occurrence in my life. Coming at me from all sides. Hopefully you aren't here to add to my burden."

"No, not this time. Came to let you know King is still hanging in there. Though he is critical. Bullet did a lot of damage."

"I hope he pulls through."

"Did you know he had a wife? Well, ex-wife and a son."

"No, I didn't. I knew very little about him. He was more a thorn in my side. Only working together because circumstances dictated it."

"Been divorced for over ten years. Kid is thirteen. Both are there at the hospital. Even though they weren't married anymore, it sounded like they were friendly."

"How old is he?"

"I think a couple years older than you. Forty, if I recall correctly."

"A shame. But I'm sure you are not here to give me a medical report and rundown on his life."

Mallard took a long sip on his coffee. He continued to look down at the table.

"Went to a reunion yesterday. Saw some family members I

haven't seen in years. Had a fun time and got some perspective being away from work. After I got home I was thinking about all the crap I go through at work. The political bullshit that keeps me from doing my job. The actual work is great. I love being a detective and solving cases, when I can actually solve them. Time in the field is taken away from me when my captain calls me in the office and says 'put the screws to that PI or else.' I wish I was in the position to tell him to fuck off, but I can't."

In a roundabout way it appeared Mallard was trying to apologize about having me booked on withholding evidence. I could have been an ass and thumped my chest, saying, I told you so. But no need to rub it in.

"Anything new on the King shooting?" I said, changing the subject.

"It appears the shooter did get hit. Some of the blood on the scene wasn't King's. The tech team said it was only a small amount. So, likely superficial. He got off one round. Probably kept the assailant from chasing after your client, though."

"If there is blood, then you have DNA."

"Yes. But only if they are in the system, will it turn up."

"What about other physical evidence?"

"King's hand had some bruising. May have gotten off a punch or two. Some hair but don't know whose it is."

"Anyone else in the neighborhood see anything?"

"A couple of cars. One appears to have been the one Lok was in. One nosy neighbor saw the car and was keeping an eye on it. Says, though, it drove away after King and your client left to go shopping. The other was your basic silver mid-size sedan. Local plates, but no number. Same nosy neighbor saw it drive by a couple of times. Didn't see it when the shooting happened. But could have been parked in the alley for all we know."

"How did they get into the house?"

"No signs of forced entry. Either a door was left unlocked or they picked it."

"I doubt King would have been that sloppy. If it was picked that speaks to someone with skills."

"I agree. Though that doesn't narrow it down much."

"No, but likely a pro of some kind. I've been running into quite a few of them so far, for a simple murder case."

"Not simple anymore. Two dead and one near death. It's time to figure out who it is. I don't care what you know anymore and don't tell me. I just want them caught. Do what you must do. I won't be a pain in the ass, no matter what the captain says."

He stood up and finished the rest of his coffee, tossing it in my trash. From his pocket he pulled out my license and gun they confiscated when arresting me and placed them on the table.

"The charges have been dropped," he said. "All the paperwork has been misplaced."

"Thank you."

"Should have never let it go that far, no matter what my captain said."

He seemed sincere, so I thought I'd throw him a bone. Whether it would cheer him up any, was the question.

"King saw what happened at Wilmar Boylan's murder," I said. "At least he witnessed some of it. He was following Cong and Lok and saw them drop off someone. He couldn't tell who it was, but decided to follow them into the building. He heard the shots but didn't get a good look at the assailant. He was broad in size and tall. That was all he could tell."

Mallard turned around. "Why was he following Cong and Lok?"

"Tony Bristol hired him to do so. Mostly at the request of my former girlfriend, who was worried."

"The brother of Don who showed up to bail them out?"

"Yes. He was also making sure his brother wasn't into something risky. Though he'd never admit it. That is what I sensed after talking with him."

"A tangled web you have gotten yourself into."

"It gets stranger. Don served papers on my client. A Cease and Desist order. Seemed she signed some document saying she wouldn't hold WANN at fault for her husband's death, in exchange for money."

"How much?"

"A lot. Five hundred thousand. Though she said that is not what she was told she was signing. Though didn't get a lawyer to go through it first. They said it was a short one-time offer if she didn't sign immediately. Barry, my lawyer, is working on it right now."

"If they served her, why try to kill her now?"

"Because she isn't going to stop, no matter what. She wants to know who the killers are and doesn't care. I think they know that and are desperate."

"Or someone unconnected to WANN is involved," said Mallard.

"Possibly. Everything so far points to them. In time I'll know for certain,"

"We are working on it too. If you have anything else, let me know. If they are truly involved, I'd like to see her bring them down. These tech companies worry me. They are gathering too much information on all of us."

Mallard headed for the door. As he started to leave, I did something I'd never done before and called him by his first name.

"Stu. Something happened at the family reunion," I said. "Something that seems to have shaken you. It is none of my business, but…"

With the door open, he turned and looked at me, sadness in his eyes.

"Found out my cousin has terminal pancreatic cancer," he said, solemnly. "Probably only has a few months to live, but he was there, enjoying the day and saying his goodbyes. He was like a brother to me at times. The news sent me for a loop. Made me evaluate things."

I said I was sorry and he was gone. Our mortality often brings us back to reality. It had happened to me many times as well. A couple hours later it hit me again, when the call came that Adam King had passed away from his wounds. One more ghostly spirit to haunt my days and nights.

Chapter 50

I had pulled myself back to the business at hand, and got reservations set for Vegas. I would arrive Wednesday afternoon, the couple of Mr. and Mrs. Mann sharing a nice deluxe room with king bed, walk-in shower and separate jetted tub for two. It felt odd when I made the arrangements and even odder when I called Lyndi back, letting her know the plan. She would be there Wednesday afternoon as well. Which would give me the evening and night with her, and I could sleep in until noon when Logan arrived. That is, if she let me sleep.

Checking in with April, all was quiet. She said Mandy was working away but still hadn't hacked in. She was determined, though, and never wavered that she could accomplish the task. I mentioned I might stop by for dinner later, but had an errand to run. After hanging up, I called to try and talk with Tony Bristol, but he was on the phone. I left a message and about thirty minutes later he called me back.

"I assume you are calling about Adam King," he said. "So sorry to hear. He did a lot of excellent work for us through the years."

"His time working, the pay you owe him. I want it put in a trust for his son. He is thirteen."

"Silly me, I didn't know he was married and had a family."

"Not married anymore but still has a kid. Set it up, please. If you feel it in your heart, add a little extra. Be good money for the kid to have for college someday."

"Do you know the name?"

"No. But I'm sure you can get it, being a resourceful person."

"Melissa can dig it up for me. Anything else?"

"Lok was waiting outside that morning watching the house. I don't think he did the killing because he doesn't use a gun, but he may know who did. Just like he may know who killed Wilmar Boylan, the computer hacker."

"Are you warning me again about Don? I told you whose side I'd be on in this."

"Yes, your brother. I was on my brother's side as well. But I also sided with his wife and daughter, who nearly were killed because of what he was into. Keep that in mind."

The line went eerily silent. I hated dead air when talking on the phone.

"Were you also aware he sent a Cease and Desist order to my client, telling her to stop pursuing WANN in her husband's murder, or they were going to sue her?"

"No, I didn't. Though I'm sure if he has legal grounds to do it, that is alright with me."

"Tony, they killed or had her husband killed. Then her business partner, and now King. Hell, I didn't like the guy, but I never wanted him to die on the job, a job I put him on. Enough of this legal mumble-jumble shit. Tell him to back away from this mess or he is going to go down too. That is my final warning to him and you. Be sure to pass it on. And don't forget the additional favor I did for you. As far as I'm concerned, you owe me now."

I hung up the call feeling better, getting it all off my chest. With little to eat in the house, I decided to do some grocery shopping and came back with three bags of food to tide me over for a while. After making some lunch I got a call from Bill down at the Denver Police Station.

"Mallard wanted me to pass on that they brought in Cong and Lok," he said. "They spoke very little and denied even being anywhere near your client's house. Don Bristol showed up shortly after and walked out with them, when they couldn't press charges."

"No surprise. Do you know what Mallard is doing next?"

"I think he is planning on making a trip to the WANN office in the Tech Center. We'll see how far he gets, but he is determined to get somewhere with them. Somebody has to know something."

"Thanks, Bill, that gave me an idea."

I hung up and went looking through my phone for a name. Mitchell Crabtree had headed out of town after his vintage Corvette was torched by the Platov boys. I did have his cell number and gave it a ring. He answered quickly.

"Jarvis," he said. "What do you want?"

"Mitchell, I hope you are enjoying your vacation."

"It would have been better if we'd left on our own terms. Have things died down?"

"The Platov boys are being detained. You shouldn't have any worries about them. Though there are others now involved. Probably best you stay away for now. But something came to mind and I wondered if you could answer me one question."

"Ask and I'll decide."

"On the night Aaron was killed, did you have anyone from your main office in town that you were aware of?"

There was a long lull, with only the crackling sound of the cell reception.

"Why do you ask?"

"Something is telling me it was someone at the home office that was engaged. Possibly even sent someone to take care of Aaron. Just looking at it from all angles."

"Well, WANN's corporate head of security had been there the day before."

"Kyle Lambert?"

"Yes."

"Do you know much about him?"

"Not really. Ex-military, I believe. Though that was true of a lot of us. WANN liked people with that type of experience on the security team."

"Anyone else?"

"Logan Albers had been there a few days earlier. Mostly to press the flesh."

"Any ideas if he met with Aaron Bailey?"

"Sorry, can't help you there. If they did I wasn't aware of it."

"Thanks."

I then called FBI Agent Price.

"Do you know anything about Kyle Lambert? He is the head of security for WANN Systems. Apparently ex-military."

Price seemed perturbed.

"Why should I help you anymore?"

"It might be important to bringing down WANN Systems. Lambert might be the one who killed Aaron Bailey. Or at least orchestrated it."

"I could care less about them anymore. I've got better things to work on, now that my boss has chewed my ass."

"What for?"

"For imprisoning the Platov brothers on trumped-up charges."

"Really, what happened?"

"That local law firm, Bristol & Bristol, got wind of them being in Florida. Got some other big-shot law team involved and before we could whisk them away, got a Federal judge to delay them shipping out. Right now, we still have them, but not much longer. Seems I was using Gitmo for the wrong reasons. Apparently, their idea of a terrorist is not mine. For now, you can do your own dirty work and find this guy on your own."

The phone slammed down. I was surprised that Bristol & Bristol had the kind of pull to get them out so quickly. When I told Tony of where they had been sent, I didn't think he'd be able to get them out. Not a smart move on my part. If they did get released, would they be coming back to get me? Sometimes I didn't think things through all that well.

The afternoon wore on and I began thinking of dinner. Since I told April I might stop by, I decided on some good old KFC chicken for dinner. I hopped in my car and was in the drive-thru when my phone rang again and this time it was Mandy. She sounded thrilled.

"I'm in," she said.

With only those words I tossed the bucket on the passenger seat, grabbed a secret recipe drumstick and headed over to April's, buoyed at what we would find.

Chapter 51

August in Las Vegas is hot. I mean, really hot. And today it was 109 degrees when the jet landed at McCarran International Airport. Thankfully I was wearing shorts and a tank top, as the heat hit me when I went outside to get a taxi. The yellow vehicle had the air conditioning running full blast, yet it was still warm inside. The drive to Caesar's was not far, and I was dropped off at the main entrance, which was busier than most airports. I gathered my bag and luggage, and after paying it was only a short walk to cool air.

As I marveled at the inside: tall oval ceiling, huge lights, marble floors and water fountain, my phone dinged with a voicemail. I checked and it was from Lyndi. It would seem she wouldn't be making it to join me after all.

"Jarvis, its Lyndi. Damn, I'm so disappointed, but I can't come out there now. My daughter got a case of the early season flu and needs her mother to take care of her. I know, it seems odd, a twenty-year-old needing her mother. But she has always come first and always will, even over my own carnal needs. If something changes, I'll let you know. You can do your detecting while I lie in my bed tonight, naked, fantasizing about what you would be doing to me. Maybe if the mood strikes me I'll send you a couple of pictures for you to ogle over. Take care."

Darn. No joy before having to go to work. I now had a day to get the lay of the land, instead of getting laid. And I probably would need it, as Caesar's Palace was the size of a small city. It was huge, with the gross national product of some third world countries being spent daily inside the borders of the complex. It would probably take me a day just to walk the entire span of the facility. If I wanted to spend the money I could take in a show and see one of the many stars who perform there daily. But for now, I wanted to get to my room and relax. Which is what I did, using the express kiosk check-in, and then taking the long trek to the Palace Tower where my room was located.

When entering the room, I found it spacious, with king bed, large sitting area, sofa and chair, and a work area. There was a marble dressing table and a refreshment center mini-bar with a choice of snacks that were a king's ransom according to the price sheet. *Twelve dollars for a bag of microwave popcorn!* The flat-screen TV was small by today's standards, with some cable options and a vast selection of pay TV, including of course adult entertainment. The bathroom was huge, with marble floor, walk-in shower, spa bathtub for two and double sink vanity. The view out of the window showed the expansive size of the Caesar's complex and my feet ached thinking about the steps they would be taking. I unpacked my things into the dresser and lay down on the pillow top mattress and closed my eyes. I was still a little worked up from my flight, so I couldn't sleep. My mind was going over the last two days.

With her persistence, Mandy had found her way into Logan's email and began downloading all that was there, caching it so it could be viewed offline. There was no guarantee any damning emails were still there, but still people often forget to remove everything, especially if there had been a long string of replies back and forth. Even when deleting, many users forget to empty that folder, as well as the Sent items. And there were options to recover even permanently deleted emails, which she did, leaving several gigabytes to comb through. She created several search strings to use to narrow the tens of thousands of messages. Once she had the entire mailbox saved offline, which took several hours, she logged off and started running the searches. What she found was interesting, to say the least.

There had been much discussion back and forth about Aaron. He had approached his supervisor in the Denver office, saying he had discovered something within the code of their switches and routers that he wanted to discuss with someone. At first, he thought it was a Zero-Day vulnerability, leaving their equipment open to attack. After reporting it and getting no response, he followed up again, and was told by the supervisor he had run it up the flag pole and was still waiting for an answer. More days passed, and this time he decided to report it to someone in the home office. Because he was making more and more noise, it was getting harder to ignore him. Emails were found where meetings were held to discuss what action to take. Finally, a memo was sent to the head of data integrity in the Denver office, to approach Aaron and talk to him. The memo outlined how to deal with the situation and him. Basically, telling him that the company was aware of the problem, but at this time weren't going to fix the issue, as it would be too costly. And to ask him to keep the situation to himself, or it would expose them to possible liabilities. He needed to be a "team player," stated one of the memos. If he continued to talk with others in the company, it would be grounds for discipline and even termination. For a while there was no more chatter about the issue. All of that changed about two weeks before Aaron's death.

Logan started sending emails to an outside Yahoo account. The emails started mentioning an issue with an internal employee, no name was mentioned, causing problems for WANN. The responses weren't addressed in anyway, so you would know whom Logan was talking with, and seemed to suggest they would do anything for Logan to alleviate the problem.

Logan: He is making waves again. Trying to access items on our network he shouldn't be.

Yahoo: How do you know this?

Logan: We've been alert to the possibility. Tracking what he is doing. Seems he is logging in via an outside IP address.

Yahoo: What can he do that can hurt you?

Logan: Leak information to the tech media. Say we've been dragging our feet. Not fixing the security issue.

Yahoo: You have, though, haven't you?

Logan: Of course. We can't fix this. It is the key to making us wealthy.

Yahoo: Will the company go under then, if exposed?

Logan: Possibly. We were a dying company before the infusion of capital saved us. Our overseas investors will not be happy. They already have their hooks in me for personal indiscretions.

Yahoo: You know I will do whatever you want me to do.

Logan: Fix the problem for me and I will be forever in your debt.

Yahoo: Will you give me your heart and soul, love and devotion?

Logan: We can see. I certainly can pay you. Give you more of a position in the company you can leverage.

Yahoo: You know I want more than that from you. Those two wonderful nights together in Vegas. Those times in your office. I need more of them.

Logan: We can talk about it once the situation dies down.
Yahoo: Promise?
Logan: Yes.

The last response in the chain was two days later, as if Logan had to think about it. There was no indication of whether it was a man or a woman, in the emails. Since he had a taste for both sexes, it could be anyone. Though it did appear it was someone who worked at WANN, as he promised them a better job. So that at least narrowed it down some. Why he was communicating with them via an outside email address, was a mystery. And it appeared it wasn't in use anymore, at least from what Mandy could tell. Test messages sent to it, would bounce back saying the address was no longer in service.

My other concern was related to Logan's comment about "making waves again." When I checked with Mandy, she explained what they had done.

"We took a break for a while after the threat on his job. We all sat down at first and wondered if it was worth it to continue. But as time went on it became apparent this was a corrupt company. We got a little greedy, thinking we could profit from it. So, Aaron, Wilmar and I started hacking into their software design matrix, going through code, line by line. We were looking for more evidence, since they were dragging their feet on a solution. At the time we didn't think they were on to us, but apparently, we were wrong. We were looking to design an exploit that we could sell to the outside world that would do exactly what they were doing to the users of their software and equipment. Once it was out there, they would have little choice but to fix the issue, as anyone could use the vulnerability. Or we could blackmail them into paying us to keep the exploit quiet. We were close to having it, when Aaron was killed. Some of the work he was doing was on his computer. Parts of it were on my mine and the rest on Wilmar's. Since they took Aaron's computer, we lost a chunk of the coding. We then couldn't chance continuing the track we were on. We were back to square one. Then came the shock when Aaron was killed. We knew deep down it was someone in WANN. And after the grief stopped, the anger took over. That is when I hired you, and Wilmar and I started up again, though more cautiously."

"Not cautious enough, as Wilmar was killed" I said. "Then attempted to kill you as well and got King instead."

"I know. And they got Wilmar's computer, though it was heavily encrypted. It would be difficult, if not impossible, to crack into."

"Did you lose more of the work you were doing?" I asked.

"Not this time, I had copies of everything."

"They shouldn't be able to track you. Find out what you are doing?"

"I'm doing all I can to prevent that. I'm good at what I do. But nothing is totally foolproof. But what we have here now, can you use it against them?"

Looking through it all, there was only one answer.

"Yes."

And now here I was, lying on a comfortable bed in Vegas, with information I could use to bust the case wide open. I just needed to leverage it against Logan. I'd thought how I was going to approach him and what to say. I had copies of the pertinent emails to throw in his face. Now all I had to do was find him in the massive facility that was Caesar's Palace. I planned on throwing the dice and laying it all on the line.

Chapter 52

I was going to leverage Neil's friend as part of my plan. I had contacted him before flying out and he was going to meet me for dinner at one of the many Caesar's Palace restaurants, Café Americano. Many of the eateries here were expensive. This one was reasonable, by Vegas standards, and provided a choice of meals I'd enjoy.

I took a stroll, admiring the Greco-Roman statues and themes that graced the entire complex. All the buildings were interconnected, a maze you could easily get lost in. I had a map to help me along, though I had to stop and ask for directions a few times. Probably looked like a tourist from out of town. It took me a while, but I finally found the café and was able to get a table for two, as the place was packed.

I ordered myself a beer, having to yell to the waitress so she could hear me, as the place was noisy, with lots of activity. Kimo Torres walked up to my table, seemingly knowing who I was. He was only about 5' 10", strong and muscular for his height. He was wearing a motorcycle jacket, while carrying his full-faced helmet and leather gloves. He draped the coat over the back of his seat, while setting the helmet and gloves under the table. He shook my hand with a powerful grasp and sat down, as he ran his fingers through his black close-cropped hair like a comb. He was in jeans and muscle shirt, which showed his natural dark brown skin. I was amazed he wasn't sweating, my body challenging the strength of my antiperspirant, for even inside it seemed warm to me, while outside it was still over 100 degrees.

"Good to meet you, Jarvis," he said.

"Same to you, Kimo," I replied. "I see you ride."

"Yep, a Ducati crotch rocket."

"I have a Harley. Though I'd find it hard to believe you can drive in this heat."

"I have a liquid cooling vest I wear on the worst days. Didn't need it today. I wear it when taking a long ride on the back roads. My Hawaiian and Spanish heritage is used to this type of heat."

"Ducati. Lots of CC's, I would imagine. Do you ride fast?"

"Over a hundred when out in the desert. Nothing like it. I love the rush."

"If you are pulled over, you just flash a badge and no ticket."

He smiled.

"I'm guessing you didn't ride all the way out here from Denver?" he asked.

"No. Took a plane ride. Needed to get here before someone."

"Neil mentioned you might need some assistance. Said to help you out."

"You called him to check up on me?"

"Of course. Like to be certain who I'm helping."

"How did you and Neil meet? I'm guessing you lived in the Denver Metro area at one time."

"Yes. Spent my teen and early twenties years in the Mile-High City. Let's say Neil and I met professionally."

"He arrested you?"

"Sort of. Since I was a juvenile, and prone to running with the wrong crowd, he kept me from a life that likely would have meant I would be dead by now."

"Gangs?"

"Exactly. Not sure what he saw in me. Maybe the doubt I had about what I was getting into. I was never comfortable in that lifestyle. Sometimes you have no choice and it's the only way to survive. He took an interest, since my dad was not there to guide me and my mother didn't know what more to do. He became a Big Brother to me. When I took an interest in police work, he helped get me the right education and training. I owe him a lot."

"Are you a detective here in Vegas?"

"Yes. Moved out here a little more than a year ago. I'm low on the totem pole, but I at least have my foot in the door. Seems like a lot of turnover out here. Not really a place people come to put down roots. But it's never boring. Robbery and murder are pretty common. And all the drunks and poor losers at gambling keep us busy."

The waitress brought me my beer, and Kimo ordered one for himself, since he was off-duty. I ordered some beer-brined chicken wings. The prices were about double what you paid back in Denver. My expense sheet was going to total up quickly. The cost of being in the gambling mecca.

"Neil says you are trying to track someone down here," said

Kimo. "A high-roller who comes to blow his money. Lots of those here in Vegas."

"His name is Logan Albers. Comes once or twice a month for four days. Likes to play poker and some blackjack. Generally, hangs with some twentysomethings, male and female. Likes the taste of young flesh, no matter the gender."

"I've not heard of him. Not surprising, as there are literally tens of thousands of people rolling through here daily. Many of which as you describe Logan. It is named Sin City for a reason."

"I need to find him. He is coming in tomorrow around noon and will be staying here. I want to observe what he does and who he is with. Then I plan on talking with all of them, separately, if I can. I have some evidence I want to show him, and see what type of reaction I get. Any connections here at Caesar's I can leverage?"

His beer arrived and he drank down about a third, along with devouring a chicken wing, which also arrived by a second server.

"These wings are awesome," he said, while licking his fingers. "There is a girl who works the front desk. We get together on occasion and enjoy each other's company. She is a hot one, who takes my breath away with her physical prowess. She is normally working that time of day. But I know they have self-check-in, so he could bypass the front desk."

"He seems the type where he wants everyone to handle his affairs for him. He is a high-level executive in a worldwide tech firm. I imagine he will go to the front desk and want someone to lavish him with praise and bellhops deliver his luggage for him."

"I'll see what I can do. At the very least we ought to be able to get the tower and suite number he is staying in."

"That would be helpful. What's it like living in Vegas?"

"Exactly what you see. Glitz, glamour, entertainment, food, booze and gambling. This place is one giant orgasm for most people coming here."

"Don't forget shopping too. Spending money is better than sex for some."

"The Forum Shops are a crowded place. Some said it wouldn't work, but it's a gold mine. I could retire on the sales tax alone they collect there."

"I see a lot of security people mulling about," I said.

"Yes. Those are the ones you see. There are plain clothes ones as well walking around. They have short fuses and little tolerance for even the slightest hint of trouble. With all the money being exchanged, they don't take any shit from anyone. I assume you aren't packing a weapon?"

"No. I didn't think they'd allow one in."

"No, they aren't legal for private citizens. Security and police are the only ones allowed."

"Hopefully I won't need one. This guy is a tech geek, and doesn't travel with security, so I think I can take him. Or least I hope so."

"If you have any problems, you can call me. I will do what I can to help."

"Always good to have an officer of the law on your side. Shall we have some dinner?"

He nodded yes and the waitress took our orders. While looking over the menu and seeing the prices, I wondered if I would look cheap asking Kimo to share a meal. I then wondered if they'd let me order off the kids' menu.

Chapter 53

The next day, shortly after noon, I was parked outside on a bench reading the paper and a couple of magazines I'd picked up at the gift shop. There was shade, thankfully, but little breeze, as the heat was sweltering. I had on beige shorts and a white Dri-Fit T-shirt that was wicking away the sweat as fast as my body could produce it. I watched people coming into the hotel, of which there were many, giving little time to read. I had Logan's face burned in my memory, so I doubted I'd miss him, even with the masses coming and going. He was tall and skinny, with a receding hairline of blonde curls. Lyndi had told me he was a casual dresser, with light-colored slacks and cotton polos, normally in red or blue variations being his most common attire. He wore thick glasses, as he couldn't wear contacts, and had a lumbering stride in canvas shoes when travelling. It was possible I'd not see him, but if I did I hoped to catch those he brought with him. I had my phone handy to take snapshots, as stealthily as possible.

The front drop-off area was as large as some airport terminal passenger-departure zones, with multiple lanes, the cabs and Uber drivers jockeying for a spot to gather and leave their riders. I had Logan's flight information, so I knew he had landed on time. Judging time to unload, pick up luggage, get transportation and make the trek to the hotel, I had a pretty good idea of when he'd arrive. Right around one I saw him getting out of a yellow Vegas cab. He had a carry-on bag and large wheeled luggage the driver retrieved from his trunk. He lumbered towards the entrance, alone, dressed almost exactly as Lyndi had said, other than the San Francisco Giants ball cap he was wearing.

I followed him at a safe distance, through the foyer with cathedral ceiling and marble pillars, to the massive curved check-in counter. He went to the first open space and I tried to stay as close to him as I could, so I could hear what he said, while trying not to look out of place.

"Checking in," he said, while handing over his driver's license and credit card.

"Yes, Mr. Albers," responded the male guest-services employee. He looked at his screen. "So glad to have you back here again." He was typing away and swiping the ID and credit card. "Your two connecting rooms are ready to go in the Octavius Tower."

"Have my guests checked in yet?"

"Ms. Sun and Mr. Pittman have not arrived yet."

"If you can give them their key cards and send them right up when they do."

"I certainly will. Do you need any assistance with your bags? Do you know where you are going?"

"Help with my bags would be wonderful. And yes, I know where I'm going. Come here every few weeks. Like a second home to me."

Logan moved on, standing and waiting for a bellhop to arrive. I jumped to the counter to speak.

"I'm wondering if Tess Border is working today."

"Yes. She is four stations down. Blonde hair in pony-tail."

I said "thanks" and I slid down to her location. She was finishing up with a South American couple, who didn't appear to speak very good English. It was a struggle, but she finally finished up with them. She smiled at me as I took their place.

"Tess Border," I asked.

"Yes. How can I help you?"

"We have a mutual friend, Kimo Torres."

"You must be Jarvis."

"I am. Mentioned you could assist me. He also mentioned you were beautiful and took his breath away when you are together. I can see why."

I left the part out about her physical prowess, yet she blushed at the words.

"Kimo is a doll. We always have an enjoyable time together."

"Can you help me?"

"For Kimo, I would do anything. What are you looking for?"

"Room numbers for Logan Albers. Staying in the Octavius Tower. Has two rooms with two other guests coming. A Ms. Sun and Mr. Pittman."

She typed away on her keyboard, retrieving the info and giving me the room numbers.

"Do you have the first names of his guests?" I asked.

"Miya Sun and Liam Pittman. Shows they haven't checked in

yet."

"Anything else you can tell me about their stay?"

"Both Miya and Liam have pool time scheduled for this afternoon and tomorrow morning. They've reserved a shaded cabana between the Fortuna and Venus Pools. Fortuna being the adults' only pool. Logan has reserved a seat in the Poker Room for tonight and tomorrow afternoon."

"Any open Cabanas next to them?"

"No, they are all full."

"Any chance of double-booking in theirs?"

"Are you planning on causing a scene? If so, security will come down hard on you."

"Not at all. It will give me an opening to talk with them. Use my charm."

Her eyes met mine, with a hint of intrigue.

"Does your charm always work?"

"I have a good track record. Though it's not a hundred percent effective."

"From what I've seen so far, it would work on me."

"Thank you," I said with a chuckle. "The percentages often are lower with the ladies. Any chance you can text me when Miya and Liam show up?"

"Sure. What is your number?"

I handed over one of my business cards.

"Not the first private detective I've met. You are not like the others I've seen."

"Hopefully I'm better."

"You are. The others seemed sleazy. You at least are easy on the eyes. And charming!"

"So are you. Can you do me one more favor?"

"Will I need to smoke a cigarette afterwards?"

I laughed and then handed her my room card and some money.

"Nothing that physical. I read on the Internet that if you hand a twenty-dollar bill to the guest services person, they will upgrade you to a better room. Any chance of a better room in the Octavius Tower near these folks?"

"Is your current room not up to standards?" she asked.

"Not what I was expecting. I was pretty disappointed."

"I will see what I can do."

She pocketed the money and then typed away. She was able to get me a nice room just down the hall from where they were staying. A definite upgrade. She made me a new set of room keys and handed them over.

"I see here listed a Mrs. Mann. Too bad, though, I don't see a ring on your finger. I'd ask you for a drink later if you weren't tied up detecting."

"I'm sorry to say, yes. Though she hasn't arrived yet. Home taking care of a sick child. My ring is tucked away safe when I'm working. That way it doesn't distract the ladies from my charms."

"A shame. Is there anything else I can do for you, Mr. Mann?"

I reached out my hand and she slowly shook it.

"Have Kimo take you to a nice dinner the next time you get together. It is on me. Sky's the limit. Though in Vegas the sky is pretty high."

She laughed while handing me her card. "If you need anything else, let me know. I will help however I can. If the wife fails to show up, give me a call if you need some company. I always enjoy charm over drinks."

I walked away happy I had some inside help, and another offer of companionship. I'd never do that to Kimo, especially since he carried a gun. But it was always nice to be asked.

The Forum Food Court was close by, so I grabbed a late lunch, found an open seat and waited. The place was loud and crowded, but that seemed the norm for the entire facility. Looking around I saw the melting pot of people, walking by, from all over the world. Most dressed casually, enjoying the good life. Being away from the arduous work and horrors on the outside. It was a paradise of sorts. Most would lose money at the gaming tables and slot machines, but wouldn't care. A small portion would go home a winner, having been the lucky one to hit a payoff. As I finished off my burger and fries a text came in. Logan's guests were checking in.

I headed back to the lobby near the check-in counters, hoping to spot them. If they were to head straight to their rooms, I should be able to narrow it down, since I knew the direction and floor they were taking. In about five minutes I saw what I thought was them. A smallish Asian woman, about 5' 5", holding hands with a six-foot or so tall white man. Both were about the age I was looking for. Late teens and early twenties. I took a couple of snapshots of them with my phone for reference later. They headed down the long hallway towards the Octavius Tower elevators. I had scoped out the various paths the day before and this morning, so I knew my way around. I kept my distance, though close enough that when we got to the elevators I jumped on with them. They pressed the button for the floor I was expecting, while I pressed the one above them. There were two other people riding up, so they didn't pay me any mind. After they got off, I did the same on the next floor and then walked the stairs down one level. I strolled down the huge hallway, passing both rooms. I knew who I was after, so now I had to put the rest of my strategy in motion. Since they planned to go swimming in a couple hours, I would head towards the Venus Pool as well. I had packed some swimming trucks, fortunately, so I was prepared. I took the elevator back to the main level and made the trek to my room in the Palace Tower, to pack and move on to my upgraded accommodations. I would be sleeping among the kings and queens tonight.

Chapter 54

Since I knew what time they planned on going to the pool, I listened at the door of my new room and could hear and see them leave as they walked past on the way to the elevator. I gave them about twenty minutes and headed down myself, in my red, white and blue swimming trunks, clean yellow Dri-Fit shirt and tan sandals. I had lathered up with some sunscreen and soon was outside, marveling at the extraordinary liquid facilities before me.

The Garden of the Gods Pool Oasis is a series of different pools. As with the hotel it keeps the Roman theme, with statues, pillars, and sights and sounds of water fountains everywhere. Around the outer edge there were a few palm trees and a garden. The pool area was crowded, though not overwhelming. Most of the blue crushed velvet padded lounges were taken. Bikini-clad women laying out, working on their tans. Most of the men, thankfully, were wearing loose trunks. I saw only a couple of Speedo-clad gentlemen, which my senses automatically averted. I went over to the Cabana, ready for the confrontation. I walked in and saw the two of them relaxing, still holding hands.

"Oh my," I said. "It looks like you are in my cabana. I have a reservation."

"Are you certain you have the correct one?" said Liam, who stood up and walked over.

"Yes."

I showed him the paperwork Tess had given me. He pulled out his own and showed it to me.

"It looks as if they double-booked us," I said.

"Yes, it does. Let me go and see if I can straighten this out," said Liam. "I will be right back."

I smiled at Miya. She was wearing a skimpy flowery bikini, covering just enough of her body to be legal. She smiled back at me. *Now time for the charm.*

"I'm so sorry about this," I said. "I feel terrible this happened."

"Not your fault," said Miya. "I'm sure he can get it straightened out. We come here pretty often."

"I haven't been here before. Just wanted to stay out of the sun when I wasn't in the water. I worry about skin cancer."

"Put on enough sunscreen and you'll be fine"

"SPF 80 in my pocket. Hopefully it will do the job. I'm Jarvis, by the way."

"I'm Miya. And that was Liam."

"Are you two here on business or pleasure?"

"Pleasure," she said with a joyous grin.

"Are you two married?" I asked.

"No, just close friends. We enjoy each other's company and companionship. What about you? Are you here for business or pleasure?"

"Some business, but mostly pleasure. Though I'm alone for now. I hope before the weekend is over I can hook up with someone. Any thoughts on where to meet people here?"

"I'd try the Seahorse Lounge. A good-looking guy like you shouldn't have any problem."

Liam returned, with the unwelcome news.

"Well they are all booked. They said they'd refund both of our monies. Says it happens sometimes. We can share it or one of us will have to do without."

"You two can go ahead," I said. "You are a cute couple, who seem to be enjoying yourselves. I will take one of these lounges here and keep myself covered up when I'm not in the water. Sorry to be a bother."

"Not a problem," said Liam. "Enjoy the rest of your day."

Miya grabbed Liam by the arm and looked deep into his eyes, as if to speak telepathically.

"Oh, Liam, can't Jarvis join us. There is plenty of room. He seems like a pleasant person. And he is worried about being in the sun too much. You never know, we could become friends."

Liam looked over at me, seeming to size me up. I used my overwhelming and charming smile to seal the deal.

"I suppose it would be OK."

"Sure it would," said Miya. "We've been talking, and Jarvis is looking to meet someone this weekend. Maybe we can help him find that special man or woman. I suggested the Seahorse Lounge."

"Yes, there are plenty of single people there. You shouldn't have any problems. Are you married, Jarvis?"

I hesitated.

"No comment."

"Looking for a little something on the side," said Liam.

Stalling to answer, I did my best to blush, as if embarrassed by why I was truly there.

"I'd say different. Hoping to experience life in innovative ways. I came to Sin City to see if the label was true."

"We sin here quite often, don't we, Liam."

"Yes, we do. A little drink, a little smoke and then we stroke."

We all laughed at his humor. I was making headway, which was good.

"Do you gamble?" I asked of them.

"No," said Liam.

"I like to shop," said Miya. "Liam helps me pick out some clothes to wear and then not wear."

"I hear there is a Victoria's Secret here," I said.

"Yes, my favorite. I always go there to find something new."

"Maybe I should go with you and find something for…the little lady. In case I'm bad here, I can get her something to ease my conscience."

"I think jewelry would be better. Plenty of options there, too, at the Forum shops. But I always like another man's point of view on my sexy apparel."

"We can both help each other. What about you, Liam? What can you help me with?"

Liam sized me up again. I was auditioning, it would seem, for them. The part I was playing was working as I'd hoped.

"Time will tell. But I'm certain I can think of something."

"Well, time for a swim."

I peeled off my shirt. I wasn't Adonis, but I was in good shape, and would only appeal to them more, once they'd seen additional skin. I headed for the water and hopped in. It wasn't really enough for a hard swim, so I just floated around. The water felt warm from the heat of the sun. I looked back and saw them talking, all the time watching me. I had made progress; the seduction had begun.

Chapter 55

We were the best of pals when our time at the pool ended. They invited me to dinner, with a friend, but I declined. I figured it was Logan and couldn't take the chance he'd recognize me, so I made up the excuse that I had a previous engagement with a potential client. We agreed to meet at around seven at the Forum Shops, since their friend was going to enjoy some poker. We'd do a little shopping, assist each other in some purchases, and afterwards maybe head to the Seahorse Lounge.

I returned to my room and changed into some workout clothes and headed to the hotel gym. It was huge, like everything else at Caesar's. I found the nautilus equipment and treadmills were excellent and pushed myself hard. Once done I was back in my room and sat in the jetted tub to ease my soreness and relax, before getting dressed and making the long trek to the Forum Shops that was on the far end of the Palace property.

I had not shared with Miya and Liam that we were staying on the same floor or even the same tower. I did my best to avoid them, trying to leave after them or taking the stairs. We had said we would meet up at the south end entrance near the Colosseum, where all the concerts were held. I was early, so I took a seat and waited, reading about world events and sports on my phone. Football was in preseason mode, while baseball was in the home stretch of their regular season. I thought of Dennis Gash and his last year of high school football, and hoped he got the scholarship he deserved. People of all ages passed me by while I waited. I was wearing shorts and a tank top, along with my Nike running shoes. I was looking good for my approaching new friends, who I stood up to greet. Miya was wearing a short-flowered skirt and halter top to match. Liam was in shorts and a polo. Both smelled of perfume and cologne, with just a whiff of marijuana smoke and alcohol. Each looked a little glassy eyed as well, but happy to see me. Miya even hugged me, and I could feel her braless chest and hard nipples pointing into my stomach. I was glad he didn't hug me, as who knows what hardness I'd feel from him.

"I've got my credit card. How about you?" said Miya.

"My plastic is ready to go," I replied.

And we were off. The Forums area was as big as any mall I'd ever been in before. There were sections that were three levels high, with spiral escalators to glide you up and down. Roman statues, pillars, and artwork were everywhere. Other sections were only a single level, with a blue-sky ceiling. The shops ranged from common, like Apple, Gap and Nike, to the high end like Armani, Gucci and Versace. In some of the stores my credit limit probably wasn't high enough to buy anything. Which was OK, as I had no intentions of splurging. Just acting like I was. Miya had us heading straight to Tiffany & Co. She was determined to find me the perfect jewelry for my wife back home, who didn't exist. *Where was she when I needed to buy something for Melissa?*

"Here is a beautiful necklace she'd enjoy," said Miya, pointing through the thick glass case.

"Ten thousand," I replied. "A little out of my price range, unless we can haggle them down on the price about ninety percent."

The sales lady shook her head. "Don't have that much mark-up."

After looking around some more, Miya found something else.

"How about these diamond earrings?"

"Still twenty-five hundred. Not sure I even have that much limit left on my card after this trip."

She was determined, but couldn't find anything, as everything was over a thousand that appealed to her.

"We'll keep looking."

Which we did, going up and down the Forum shopping area. When we hit the Victoria's Secret & Pink shop, Miya turned her attention to herself. Going from rack to rack, she found a couple of sheer teddies and held them up to her body.

"What do you think," she asked of Liam and myself.

"Fabulous," answered Liam.

"Hot," I replied. "Try it on and see what you think."

"Care to join me in the dressing room?" she said.

"Tempting. Though I'm sure they have cameras in there."

"All the better. Liam has been in there with me on many occasions. It is quite a rush."

"I'm not good in public. But behind closed doors, and I could give it go."

"You might get your wish. Let me try these on."

She went into the dressing room, alone. While in there Liam walked over to me and put his hand on my shoulder.

"You realize she is hot for you," he said.

"I'm getting that impression. Hopefully you don't mind."

"Not at all. I don't mind sharing. Could be an enjoyable time for all of us, if you know what I mean."

"I think so. Though I've never had a three-way before. I might need a little help."

"We have lots of help back at our room. Weed, pills, alcohol. All the right stuff to get you in the mood. Are you interested?"

"I'd be willing to come up and see what develops. I'd even enjoy watching you two. It would be like live porn."

He put his arm around me now.

"She is a wild one, too. Nothing she won't do. We can demonstrate and see if you'd care to jump in."

"Sounds like fun."

Liam walked over to the dressing room door and knocked. Miya opened it and he stepped in. About ten minutes later they both came out, her hair a little bit messy now. She walked over to the sales desk and threw down her credit card. Liam adjusted himself as he walked over to me.

"She can't wait to get back to our room and get started."

After paying we walked back taking our time. She held both of our hands, as Liam and I both walked on either side of her. I could feel her fingers caressing my palm and at times she rubbed up against me, her hand in mine rubbing my thigh. It was a crazy game I was playing, but I hoped once inside I could get away and search the other room. On the elevator ride up, we were alone. Miya leaned in, raising my shirt with one hand and kissing me on the chest, the other hand cupping my butt. I saw Liam watching us, getting aroused at the sight. It wasn't my thing for a man to get off on my pleasure, but I played the part as best as I could. When we got into the hotel room, Miya left to put on one of her new teddies.

"Care for something?" said Liam. "Like I said, we have weed and some uppers that will put a smile on your face and a rush of blood to your groin."

"I will take a pill or two and some beer," I said.

He went into the adjoining bedroom and was back with a few pills, He handed me two, while downing two of his own.

"Grab a beer from the mini-bar. I'm going to light up and take a few hits."

I pulled out a Bud Light and popped the top. I took a long draw and with some sleight of hand, dumped the pills in the trash with the bottle cap. I then pretended to put the pills in my mouth and drink down another long sip.

"Best seven-dollar bottle of Bud I've ever had."

Liam laughed as he took a long hit on his bong that he had going now, while sitting on the sofa. I could smell the marijuana, but if I kept my distance I would be fine. I took a chair near the window where the air conditioning was blowing, keeping some fresh atmosphere to take in.

Out came Miya in her sheer white teddy. The material hid nothing, as I could see her naked body now. She grabbed a couple of pills from Liam and swallowed them down without any liquid. She took a long draw on the bong and then came over and stood in front of me.

"How do you like it?"

"Wow. Better than I imagined."

She came and sat on my lap and put her tongue in my ear. It had an immediate effect on me, which she could feel.

"Someone, or something seems to be perking up," she stated with a whisper.

"The pills must be kicking in."

"Can I do anything to relieve the pressure?"

"Jarvis here likes to watch," said Liam.

"Yes, you told me in the dressing room. Too bad you didn't join us as well. While Liam was telling me about you and what you desired, he put his hands between my legs and got me all excited."

"How about you two going into the bedroom and getting things started?" I said. "I will watch and when I'm ready I can join you."

"Sounds hot," said Miya.

She got off my lap and went over to Liam. She took two more draws on the bong and then pulled Liam to the bedroom. I followed and stood outside watching the activities. It didn't take long before clothes were removed and the moaning began. About five minutes in they had forgotten all about me, completely engrossed in each other. I slipped away and went to the door that joined the two rooms. I slowly opened it, finding the room dark. I found a light switch and lit up the space, watching for any sign of someone there. But the room was empty other than for the contents of the person staying there.

The door had opened into the living area. Once there I found a notebook computer sitting on the table. It was powered off, so I powered it on to see if I could log in. Mandy had given me Logan's password, at least the one that worked to access his email, and in this case the same to unlock his computer. It had automatically logged into the hotel wireless, so I grabbed my phone and made a quick call.

"I'm at his computer," I said to Mandy who answered her cell phone. "Tell me what I should do?"

She gave me a web address to go to, LogMeIn.com. It was a remote access site that you can connect to, and allow a technician to take over your computer to troubleshoot. Once connected, she gave me the six-digit code and after a couple of other clicks she was in control.

"I'm in. Let me do my thing."

"Ok. I'll hang up and keep searching his room. Call when you need me to disconnect."

In the living area I found a briefcase, but it had nothing other than papers, none of which were of any consequence. I checked the hallway closet, but found nothing there, other than the normal hotel items. In the bathroom, I went through his toiletries and the various medications you'd find for a man his age. Two different blood pressure medicines, antacids, allergy and Viagra. It would seem the sex machine needed help in the erection department.

From there I went into his bedroom and found some interesting items. In one of his bags were various sex toys. Toys for women and for men. You name it and it was there. Along with various oils and lubricants to keep the action going. Plus, there was some bizarre clothing that lead me to believe some wild role playing would be enjoyed this weekend. And more pills, marijuana and some white powder that had to be cocaine. I took pictures of all it, as evidence to show him.

I went through the room some more, finding nothing else of value, except for one thing. Sitting on the dresser was the envelope they give you when you check in. They always give you two key cards and since Logan was in the room by himself, the second card was there. I grabbed it, sticking it in my back pocket, leaving the envelope where it looked as if it had never been moved. He likely would never miss it and I now had access to his room. I walked back through, and Mandy called me.

"I got what I need."

I said "Good" and ended the call. I powered down the machine, leaving it the way it was. I went through turning off all the lights and then back through the connected door. I could still hear moaning coming from the bedroom, the smell of marijuana still strong. The drugs would keep the action going for some time. I went over to the table in the living area and wrote out a quick note.

Sorry I had to leave. I got embarrassed and found I couldn't go through with joining you. I hope you enjoy the rest of your stay.

I didn't sign it, as they should know who left it—if they remembered any of the evening, since they were so high. I snuck out, holding the self-closing door so it didn't slam shut, and headed back to my room. Into the bathroom I went; a long drenching under the rainfall showerhead was needed to wash off the stench and sleaze of the night. The plan was to go to sleep, hoping to dream of happier times other than the two naked bodies I'd manipulated to an end I needed, to force Logan's hand. Believe it or not, I slept like a baby for the first time in a while.

Chapter 56

The next morning, I had room service deliver me some breakfast. Eggs, bacon, English muffins and some juice. It cost an arm and leg, but I didn't mind. I was sleeping in ready for the big day ahead. After finishing, and showering, I called Mandy to see what she found when logged into Logan's notebook.

"He had an email archive that wasn't cloud-based. I got a copy of that and I've been looking through it. I found where he had been emailing some Chinese gentlemen about what to do about you snooping around. He wanted them to try and buy you off. If that didn't work, hurt you to try and scare you off. Were you aware of this?"

I had not told Mandy of what had happened the first time I'd met Cong in my apartment. I looked down at my hand, which was still a little sore, but mostly healed now.

"Lived it. They offered me cash, which I refused and then dislocated my fingers."

"You didn't tell me."

"No. Would have only worried you. It's my job to handle those situations."

"Found some other emails to that mysterious Yahoo account. Whoever he was emailing was warm for his form. Not sure why. Seems sleazy to me."

"He is. But some like sleazy. Plus, he is a big-time executive with money. Sometimes that is all anyone wants."

"There were communications to their legal department on how best to handle, including one where he told them to write in the cause for the agreement I signed about not pursuing WANN in Aaron's death. Said to make it vague and not apparent. Specifically, he said, and I quote 'Don't tell her any of this. Only say the money is for compensation for wages lost.' Then later in the email he said, 'If they didn't get me to sign it, he was going to find himself a new legal team with the balls to do the job.' The man is a corporate vulture."

"Be sure you are sending all of this to Barry. We need him to have copies of everything, just in case."

"I have been. He was salivating over these last ones I sent.

Figures he can get a Stay on the Cease and Desist order."

"Barry is a hawk in the courtroom when he has the evidence to back him up. Did you find anything else useful?"

"Nothing yet. But I'm still looking. Still trying to find a smoking gun about the coding issues. They were smart and removed those emails. Or everything was communicated verbally."

"Keep digging. His ties to the Chinese and Russians are crucial. Be sure you are including that in your search parameters. Can I talk with April?"

After a couple of minutes, she came on the line.

"Enjoying yourself in Sin City?" she asked.

"Not really. I may need a delousing from all the sleaze I'm neck-deep in. But I've made progress and will have a big showdown this afternoon. I might even see about coming back a day early if all goes well."

"Be good to see you again. So far all is quiet here. Neil and I mostly sit around reading, while Mandy works away on her computer. She's only been sleeping about three or four hours a night. Nearly working non-stop. She wants these people in a bad way."

"So do I. Just keep a lookout. Tell Neil thanks again for using his vacation on this. If I end up coming back tomorrow, I'll let you know. If not, I'll be in by ten Sunday morning."

Logan's poker match was starting at 1 p.m. Tess had told me they generally lasted a few hours, depending how quickly people get knocked out and how aggressive the bettors are. My intent was to walk down there close to two, and see how he was doing. I didn't expect to see Miya or Liam there, as they had a pool day scheduled and told me they hated watching Logan gamble. Since I had time, I lay down in bed and set the alarm, falling asleep to some music playing on my phone.

After the annoying buzzer went off, I was up, alert and raring to go. Down the elevator and on the ground floor, I walked and walked and walked some more. At the very least I was getting exercise for my legs and feet. I found the poker room and stepped in. There were sixteen tables, all of which were being used, with as many as twelve people at each one, one of which was the dealer. If you were claustrophobic, you'd freak out, as everyone was tightly packed together. My eyes scanned the room and smack-dab in the middle was Logan, sitting at the end, checking out his cards. There were eight other men and two women playing, with stacks of chips in front of each of them, some with more than others. Logan was right in the middle, but had just won a hand that put him among those with the higher amount. There was nowhere to sit and watch. There was a small bar, so I went there and got a drink that cost a king's ransom. I was wandering around when a security person came up to me.

"What are you doing, sir?" he said.

"Looking over the room. Amazing all the people in here. Wanted to see some of the action."

"Some people get nervous when they see someone walking around, watching the tables and not playing."

"I'm considering playing, just needed to see what games are going on. Looks like Texas Hold 'Em at many of the tables."

"Yes, that is the main game that is played, though some are more traditional poker games. If you want to stay in, you need to buy into a game or you can play some of the slot machines."

I thanked him and then found a slot machine with a decent view and took a seat. I had no change to play with, so I just sat and watched. It was hard to see, but Logan seemed to be winning. I killed about forty-five minutes and then headed back out to grab a sandwich at the food court. Once I ate I walked back again and found Logan's table was down to him and two others. The end was in sight. I went back to our tower, and with the key card, entered his room and took a seat in the dark, waiting and reading. I pulled out some printed papers I'd retrieved from my room and placed them on the table next to me. Time can go slowly when waiting for someone, but I was a patient man. I had made sure the connecting room door was locked, so if those two returned, they wouldn't walk in on me. I heard the door handle twist and in lumbered Logan. Since the shades were closed it was dark enough that he couldn't see me. He made a trip to the bathroom first, and after the flush of the toilet he walked in and turned on a light, startled to see me.

"Who the hell are you?" he said.

"Have a seat, so we can talk," I replied.

"I'm calling security."

"No you aren't. All the phones have been unplugged. Please

hand me your cell phone."

"Why should I?"

"If you don't, I'll dislocate your fingers." It was an idle threat, but payback would have been sweet. "Now do it and have a seat on the sofa."

He was caught off guard and uncertain what to do. I stood up and pushed him up against the wall, hard. Twisted one of his arms behind his back and took his iPhone. I then spun him around and pushed him down on the sofa. He was flexing his arm, trying to get the feeling back.

"You didn't have to do that," he said.

"You were hesitating. Trying to decide what to do. You are a tech geek and anything stupid would have gotten you hurt. I wanted to make sure you understood you were out of your league when going up against me."

"I'll ask again, who the hell are you?"

"Jarvis Mann." I pulled out my ID and flashed it at him. "I believe you have heard of me."

"You are the detective that bitch hired."

I waved my index finger at him.

"No need to call her names. Mandy Bailey or Mrs. Bailey is what you should call her."

"I call that bitch whatever I want. What are you, the etiquette detective?"

"I am with you. Call her that again and you'll be missing some teeth."

He thought over his options. He may have been smart in the computer world, but not street smart. Still he had to know he was overmatched.

"What does Mandy Bailey want from me?"

"To know why and who killed her husband, Aaron."

He laughed. Not really sure why. Didn't seem funny to me.

"I don't know. The police said robbery."

"No. You had him killed because of what he found out about your company and how it is stealing from your customers."

"Silly notion. Why would we do such a thing?"

"Because it was the only way you could stay profitable. And because you were stupid."

"How so?"

"The excesses of a wealthy man. You had a great deal going for you. A wife and daughter, a huge home and nice car. A life most could only wish of having. But it wasn't enough. You had a taste for gambling, some drugs and sex with young men and women. Like Miya and Liam who are staying next door. Your wife found out and divorced you. Then maybe others found out and blackmailed you. Even leveraged you as a way to not only get a piece of the company profit, and steer it to try something illegal to save it from going under. Russian mobsters, and Chinese government enforcers."

"You have it wrong. My wife was unfaithful to me."

"I know different. I've talked with her. What keeps it friendly are the large alimony checks you send her way. You were a cheating bastard. They just needed to be young enough."

"You don't know shit."

"I've seen your bag of toys. The pills you take to keep it up. Even have taken a picture of all it. Also got to know Miya and Liam. Seems with the right amount of drugs and dirty talk, they will screw anyone."

Logan was getting nervous. You could see he was contemplating something. He got up and made a dash for the door. I, though, was quicker and stopped him. This time I popped him in the stomach and doubled him over. Once he got his breath, I moved him back to the couch and dragged the chair to block the way, so his only option of escape was out the window.

"How dare you hit me," he said, after a few minutes of composing himself.

"Need to work on your abs," I said. "I didn't pop you that hard. Next time it will be worse."

"Do you realize who I am? I will sue you for everything you are worth!"

"No you won't, because of this."

I grabbed the emails and sat them on the coffee table in front of him. Flipping through them one at a time, I could see his mouth moving while he read them. He straightened up the stack and laid them back down.

"How did you get these?"

"How do you think? We hacked our way in and got them. Mandy is a pretty resourceful computer hacker."

"The bit… I mean, Mrs. Bailey is a computer hacker?"

"Yep. She was the computer genius in the family. Aaron was good, but she could run circles around him. You were going up against a two-headed monster, or maybe even three-headed if you count Wilmar, whom you also had killed. The problem is, one head still remains. And it's coming to get you."

"What do you want? I can pay you. Name your price."

"Money won't buy me or Mandy."

"How about drugs? I have anything you can image to brighten your day. Or sex. Miya can please you any way you want."

"Been down that road with her. And she doesn't interest me in the least bit."

He looked shocked that anyone would refuse living a sexual fantasy.

"What, then?"

"We want who killed Aaron. You need to turn yourself in and confess to the crime. And then get your management to agree to fix your code so you no longer are stealing from innocent people."

"We aren't stealing. We are only data gathering."

"Yeah, right. Data gathering people's identity and ruining them."

"Even so, I didn't kill Aaron. I won't confess to something I didn't do."

"You did it and you know who did. Maybe you didn't pull the trigger, but you orchestrated it. If you don't confess, then we will bring the whole company down."

"How?"

"By leaking code that will have hackers tearing down your front door, blasting through your firewall and stealing all of your company information. Employees, your clients and their credit card info. All of it out on the Web for anyone to access. The lawsuits alone will shut you down."

He put his head in his hands, trying to decide what to do.

"You will also stop this silly legal action against Mandy and continue to pay her what you promised."

"I need time to think this through. You put me in a no-win situation. There are pressures from dangerous men if I do this."

"It is your call. You will be brought down one way or another. I will give you until Monday, at noon. If you don't turn yourself and the killer in to the authorities, it all goes out on the Web."

"You don't know what you've done."

I pulled out the key card to his room and tossed it on the table.

"Actually, I do know. Monday by noon, or else."

I walked out of the room feeling stoked. He would have to do something. He had no choice. A smart man would turn himself in and save all that he had built. But he didn't seem all that smart and someone in a panic can do stupid things. I was prepared to face whatever he threw at me. When I got to the room and opened the door to my suite, I sensed I wasn't alone. Letting the door close I put my hand in a fist and stepped into the bedroom. On the bed was Lyndi, dressed in nothing but a smile, drinking some wine from a large bottle she had brought with her.

"Hello, Jarvis," she said in a sexy voice. "I believe we still have some time to get better acquainted."

"Your daughter is feeling better, I assume," I asked.

"Much better and so am I. As soon as you remove those clothes and demonstrate the proper time you claimed you needed to satisfy me."

I was thrilled at what I had done, and aroused at the hot woman on the bed before me. I removed my clothes, so she could admire all of me. I walked over to the bed, grabbing her right foot and started kissing and sucking her toes, then working my way up her leg, kissing and licking every crease and fold, as she threw back her head in desire. I was a man of my word, as she was soon screaming in a heated desire that would last for another twenty-four hours.

Chapter 57

Because of Lyndi, I didn't make it back to Denver a day early. I had texted April and Mandy that something had come up, literally and several times, so I would return at the planned date. Sufficiently refreshed and relaxed, Lyndi and I said our goodbyes, with talk of sexual rendezvous at another time when the mood stroked us. She went off to California, while I headed to Denver. The takeoff and landing were all that one would hope for and I was back at my place by midday, the late summer heat still in full-on intensity.

When I opened my front door, two men were waiting for me. One was Lok and the other Cong. Cong pointed a gun at me and told me to turn around, while Lok frisked me. I wasn't armed, so I was defenseless. Lok turned me back around and stepped back.

"Well, at least you left the door closed this time," I said. "No flies for me to try and kill. There must have been fifty I had to swat from your last visit."

"You are a funny guy, Jarvis Mann," said Cong. "Sorry we have to ruin your mood. Would it be a cliché to say we are going to go for a ride?"

"Well, if you were taking me to the zoo, to see the animals, then no. But if it's a ride to my death, then yes it would be."

"No death, if you give us what we want. Please go change into some workout clothes before we get in the car. And don't be silly and try retrieving your gun from your safe. It will only force me to hurt you sooner."

"Workout clothes, you say. What type of workout should I be expecting?"

"A little kick-boxing. Something to loosen up the muscles and the tongue."

I went into my bedroom and changed. Gym shorts, Dri-Fit tank top and my good running shoes. Lok was watching me every step of the way, so no chance to snatch a weapon. Once I was done I was allowed to grab some water and we were in their car, Lok behind the wheel, Cong in the back with me, gun still pointed, heading to who knows where.

"I guess I should say I'm surprised you are here," I said. "But

I'd be lying. I thought maybe Logan would think this through and come to his senses."

"Logan?" said Cong, his eyes focused on me, the gun still pointing.

"Oh, come on, Cong. We know Logan Albers is the one who brought you in on this, in an attempt to save his precious empire."

"You think you have it all figured out."

"Not completely. Just a pretty good idea. The one thing I can't figure out is why he brought in the Russians first and then you."

Cong said something in his native language. I wasn't sure, but I assumed it was a curse word.

"Those monsters are uncivilized. When WANN was circling the drain the first time, they came in, provided cash and a new direction. They weren't disciplined enough to keep WANN or their own people in line. We got wind of what they were doing and came in to save them again, this time getting them on the right track. Less waste of money and resources. We attempted to work peacefully together with the Russians, but it hasn't been fruitful. We tried to buy them out, but they wouldn't budge. We had to find a way to free ourselves from them. That process has started."

"Did you blackmail Logan Albers to get your foot in the door?"

"Of course. He was an easy mark."

"Is Miya one of yours?"

"No. We had someone before her. A female he couldn't refuse."

"Underage?"

"Of course. She was still sixteen. She got to live the high life, get out of China and enjoy the fruits of the American way. Once we sufficiently had the evidence against him, we pulled her out and sent her home. We had him by the balls, as they say. He let us in on their secrets and we've been working with them ever since."

"And you hope to make headway, getting the US government to use their network equipment and software, so you can now more easily hack us."

"Something like that. We hack in now. But this would make it so much easier to do. And we'll be smart about it, and only use it when necessary so as not to cause any undue concern from your security agencies. One can't be greedy about these things."

"Sounds like you have all that you need. What do you need me for?"

"Answers to questions we don't have."

The ride took us to the southwest side of the city, past County Line Road and Wadsworth. There was a site where construction work was going on, building what looked like a new shopping center. On the edge was a building that was nearly completed by the looks of it. It was a Fitness Center, it appeared from the partial sign that was in place. Since it was a Sunday, no one in the area was working. We pulled right up to the front, where Lok got out and opened the door for me. I stepped out and was led inside. Everything looked new, and ready to begin operation, yet no one was there. We walked past the front counter, through a couple of sections and into an open room. Pictures on the wall of various martial artists through the years, told me what the space would be used for. Towards the back was a competition ring, complete with four supports, ropes, padded corners and foam padded flooring. Lok moved away from me and began removing his pants and top, to reveal his workout shorts, but no shirt. He looked strong and powerful, with more tattoos over most of his upper torso. He ducked through the ropes and began warming up. It was obvious we were going to be matched against each other.

"Place looks brand-new," I said.

"Will be opening next week. One of our investments. Give us a chance to break it in tonight. Please join Lok in the ring."

"Be a shame to get sweat and blood all over it before opening."

"Nothing that can't easily be fixed," said Cong, while waving me on.

I did as I was told, as Cong walked over to a storage cabinet on the wall and pulled out two sets of padded mixed martial arts gloves. One for me and one for Lok. We each put them on, the size fitting perfectly. I wasn't liking where this was headed.

"Are we going to spar?" I asked.

"Shortly. But first you need to tell me where the girl is."

"So if I do, then I get to walk out of here, no harm done?"

"No. You still will fight Lok. Logan made it clear he wanted you, how did he put it, pulverized."

"So why should I tell you then, if you are going to pit me against Lok?"

"The difference between living and dying. If you tell us, you get to live another day, though in pretty rough shape. Though you will heal in time. If you don't, then you will likely die. And who knows, before you die you may tell us anyway, when the pain gets too great. So why not tell us now and live to detect another day."

"You seem confident I won't win."

"Lok bested you before. Though I've been told you are pretty good, I don't see you coming out on top. If you do, I will gladly let you walk away."

There was little I could do but fight it out with him. Removing my shirt, so Lok had less to grab onto, I began loosening up, stretching my arms, back and legs. I would need all my skills and a lot of luck, falling back on the few lessons I had taken. And maybe some help from the great martial artist in the sky.

"I guess this means you won't tell me where she is?" said Cong.

"Not going to happen. You might as well shoot me now and save some wear and tear on Lok's body and face, because I'm going to bring it."

Cong stepped back and found a chair, sitting down, resting the gun on his leg. He waved for Lok to begin.

"It's your funeral."

Chapter 58

Lok would be a handful. I knew that from the talent he had exhibited at my place. My fingers were still sore, but functional. He was extremely quick, but small in size. I had a height and weight advantage I needed to use to somehow best him. I had some martial arts skills, a couple of lessons recently from the studio April had used. But I was better at boxing. From what I knew he was an expert martial artist, but not a boxer. Time would tell, but I had to bring all I had to this confrontation.

"Rules?" I asked, before we began.

"No referee, no rules. But if you try to leave the ring, I will shoot you."

"Does that include Lok, if I happen to knock him out of the ring?"

Cong laughed. "I'm glad you haven't lost your sense of humor, in the face of defeat. I will miss our little chats."

"Yes, we should have exchanged phone numbers. Could have been pen pals."

I too laughed, at myself. Levity had gotten me through some tough situations and today was no different. I faced Lok and bowed to him, like you'd see in any martial artist competition. He hesitated and bowed, too, so I kicked him in the face, knocking him back into the ropes. It was a cheap shot, but I needed whatever advantage I could muster.

"No rules," I said, while holding up my hands.

Lok's nose was bleeding, but it didn't faze him. Using his speed, he came at me with a flurry of punches, mostly to the body. I covered up as best as I could, but still felt them. I struck back with my own right and left jabs, but it didn't slow him. He spun and kicked high at my jaw. I twisted and got my left arm up, taking the blow to the shoulder. There was immediate pain, that ran down my arm, it going numb. I backed up into the ropes to bide time, yet he came and attacked more. He went low to my leg with another kick, but missed my knee, getting my thigh instead, which hurt like hell. He pounded me with two more shots, this time landing on the side of my head, and I was down on one knee. He stood over me, letting the blood from his nose, trickle on the floor before me. My head was spinning some, but I still had my wits. He went to kick me and I caught his lower leg, turned and twisted it, putting him off balance and down to the floor, as he cushioned his fall with his hands. I held his leg as long as I could and came crashing down with my elbow on the side of his knee, the popping sound filling my ears. He let out a groan, for I had hurt him. I was back on my feet now, doing my best boxing dance.

"Not bad, Jarvis," said Cong. "This is making for some exciting entertainment."

I glanced over and saw he had his phone up and was recording the battle. I hoped I'd live through the event to watch it someday.

Lok was back on his feet. He was doing his best not to show it, but you could tell I'd done a little damage to his knee. I came towards him and pressed on. We each went toe to toe, throwing punches. I'd land one and he'd land one solid shot out of three that were thrown. I'd backed him up against the ropes using my height and strength, going for the head, but still pounding at his firm body, hoping to soften it some. I was tasting blood and hoped it was my own, for he was still bleeding as well. I had hit him good and he seemed to stagger, but then out of his daze he popped me straight in the nose, and I stumbled backward, and onto my butt.

"Got cocky, didn't you Jarvis," said Cong.

"I don't need a Jim Lampley–style commentator," I said, gathering my senses and then spitting out blood.

My nose was most likely broken. I'd had a couple through the years, so knew what to expect. But it would make things more difficult and it would be hard to breathe through it now. But I didn't have time to reflect, as Lok pounced, coming at me with his feet. I rolled and took a shot to the ribs and another to the hip. I would feel all of this later, but adrenaline was in charge now. I came up swinging with a left that crashed into his thigh, blocking another leg kick. He now stumbled off balance and I attacked again, four solid body shots that lowered his arms and two straight punches to the face. He was in the ropes, trying to gain time, but I didn't let up, using fists, forearms and elbows, blocking and striking him, until he slumped to the floor. I continued to punch and batter at his head, not wanting to stop. I don't know how much time passed, but soon his body was limp and prone on the canvas. I stood up and walked to the center of the ring. I wanted to do a

Rocky Balboa and jump up and down, with my arms in the air, but I was too tired. I took one more step and collapsed to one knee and then finally, lay on my side and then rolled onto my back. I was doing my best to take in oxygen, my heart pounding as hard as it ever had. I may have won, but I didn't feel like it.

Cong had stopped the recording and put away his phone. He grabbed the gun and stepped through the ropes into the ring, and soon he was standing over me, pointing the gun at my head.

"Can I get a copy of the recording?" I said, between breaths.

"Always the jokester."

"Or you could post it on YouTube, so the world could share in my triumph. A few thumbs-up from the adoring audience."

"You never stop with the humor, do you?"

"Burn it to a DVD and sell it. We can split the profits."

He'd grown tired of my jests.

"Tell me where she is, Jarvis, or you die."

"You said you'd let me go if I beat Lok," I said, while pointing at the unconscious body a few feet away. "I think that qualifies."

"I lied. Now give me the answer or I will shoot you in the leg."

"Could you make it in the left shoulder? I think it is already fucked up. That one kick of Lok's was a killer. If I was left handed, my pitching career would be over."

"Mandy Bailey or else."

"I think not," came a voice from behind.

Cong turned around and saw the two Platov brothers. Both were armed. Aleksi with a big 9mm, and Petya with an AK-47 pointed towards him. My first thought, was oh shit. Now I had two sets of criminals out to kill me. I continued to lay there, trying to refuel for one last battle.

"This is not your business, Aleksi," said Cong.

"I'm making it my business. Put the gun down or Petya will drill you several times before you can even blink."

Cong looked around, and saw no one was going to help him. Lok was still out cold and I, of course, could care less if they shot him. He put the gun down slowly and then kicked it away. My only concern: was I being rescued by them for an even worse fate?

"Why are you saving him?" asked Cong.

"Because I choose to. Hard not to be impressed with him beating your man Lok. I'd have thought his chances were slim, yet he prevailed. It was quite a show to behold."

"Yay for me," I said, finally getting my right hand in the air.

"Jarvis, you can get up now," said Aleksi. "We have business to attend to."

I hoped the business was a hot shower and some clean clothes, but I wasn't holding out much hope.

"I'm trying my best. I have a lot of parts on my body not working at one hundred percent. But I'll get there. You didn't happen to bring a wheelchair, did you?"

If anyone laughed, I didn't hear them. As I rolled onto my right side, I pushed up and onto my knees. My left shoulder was definitely messed up. Broken nose, split lip, cut cheek and a few loose teeth. Blood covered my face, chest, shorts and legs. I finally was able to stand and saw some signs of life from Lok. He was breathing, his body twitching, eyes trying to open. I hoped he felt as bad as he looked. I made it to the ropes, grabbing them for a minute for balance, and stepped through. I found the chair Cong had been using and sat down.

"You realize I want to know why?" I asked.

"Like I said, I choose to. I don't like Cong and his Chinese bosses. We've been in competition for some time now, and I've grown weary of it. Time for it to end."

Petya, with those words, walked over to the stirring Lok and shot him in the head. If I hadn't been so tired, I'd have jumped out of the chair in horror. I wondered if there were bullets in the AK-47 for Cong and me.

"Am I next?" asked Cong.

"No. We are going to take you away and ask some hard questions. After that, it depends on my mood."

"And what of me," I asked. "Am I going to be asked some hard questions too?"

"No. You are free to go."

"Really. I doubt I can walk out of here. Can you drop me somewhere?"

"No, but I can call you a cab."

"How about an ambulance."

"No. We have some cleanup to do here. But I'm sure they will take you to the nearest hospital."

"That would be swell of you. But again, I have to ask why?"

"Let me say an acquaintance hired me to watch after you."

"Who?"

"I'm not at liberty to say. We were to assist in any way we could."

I thought about it for a moment, a request coming to my bloody tongue.

"Does that include you getting me some answers?"

"Ask, and we will see."

I stood up slowly and walked over to him, whispering my request.

He smiled while looking at Cong, still standing in the ring, and nodded his head convincingly.

Chapter 59

We were sitting in a meeting room, designed by a male who was compensating for a lack of a certain physical prowess. The room was huge, with long rectangular marble-top table, with thirty chairs, and acoustics to amplify the sound in the room so everyone could hear those speaking in the other zip code. Mandy was sitting to the left of me, Barry to the right. Both had their computers out and were typing away. I felt quite low-tech holding my smartphone in my right hand, checking on baseball scores. The Rockies weren't in the playoff chase again this year, which bummed me out.

I was working the phone one-handed, as my left arm was in a sling. The damage was bad, but repairable, either with time or possibly surgery. A shoulder socket dislocation and rotator cuff tear was the prognosis. My face was still bruised and swelling in places, cotton and tape no longer needed for my broken nose, which was slowly healing. Other parts that didn't show, much the same. I was walking stiffly, though Ibuprofen helped. I'd spent twenty-four hours in the hospital, twenty-four more than I cared for. The only good thing about the stay was the pain meds, which helped me sleep. I had lived through the battle to carry on another day, though I'd wished it had been less painful. More than I could say for Lok, whose body had been disposed of, who knows where. No news of it ever being found. When I was delivered to the hospital, when they asked what happened, I said I'd been in a fight, but couldn't identify who it was. When questioned by the local Littleton police, they took the statement, but you could tell they didn't believe much of it. Another local civil service department that would have a file on me, with little or no detail to work with. I'd soon be flagged in all the state-wide systems. A don't ask, for he won't tell designation.

For now, we sat by ourselves waiting, a pitcher of ice water to keep our glasses filled. Mandy was outfitted in a long blue skirt, with white boots, and white silk short-sleeved blouse. Barry was in expensive black suit, with yellow tie, white shirt and mirror polished black shoes. Next to them I looked like I was slumming it, with green polo, white slacks and less than polished white Nike running shoes. We had a meeting with the power structure of WANN Systems. We were going to state our case and hopefully bring this whole situation to a conclusion.

After about a thirty-minute wait, in walked a parade of WANN power management. *Don't all big executive types make the little people wait?* There were four of them altogether, two I knew and the other two I didn't. The two I didn't know dressed more upscale than the two owners. They took seats on the opposite side of the table, each pouring their own ice water from another pitcher within their reach. They all got settled into their cushiony chairs, and I felt the cold stare of Logan across the table. No doubt remembering me even with my black and blue face.

"I am Maddix Bishop, the lead counsel for WANN Systems," said the third man from the left. "Immediately to my right is Chief Security Officer, Kyle Lambert. To my left is Logan Albers and to his left Burton Waterton, both the founders, owners and co-CEOs of WANN Systems."

"I am Barry Anders, representing Mandy Bailey, the beautiful young lady to my far left. And the gentlemen next to me is private detective Jarvis Mann."

"Since this is an informal meeting," stated Maddix, "we will not be recording any of the proceedings. If at any time any of the parties are uncomfortable with this, we can begin recording, if all parties agreed."

Barry nodded his head.

"Counsel Anders, you called this meeting," continued Maddix. "What do you want to discuss?"

"Jarvis has been leading this investigation," said Barry. "I will let him have the floor to spell out what he has discovered."

I would have loved to stand up and walked the floor, giving a summation like the best lawyers you see on TV, but I was too sore.

"Good afternoon, gentlemen," I said. "I will begin with a short synopsis of how all of this began, for anyone not familiar. A few months back Aaron Bailey was found murdered in the parking garage of your Denver office facility. Aaron was a software engineer, who was beaten, shot in the leg and then in the chest, which killed him."

"All ruled a robbery gone bad by the police," added Kyle.

"Exactly. Mandy, the widow of Aaron, did not believe this to be the case. She hired me to investigate. When I first looked at the case, I found one odd item, and that being the fact that the security system was offline at the time of the shooting. If it had been working, the culprit would have easily been identified."

"Purely coincidental," said Kyle. "Computer systems go down like that all the time."

"In fact, that is not the case for this system. It had a record of being nearly hundred percent operational."

"Who did you hear this from?" asked Kyle.

"The Head of Security of the Denver office, Mitchell Crabtree."

"Former head. He was fired for his incompetence."

"Then he is to blame?"

Kyle gave me a hard stare now that rivaled Logan's. The combo would keep the ice in my glass from melting.

"We are not saying that," said Maddix. "No one who worked at WANN is directly responsible for Aaron's death. But being the Head of Security, he should have made sure the system was operational."

"Even though he wasn't working at the time? Come now, gentlemen, we know he was a scapegoat you could blame to take the heat off all of you. You even paid him to keep his mouth shut."

"Where did you learn this?"

I just shrugged my shoulders.

"Any agreement we had with Mitchell is between us and him," said Maddix.

"Sure it is. And after talking with him, three Russian men paid him a visit, attacking him and fire-balling his classic Corvette. A damn shame, as well as a crime to destroy such a pristine vehicle."

"Do you have witnesses to prove this?"

"Not directly. Mitchell went into hiding along with his family, in fear for their lives. Those three men later attacked me outside of my favorite watering hole, wanting to know who hired me to investigate the Aaron Bailey murder. Fortunately, a police officer friend stopped by and kept them from beating me senseless."

"There must be a point in all of this," said Kyle.

"Oh, there is. A conspiracy to prevent me from finding out who actually murdered Aaron Bailey for knowledge he was about to spill about a WANN Systems software security issue, which was allowing them to steal information from their unknowing customers."

"Ridiculous," said Burton. "Our software is as secure as any on the planet."

"Really. Is that true, Mandy?"

"No, it's not," she said. "With the security vulnerability I have discovered, I can shut your entire network down. If you were to buy something I would be able to steal all the information in the order."

"Why should we believe you?" said Burton.

"Because she is the computer genius in the Bailey family," I said. "Watch what happens when Mandy takes over your network. Go ahead, Mandy, demonstrate."

Since Mandy had hacked back into the WANN Systems she had been working on coding to take advantage of the computer vulnerability. It was a Trojan horse that once inside could do most anything she commanded. It took her a whole five minutes to activate it.

"Check with your tech people," she said. "I just rebooted several of your main routers and firewalls, telling each to block all incoming and outgoing traffic for ten minutes. I made it think your network was under a denial of service attack, so it's shutting down everything until the attack ceases."

The four men looked at each other, trying to decide what to do. Kyle got up and went over to a phone on a small credenza. When he couldn't get a dial tone, since the phone system shared the same network, he pulled out his massive iPhone and called. He spent several minutes talking, getting angry at what he was hearing. We caught him saying "fix it or else" and then he hung up the phone. Once back in his seat he confirmed what Mandy had done.

"Hacking into a network is illegal," said Kyle. "We should call the cops or, better yet, sue you."

"You already sued her," said Barry. "But we have a judge looking at it right now. From emails we obtained you manipulated her to sign that settlement agreement. That judge has now suspended the Cease and Desist order. We plan on countering with our own legal action."

Barry pulled out some copies of the emails and tossed them in front of Maddix. He went through each one, before passing them on to the other three. All read them, accept for Logan. He didn't need to because he already knew what was in them. When Burton read through each one, he turned and gave Logan a nasty look. Burton got up and walked over to Maddix and whispered in his ear.

"We need a few minutes to discuss some things," said Maddix. "Could you please step out and we'll call you when we are ready."

Mandy and Barry closed their computers and the three of us walked out. I had grabbed my water and took a long drink while we stood, waiting.

"How do think it's going?" asked Mandy.

"They are sweating bullets," answered Barry.

"What do you think they will do?"

"What do most big companies do when in trouble? Buy their way out of it."

"How will we respond?" I said.

"I want Aaron's killer or killers brought to justice," stated Mandy. "And a big payday would be a nice bonus."

"The plan was to get both," Barry replied. "We'll see what they have to say."

It took about twenty-five minutes before they called us back into the room. When we reached our seats, the power quartet looked worried but confident they could deal with us. Barry insisted on recording the proceedings now, as he wanted it on record. After a long discussion among themselves the four of them agreed. Barry pulled out of his briefcase a high-end digital recorder and placed it at the center of the table and pressed record.

"What will it take for this to go away?" said Burton.

When flying out we had discussed figures and what we would ask for, looking at Aaron's income potential for the years he had remaining. The pain and suffering for the loss of a loved one. And let's not forget the fees for Barry and myself. We came to a significant number.

"Twenty million," said Barry.

"You've got to be kidding me," responded Burton.

"No, I'm not. Mandy's pain and suffering, the jeopardy her life has been in since she hired Jarvis, and the income potential that has now been lost with Aaron's murder. You are lucky it's not higher than that. And we want all the money up-front. And not paid out over time."

"Not a chance," said Logan, speaking for the first time.

"He speaks," I said. "Logan, you know we have you. In the end you will deal. But there will be one stipulation. And that is the murderer of Aaron Bailey will be brought to justice. Of this there will be no negotiation."

"We don't know who killed Aaron," said Kyle.

"You may not know, but Logan knows, for he manipulated this person into doing his dirty work for him. You see he has an issue with sex that others have used against him, to gain a foothold in this company. I know Burton knows of his problems and has tried to cover for him for years now. But it allowed you both to keep the company afloat. Both the Russians and the Chinese gave you money to keep the gravy train running. Even twisted you into designing your hardware and software so they could steal from those using it. Identity and credit card theft are big business. And the Chinese hoped with your rising market share that you would be able to sell your products to the US Government. Buy your firewalls, switches, routers and software, giving them the ability to infiltrate and snoop on what our security agencies were doing. Hell, there is a lot of money going across the government network they could access, intercept, and possibly steal."

"You are full of it," said Logan. "You have nothing to link me to his murder."

"Oh, I do. And not only Aaron's murder, but Wilmar Boylan's and Adam King's. They were all murdered by the same person. A couple of Denver police detectives flew out here with us. They got a warrant to search the home of the suspect. We should be hearing from them shortly."

Logan was now getting nervous. He looked around the room and got up to leave. I jumped up and beat him to the door. Even with one hand I would have no issue with stopping him.

"Sit down," I said with some vigor. "Or I will sit you down myself, as I did once before."

His hand went to his stomach, as he remembered the blow to the solar plexus I given him in the hotel room. He turned around and sat back down, this time next to Maddix.

"Ten million," said Burton.

"Fifteen, and not a penny less," countered Barry.

Burton paused, not sure what to do. It was a lot of money, but his company was worth it, and could afford it, as least for now.

"Alright. Fifteen million. Do we have a deal?"

"Sure," replied Barry. "Other than Aaron's killer. Once the police have them in custody, then we can sign some paperwork. They are not part of the deal."

"You can have him," said Burton. "I'm tired of cleaning up his messes."

"You son-of-a-bitch," said Logan. "You'd be nothing without me."

"I suggest you both shut up," said Maddix, while pointing at the recorder. "Before you say something that you both will regret."

Logan was angry and didn't care. He stood up to go after Burton, but I stepped over and punched him once in the kidney. He buckled to the ground to one knee in pain.

"You asshole," he said, while trying to speak through the agony. "I will have you arrested for assaulting me."

"Actually, I think I was saving your partner from you assaulting him. And I imagine he would testify to it."

Kyle stood up, thinking he should do something. He was the Head of Security, but didn't appear to be in charge of anything on the security side at the moment. He walked over and helped up Logan, telling him to sit down. He stepped over to me, trying to look tough, but I wasn't fazed. I waved my finger at him as a warning, when my cell phone rang. It was Dan Cummings. After I heard what he had to say I went to open the meeting room door. Stu Mallard, Denver Police Detective, walked in and showed his badge so everyone knew who he was.

"What is this about, Officer?" asked Burton.

"I will explain in a few minutes. We are waiting for someone to join us."

Everyone turned to watch the open doorway. Within a few minutes Bronwen Pearson, Director of Security for the West Region, walked in the door. She was, as I remembered, a tall lady, with broad shoulders and thick hands. She was dressed in black slacks and a peach blouse. Her black hair was cut short, parted in the middle and combed straight back. From a distance, in the dark, most would not think she was a woman.

"What the hell is this?" she said.

"Are you Bronwen Pearson?" asked Mallard.

"Yes."

Mallard walked over to her and handed her some paperwork.

"If you want to read that, it's a warrant to search your home. We've already executed it and are there now."

She looked down at the paperwork, looking over the details, trying to make head or tails of it.

"What are you looking for?" she asked.

"Guns. Specifically, the guns which killed three people."

Her eyes glanced over at Logan and then back again at Mallard.

"I haven't killed anyone."

"Actually, we think you have. We found at least one of them. Once we test it, we'll know for sure." Mallard then recited her Miranda rights.

"What did you do to your left arm?" I asked, pointing to a bandage above the elbow.

She looked at it for a second but didn't respond.

"Maybe a flesh wound from a bullet, from Adam King's gun," I added. "Enough to leave blood and DNA at the scene."

Her expression changed, from innocent to a look of guilt.

"I did what I had to do."

"Probably should keep your mouth shut," said Maddix. "Anything you say can be used against you."

"You think you're my lawyer now," she said back to him, with anger. "What the hell do you know? What all I've done. What I've been through."

Kyle walked up to her.

"Bronwen, shut up. Maddix is right. You are only making it worse."

"You limp dick. You wouldn't do anything about the problem. Had to delegate it to me for handling. You wouldn't suck his dick like I did. Hell, he was going to give me your job after all of this. I was tough enough and man enough, where you sat behind your desk playing video games all day. I cleaned up his mess, and what did I have to show for it. Did he love me? Hell no. He'd fuck me alright, like his other sex toys. Hell, we did it in his office, my office and even on this table. He promised me the job. He promised me lust. But not his love."

Mallard had heard enough. "Bronwen Pearson, you are under arrest. Put your hands on the table and spread your legs." He went to reach for her, but she resisted.

"Oh, hell no," she yelled. "You aren't going to fuck me in the ass, like he did!"

With that she turned around and punched Mallard with a haymaker and he went down. She leaned down and pulled a small gun from an ankle holster and pointed it at Logan. Possibly the gun that killed Wilmar. Everyone in the room ducked down. Barry lunged on top of Mandy and hit the floor. Burton, Maddix and Kyle ran to the other side of the room. Logan yelled and was standing, uncertain what to do. He backed up and pleaded for his life as she stepped towards him.

"How could I have been so stupid," she said. "To think you would ever love me. But you knew the right buttons to push me to a place I'd never been before. I killed and killed, and killed again for you, only to hope you'd see what we could be together. But now it's clear I need to kill again. But first I'm going to make sure you don't stick that cock of yours in anyone else to manipulate."

With her gun she fired straight into his crotch. He dropped down clutching his groin, screaming. She walked over and aimed again. I didn't have my gun, so I grabbed Mallard's from his holster and pointed.

"Bronwen, stop or I'll shoot," I said.

She wasn't listening, so I fired, one in the shoulder to stop her. She clutched at her collarbone, leaning forward, looking at her blood. She was so mad it didn't seem to faze her. She turned around and aimed the gun again at me, about to fire.

"Bronwen, don't or else!"

She didn't care; rage had overtaken her. I wasn't about to die and this time I went center mass, a direct shot to her chest, backing her up a few feet before she slumped to the ground, dead. I walked over and checked to be certain and slid the gun away. Logan was crying and moaning in pain on the ground. I had never killed a woman before and the shock of what happened would overwhelm me later, but for now I was mad as I stood over Logan.

"I should have let her kill you," I said. "Because your pitiful life isn't worth saving."

I went to check on Mallard, Barry, and Mandy, pushing aside the horrible memories waiting to haunt me.

Chapter 60

I ended up staying an extra day on the West Coast with interviews and statements to be made. Once released I had to promise to return to testify, if it ever came to that. The shooting was justified, everyone in the room knew that, so I wasn't in any trouble with the law. It didn't make me feel any better, or help me sleep, but I was satisfied I'd done all I could for my client, which in the end is what mattered.

Before leaving town, I needed to pay one more visit. As I stood in the living area, Lyndi walked down her staircase in a long evening dress, sparkling from sequins, plunging on the back to just above her hips and clinging to her chest enough to tease any man into wondering what was underneath. She was not dressed for me, but dressed for a night out. I stopped by to say hello and likely goodbye.

"Wow," I said. "Someone is going to turn heads tonight."

She reached the bottom stairs. In her hands she held her high heels, which she reached back to put on. Once done, we were eyeball to eyeball, as she kissed me softly not to mess up her makeup.

"Fundraiser tonight. At twenty-five hundred a plate, for a children's charity. Going with a wealthy man, who is willing to pay for my company."

"He is getting his money's worth."

She looked at my face, seeing the healing bruises and my arm in the sling.

"What the hell happened to you?"

"Long story. But in a nutshell, your ex-husband sent some men after me to get even for Vegas."

"You look terrible. How did they end up looking?"

"One dead, the other I don't know for certain. A pair of Russian men took him away."

"Russian men. Didn't you tell me about some Russians who were trying to kill you?"

I nodded. "Yes, those same men."

"Why did they save you this time?"

"I'm not completely certain. Said they had been hired by an

acquaintance to keep tabs on me. I never got an answer."

"Nice to have friends in high places. I had heard about the situation at WANN on the news. They didn't give your name but I wondered if you were involved."

"I was. I've been tied up with the police. I'm sure you heard the gory details."

"Yes, poor Logan. What will he do without his penis to think with?"

I laughed, which felt good. I had not laughed much this last week.

"With any luck they will castrate him and the boys in prison will fuck him as he fucked over others," I said. "Too many died over his lustful ways."

"I've said plenty about his twisted sexual habits, but when we were first together he was as good as I've ever had. I don't know where he went off the rails. Maybe it was always there and came to the forefront when he became successful."

"Better than me?" I asked.

"No. That is one twenty-four hours I will never forget."

"Nor I. I'm sorry I may have put an end to him and his business. I know it will affect you financially."

She put her hand on my face.

"Don't worry about me. I have plenty of money and will have for some time. I don't think I told you I had a lot of stock in WANN that he had paid me with over the years. After what you revealed about Logan, all the cyber theft going on and what you had planned for him in Vegas, I sold it all for top dollar. Good thing too, as their stock has taken quite a hit."

"Would that be considered insider information?"

"Not at all. I was only being a smart businesswoman. Besides, the only insider information you gave me was you being inside me in a pleasurable way."

Her hand went down to grab my right hand, squeezing it tightly.

"Will I ever see you again?" she said. "I know it would be tough to repeat that night in Vegas, but it would sure be fun to give it a try."

"If there is a trial I will have to come back and testify. If the leeching lawyers don't drain me of all my bodily fluids, I'd be up for some more Lyndi time."

"Good. Now go before I tear off this thousand-dollar dress and take you right here on the stairs."

I took her hand, kissing it passionately, as if I was kissing another part of her body. Leaving a wonderful memory behind and a hope of another Silicon Valley trip sometime in the future.

Chapter 61

I was back home enjoying an evening stroll with April, on a warm early September night. She was doing better, walking nearly at full strength, with only a little bit of pain. Doctors said in a couple of weeks she could go on light duty again, with full time coming shortly after, if there were no complications. A job as a street cop was waiting for her, riding with a veteran trying to keep the peace from someplace other than behind a counter at the station. She was excited about the new opportunity.

We walked at a good pace, being quiet for now. She reached out her hand and grabbed my left gently. Though no longer still in a sling, my shoulder remained sore and on the mend. Her fingers and palm felt warm and inviting. We had grown close over this last month or so. I worried I'd do to her as I'd done with Melissa and hurt her, so I was cautious. Still, there was an attraction there that was hard to ignore. I clung to her hand, happy to have someone to touch.

"You are strangely quiet tonight," I said.

"I know. I'm normally going a mile a minute. Miss Crude and Rude."

"I've always liked that about you."

"Been one of the guys most of my life. That is how I fit in."

"You may talk like one, but you don't look like one."

She squeezed my hand a little harder, and carefully pulled me against her.

"You realize I'm almost completely healed. To the point where I can consider some adult pleasure."

"Really, what did you have in mind?"

"Keep it simple at first. Maybe a naked man sleeping in my bed and see what develops."

"Is there a certain man you had in mind?"

"Well, normally I'm not all that picky. But yeah, there is one I wouldn't mind getting a peek at. I've had this fantasy of what he looks like, but would prefer to see how it matches up to the real thing."

I turned and kissed her. It was soft and passionate. There was a worry about what would happen deep down, but I'd regret it if I didn't explore the options."

"You know I'm not the best boyfriend," I said. "My history has been poor when it comes to relationships."

"I've not been the best girlfriend either in my lifetime. I've gone through men pretty quickly with nothing long-term to show for it. Sometimes it was me, other times it was them. Right now, I'm looking to find a lover to fill a need. I don't expect you to be a one-woman man, so long as you don't expect me to be a one-man woman. What I expect, is that when you are with me, you are all into me and not someone else. What you do on your own time really doesn't bother me."

Had I struck pay dirt and found a woman who understood me? The person I was and the life I led? Only time will tell. For now, it seemed I had nothing to lose. As we continued our walk, this time our bodies brushing against each other, a black SUV pulled up beside us. I felt April tense up, when she saw Aleksi Platov step out the door. She was tough, though, and didn't cower, expecting a confrontation. He walked over with a happy look on this face.

"I'm sorry for interrupting," he said. "I see you are enjoying this pleasant late summer Colorado evening."

"What do you want?" said April. She still didn't trust him, even though I had explained how he had helped me.

"April, I'm happy to see you up and moving around. You are looking well."

"Thank…you," she answered, surprised at what she heard. "Yes, I should be a hundred percent pretty soon."

"I wanted to stop by and say I'm sorry about Jasha shooting you. It is not in my nature to hurt women and I warned him against doing so. They are to be loved and cherished. Jasha let his emotions get the best of him. In our line of work that can be a hindrance. In this case it cost him his life."

"Emotions can do that to you."

"There is nothing for you and Jarvis to worry about from me. All water under the bridge, as they say."

"Are you leaving town?" I asked.

He nodded.

"I have other matters to attend around the world. I've been here far too long."

"So, your business here is finished?" I said. "Does that mean

Cong is finished too?"

"Not to worry about him either. He will never bother you again."

I was happy he would not be bothering me, which I was to assume meant he ended up buried next to Lok. But not before he spilled the information Aleksi and I was looking for.

"I hear you found the killer of your client?" stated Aleksi

"Happy to say we did. Everything you got from Cong helped us find out who it was. Unfortunately, I had to kill her."

"Do not lose too much sleep over it. Justice sometimes works more swiftly when at the end of a gun. And your client got a big payoff, which I assume means you will as well."

He seemed to be well informed of the situation. Money for Mandy, Barry, myself and even the King family.

"It was a nice check for all, cashed and deposited. Are you still tied to WANN Systems?"

"No. We have pulled all of our funding and ties to them. We have bailed from the sinking ship. They are about to collapse, as your friend in the FBI is digging in deep. We have many other avenues of revenue. We will survive."

"I'm sure you will."

Aleksi put out his hand and I shook it. He then took April's hand and kissed it. He bid adieu and headed back to his car.

"You still never told me who hired you to watch over me?"

He turned back, looking my way.

"You never told me why you told Tony Bristol where the Feds took me?"

"Seemed like a clever idea at the time. And I needed Tony's help and that greased the wheel."

"Then I'd say you have your answer, then. But keep in mind, if you ever hold a gun to my head again…"

With that he hopped in the car and drove away.

"That was spooky. Was he implying what I think he was?" asked April.

"I would say so. Sometimes fate works in mysterious ways."

We continued our walk, when I turned to her.

"Now, where were we," I said. "I believe there was some talk of getting naked and getting into bed or something like that."

"Yes, I do believe that was the conversation."

"If that is the case, we are heading in the wrong direction."

She laughed and spun me the other way. We quickened the pace, and got back to her place in record time. Then slowed the pace down to enjoy the tease of the undressing. Being naked with her felt absolutely right as we spent the night together, only sleeping, our bare skin stimulating enough for our first night together.

Thanks for reading **Dead Man Code**. I hope you enjoyed it and would greatly appreciate if you would leave a review on Amazon to help an Indie Author. It is the greatest gift you can give us!!

And check out the other books in the **Jarvis Mann Detective Series** of which there are 9 to read. Read the books in this order for the best experience: **The Case of the Missing Bubble Gum Card, Tracking a Shadow, Twice as Fatal, Blood Brothers, Dead Man Code, The Case of the Invisible Souls, The Front Range Butcher, Mann in the Crossfire and Lethal Blues**. All are available on Amazon in eBook format including two boxsets, along with paperback versions, and on Kindle Unlimited.

And you can check out my **Divine Devils** Suspense/Thriller series. Read the entire series in this order for the best experience: **The Divine Devils, Fallen Star: The Divine Devils Book 2, Sold Souls: The Divine Devils Book 3 and Divine Retribution: The Divine Devils Final Chapter.** All are available in eBook, paperback and on Kindle Unlimited.

Find all my books via this link:
https://www.amazon.com/R-Weir/e/B00JH2Y5US

If you want to reach out, please email me at:
author@rweir.net

Receive a free eBook copy of my **Jarvis Mann PI** book, **Tracking A Shadow**. All you need to do is sign up for my newsletter on my website.
https://rweir.net

Follow R Weir, Jarvis Mann, and Hunter Divine on these social sites as I appreciate hearing from those who've read my books:
https://www.facebook.com/randy.weir.524
https://www.facebook.com/JarvisMannPI
https://www.instagram.com/rweir720/

Thanks for reading. Stay Safe, Happy and Healthy!!

Made in the USA
Columbia, SC
27 November 2023